BLOOD BOND

RIDE FOR
VENGEANCE

BLOOD BOND
RIDE FOR VENGEANCE

William W. Johnstone
with J. A. Johnstone

PINNACLE BOOKS
Kensington Publishing Corp.
www.kensingtonbooks.com

Chapter 1

The school in Sweet Apple, Texas, not far from the Rio Grande, wasn't serving its usual function tonight. The benches and desks had been moved to create a large open space in the middle of the floor, and dancing couples filled that space, swirling around in time to the tunes played by several fiddlers and a trio of Mexicans with guitars. The music was loud and raucous, and so were the stomping feet and the laughter of those attending the dance.

Folks in Sweet Apple were having a high old time.

Matt Bodine leaned against one of the walls of the schoolroom and sighed. "All these pretty gals," he said, "and not one of them wants to dance with me."

"Stop complaining," said Matt's blood brother, Sam August Webster Two Wolves. "We're working, remember?"

In truth, probably all of the young, eligible women in Sweet Apple and the vicinity—because everybody within riding distance came to town for a get-together like this—would have been glad to dance with either Matt or Sam, because the blood brothers were both tall, muscular, and handsome. They could have almost passed for real brothers. Matt's hair was dark brown, while Sam's was black as a raven's wing. Matt's eyes were blue, Sam's such a dark gray as to be almost black. Sam also had the high cheekbones and slightly reddish cast to his tanned skin that he had inherited from his father Medicine Horse, a Cheyenne warrior who had been killed at the Battle of the Little Big Horn.

Unlike nearly all the other members of his tribe, Medicine Horse had been educated in the East, at a white man's university. It was there he had met and married Sam's mother, who, when Sam was a young man, had insisted that *he* receive a college education, too.

Matt hadn't gotten the benefits of such advanced schooling, but he possessed a keen natural intelligence. The son of a pioneer Montana ranching family, he had been Sam Two Wolves' best friend since both of them were very young men, no more than kids really. Matt had been accepted into the Cheyenne tribe because of his bond with Sam. They were *Onihomahan*—Brothers of the Wolf.

Although they both owned sizable cattle spreads in Montana, both young men were too fiddle-footed to stay in one place for too long, so for the past few years they had been drifting around the West, usually landing smack-dab in the middle of trouble even though that wasn't their intention. But they couldn't turn their backs on folks in trouble, nor pass up the chance for an adventure.

Which was how they'd come to wind up in the rough-and-tumble border town of Sweet Apple, working as unofficial deputies for the town's lawman, Marshal Seymour Standish. It was a long story involving owl-hoots, Mexican revolutionaries (a fancy name for *ban-*

didos), and a train car full of U.S. Army rifles. Much powder had been burned. The air in Sweet Apple's main street had been full of gun smoke and hot lead. Blood had been spilled, including a mite that belonged to Matt Bodine. But in the weeks since that big ruckus, things had been fairly peaceful in town.

Matt and Sam knew that wouldn't last. It never did.

Tonight they were dressed a little fancier than usual for the dance, Matt in a brown tweed suit instead of his usual jeans and blue bib-front shirt, Sam in dark gray wool instead of his buckskins. They both wore boiled white shirts and string ties. Matt pulled at his collar and grimaced in discomfort and distaste.

"Damn thing feels like a noose," he muttered. "This must be what it's like to get strung up."

"Are you going to complain about everything tonight?" Sam asked.

"I might." Matt's eyes followed the slender, graceful, redheaded form of Jessie Colton as she danced with one of the men from Sweet Apple.

"Oh," Sam said. "I understand now. You're mad because you haven't gotten to dance with Jessie yet."

"I saw you eyein' Sandy Paxton," Matt shot back. "Don't tell me you wouldn't rather be out there with her instead of standin' here holdin' up this damned wall."

"We're doing more than that. We're keeping an eye on the men from the Double C and Pax."

Matt had to admit that those cowboys did need to be kept an eye on. Like the men who rode for all the other spreads in the area, the hands from the Double C and Pax ranches had come into Sweet Apple for the dance. They all knew that hostilities had to be put aside at the door. That was the plan anyway. Whether or not it worked might be another story entirely.

Once Pax and Double C had been one vast ranch, owned by cousins Esau Paxton and Shadrach Colton. Matt and Sam knew that much, but they had no idea why, somewhere along the way, the spread had been broken in two and Paxton and Colton had become bitter enemies. That was the case, though, and the feud was still going on.

Since Western men rode for the brand, the enemies of a cowboy's boss became the cowboy's enemies, too. That feeling had led to more than one brawl between riders from the two ranches. Here lately, as sort-of deputies, Matt and Sam had been forced to break up some of those ruckuses.

So far tonight, the men from Pax and Double C hadn't done any more than eye each other suspiciously. Matt and Sam hoped it stayed that way.

Marshal Standish went by them, dancing with Magdalena Elena Louisa O'Ryan, the pretty little half-Mexican/half-Irish schoolmarm. Maggie O'Ryan had a big smile on her face. She was sweet on Seymour, and the feeling was returned.

Seymour glanced over Maggie's shoulder at Matt and Sam, who each gave him a curt nod signifying that everything was all right so far. Seymour looked both relieved and happy. His face was flushed from the exertion of dancing, but it wasn't as noticeable as it would have been a month or so earlier when he'd first arrived in Sweet Apple from Trenton, New Jersey. He'd been a salesman then, for the Standish Dry Goods Company, not a lawman. He'd also been pale as bread dough and just about as courageous. In fact, he'd been known for a time as The Most Cowardly Man in the West, a tag slapped on him by the local newspaper editor.

Nobody thought of him that way anymore, not after he'd stood up to the fierce outlaw Deuce Mallory and Mallory's bloodthirsty gang, as well as the vicious bandits led by Diego Alcazarrio. Seymour was still slender and a little pale—although he was starting to tan a little—but he carried himself with more confidence, and with tutoring from Matt and Sam, he was getting better every day with the six-gun he now packed in a holster on his hip.

A couple of well-fed, middle-aged gents sidled up to the blood brothers. Abner Mitchell was a local merchant and the mayor of Sweet Apple; J. Emerson Heathcote published the newspaper and served on the town council with Mitchell and some of the other businessmen.

"It appears that everything's under control," Mitchell said as he hooked his thumbs in his vest. Even when he wasn't trying to make a speech, his words came out with a certain blustery quality to them Matt supposed that Mitchell was just a natural-born politician. He'd probably launched into an oration for the first time when the midwife slapped him on the ass after birthing him.

"I see that everyone from the Double C and Pax came into town tonight," Heathcote said with a worried air.

"Of course they did," Matt said. "It's a dance. Everybody comes to a dance."

"If there's trouble, perhaps in the future the ranches could alternate—"

"No offense, Mr. Heathcote," Sam cut in, "but you're getting ahead of yourself. Everybody knows the rules. No matter what happens out on the range, when you step into a dance you leave all that behind."

Heathcote nodded. "Yes, yes, I know. But some of those young cowhands are pretty hotheaded—"

"If anything happens, we'll take care of it," Matt said. He moved his coat aside a little to reveal the walnut grips on the butt of the gun holstered at his right hip. A matching Colt revolver rode on his left hip, covered up at the moment by his coat.

It was pretty obvious what he meant. No matter how reckless and impulsive they were, folks tended to listen to Matt Bodine, because he was known from one end of the West to the other as a gunfighter. He was deadly accurate with his shots, and nobody was slicker and faster on the draw than Matt except for the legendary Smoke Jensen, and maybe, just *maybe,* a youngster down Texas way named Morgan.

What was sometimes forgotten was that Matt's blood brother Sam Two Wolves was only a hair slower on the draw. Together, they were as formidable a pair as had ever ridden Western trails, a pair of Western aces if ever there was one.

Their reputation had quelled trouble by itself on more than one occasion. If more than that was required, they could certainly provide it. But nobody wanted gunplay at a dance like this, especially with the whole town in attendance and kids running around underfoot.

The musicians reached the end of a song and paused for a minute before launching into the rollicking strains of another tune. Seymour came up to Matt, Sam, Mayor Mitchell, and J. Emerson Heathcote. The marshal was out of breath and sweating a little. He had been wounded in the battle a couple of weeks earlier, too, and maybe he wasn't quite back up to his full strength yet.

"My word, that young lady can dance!" he said.

Heathcote dug an elbow into Seymour's side. "You aren't complaining, though, are you, Marshal?"

Seymour turned even redder, but he said, "Not in the slightest."

"Sitting this one out?"

"Yes, Maggie said she needed to catch her breath, and to tell the truth, so do I. I was glad to oblige her."

"Do I hear matrimonial bells in the offing? Should I save space on the front page of the paper for a wedding story?"

Seymour looked shocked. "Good Lord, no!" As the other men grinned at him, he hurried on. "I mean, that would be vastly premature. Perhaps someday . . . if Maggie and I . . . I mean, if Miss O'Ryan and I continue to . . . grow closer . . . I mean, if we decide that we want to . . ."

"Why don't you stop right there, Seymour?" Matt drawled. "I reckon we all get your drift."

Seymour took a handkerchief from his pocket and mopped his forehead. "Good." He paused, and then went on. "I saw some of the men from the Double C going out the back door a few minutes ago."

"Probably somebody's got a jug outside," Matt said.

"They'll guzzle down some of that Who-hit-John and then be back inside," Sam added.

Seymour nodded. "I suspect that you're correct. The only reason I worried was because I saw Jeff Riley and some of the men from Pax follow them."

Matt stiffened when he heard that. Jeff Riley was Esau Paxton's top horse-breaker, and he was one of those hotheads Heathcote had alluded to. He'd been involved in more than one scuffle with riders from the Double C. Matt supposed that all the jerking and jolting

Riley's brain had gotten while he was on the backs of those wild broncs might have something to do with the man's rash behavior.

"Maybe we'd better go take a look, just to make sure nothing's brewing," Sam suggested.

Matt nodded. "The back door, you said?" he asked Seymour.

"That's right," Seymour replied. "I'd better come with you."

"That's all right," Matt said quickly.

"We can handle this," Sam said. "Might be better for you to keep an eye on things in here, Marshal."

"Oh." Seymour blinked. "Of course. I'll stay in here while the two of you see what's going on outside."

Seymour was trying to sound decisive, but it didn't really come across that way. Matt felt bad about the way he and Sam had contradicted Seymour's decision to come with them, especially in front of Heathcote and Mitchell.

But even though Seymour had come a long way and nobody questioned his courage anymore, he was still pretty inexperienced when it came to gun trouble. Matt and Sam were both confident that they could handle anything the Double C and Pax crews might come up with, but it would be easier if they didn't have to worry about Seymour accidentally getting in the way of a bullet.

The blood brothers didn't seem to hurry as they crossed the room, skirting around the dancers. But there wasn't a wasted movement between them, and they arrived at the rear door pretty quickly.

Not quite quickly enough, though, Matt saw as he and Sam stepped outside. The moon and the glow of lamplight that came through the windows of the school building provided enough light for them to be able to see the two compact groups of men facing each other. The cowboys crouched, their hands hovering over the butts of their guns as they stood ready to hook and draw.

In the next breath, the next heartbeat, shots would roar out, Colt flame would bloom in the night, and men would die.

Chapter 2

Matt's eyes took in the scene instantly, and he reacted just as fast. He saw Jeff Riley standing out in front of one group, while facing him was Tom Danks, one of the Double C's top hands—and just as big a hothead as Riley.

Without thinking about what he was doing, Matt launched himself in a dive from the little porch at the top of the three steps leading down from the rear door of the schoolhouse. He tackled Riley and drove the bronc-buster off his feet. Both men crashed to the ground.

"Hold it, Danks!" Sam's shout sounded loud and clear in the night. "Get your hand away from that gun!"

The hard-edged menace in Sam's voice meant that he had his own Colt out and had the Double C hands covered.

Meanwhile, Matt had rolled away from Riley and come up on one knee. His fast action had shocked the cowboys on both sides into immobility for a second, and that had been long enough for Sam to draw his gun and take control of the situation. Nobody wanted to slap leather when faced with a Colt that was already rock-steady in Sam Two Wolves' hand.

Riley pushed himself up and yelled, "What the hell!"

His eyes fastened angrily on Matt. "Why'd you jump me like that, Bodine?"

"You and Danks were about to draw on each other, weren't you?" Matt asked as he got to his feet.

Riley scrambled up, too. "What if we were?" he demanded, his voice hot with rage. "That's our own business, ain't it?"

"Not tonight," Matt snapped. "Not right outside a schoolhouse where there's a dance goin' on. There are a lot of innocent folks in there, Riley. Some of 'em could've gotten hurt if lead started to fly out here."

Riley, who was a wiry man with a lean, foxlike face, sneered at him. "For a gunslinger, you're mighty concerned about innocent folks gettin' hurt. You always think about that every time you slap leather, Bodine?"

"Not always," Matt answered honestly. "Sometimes, there just isn't enough time for that. But I don't go out of my way to endanger anybody either."

"The two o' you struttin' around town all high-and-mighty," Riley sputtered. "You make me sick. You ain't even real deputies. You got no right to tell me what to do."

There was a jug being passed around somewhere outside the school, Matt thought. That was for damned sure, because Riley was already half-drunk.

Tom Danks spoke up. "Bodine, why don't you go get the marshal? I want Riley arrested."

"Arrested?" Matt repeated. "For what?"

"Slander. He called Shad Colton a rustler."

An ugly laugh came from Riley. "That's what he is."

Sam said, "Nobody's going to get arrested for slander. Why don't all of you either go back inside and enjoy the dance, or else get your horses and go home. Either way, there's not going to be any gunfight out here tonight."

Riley laughed again. "I'm sure as hell not takin' any orders from a filthy redskin. I don't care if you *are* wearin' white man's clothes, Injun."

Sam's mouth tightened, but he didn't say anything. He had long since heard every slur that could possibly be directed toward his mixed white and red heritage. He didn't let them bother him.

Matt knew that, but he knew as well that Riley had no call to be saying such things. "Shut up," he said. "You've done all the dancin' you're gonna do tonight. Get the hell out of my sight, Riley."

"What are you gonna do if I don't?" Riley swayed closer to Matt. "I'm not gonna draw on you, Bodine. I know you'd kill me." His hot breath reeked of whiskey as it gusted in Matt's face. "So how are you gonna make me leave?"

Matt stared at him for a moment, narrow-eyed, then muttered, "The hell with it."

His fist came up and shot out with blinding speed.

The punch didn't travel more than six inches or so. It landed squarely on Riley's jaw with enough force to send the bronc-buster flying backward. Some of the other Paxton riders might have caught him, but they got out of the way instead and allowed him to crash to the ground on his back.

The other cowboys from Pax would have stood with Riley in a fight, but that didn't mean they liked him. And none of them wanted to go up against Matt Bodine either.

Riley tried for a second to get up, then groaned and sagged back down. The limp sprawl of his arms and legs showed that he had passed out.

In disgusted tones, Matt ordered, "Somebody put him on his horse and take him back out to Pax. When he wakes up, tell him not to come back to town until he's sober and willing not to cause trouble."

A couple of cowboys moved to do as Matt said. While they were busy with that, Sam said to the rest of the men, "Like I told you, either go back into the dance or go home. But the trouble is over, understand?"

Mutters of grudging agreement came from them. Both groups broke up, some of the men returning to the schoolhouse, others drifting off into the night.

Matt joined Sam on the porch. Sam still held his revolver, but he had lowered it to his side. "Think the ones who left will start taking potshots at each other in the dark?" he asked.

Matt shook his head. "I don't reckon that's likely. Looked like Riley and Danks were the ones who were stirrin' things up."

Sam leathered his iron and said, "I wonder what that business about Shad Colton being a rustler was all about."

"Just a drunk mouthin' off, I'd say. Riley was tryin' to get under Danks's skin."

"Yeah, I guess." Sam still sounded interested, though.

They went inside, where Seymour hurried over to them right away. "What happened?" he asked. "People are saying that there was almost a gunfight, and there was something about punches being thrown."

"Punch," Matt said with a smile. "There was only one punch . . . and I threw it."

"You were right to worry, Seymour," Sam said. "A couple of men from the Double C and Pax were about to slap leather, and if they had, the rest of both bunches would have joined in, too. It could've been pretty bloody."

"But you stopped them," Seymour said.

Matt nodded. "Yeah."

"This time," Sam added. "Somebody ought to have a talk with Colton and Paxton and see if they can't be convinced to patch up their differences and put an end to this feud."

"I agree," Seymour said, "but I couldn't do that. I haven't been here long enough. Neither of those men would listen to me."

"That's right," Matt agreed. "Anyway, I've heard about these Texas feuds. Usually the only thing that ever ends them is when one side is killed out."

"My God. That would require wholesale slaughter."

"Yeah," Matt said, "that's about the size of it."

Matt Bodine's comment was still on Seymour's mind as he walked Maggie O'Ryan back to her house after the dance was over. "Is that really the way it is here in Texas?" he asked her as they strolled along. "One family commits mass murder on another family?"

"Well, they sort of commit mass murder on each other," Maggie said. "That's why they call it a feud."

Seymour shook his head. "I've learned a lot about the West in the relatively short time I've been here, and there's a great deal I like about it. But I'm not sure if I'll ever become accustomed to the cheapness with which human life is regarded on the frontier."

Maggie stopped, which made Seymour come to a halt as well. She turned toward him and said, "It's only some of the people who feel that way, Seymour. We're not all like that. I wish there never had to be any violence at all. I . . . I worry about you being the marshal and all. Something could happen to you."

"I'll be fine," he told her with a smile. "I'm learning all the time how to handle the job, and as long as I have Matt and Sam around to help me—"

"But that's just it," Maggie interrupted. "Mr. Bodine and Mr. Two Wolves won't be around Sweet Apple forever. They're drifters, Seymour. You'll wake up one morning and they'll be gone."

"I know," he said. "Matt warned me that they were . . . violin-footed, I believe was his word, although I'm not quite sure I understand the derivation of it."

Maggie couldn't help but laugh softly. "Fiddle-footed, Seymour. I'm sure he said fiddle-footed."

"Oh. Yes, I believe he did. I suppose that makes a bit more sense. But at any rate, I know that the time will come when I have to maintain law and order in Sweet Apple by myself. I'm confident that by then I'll be up to the job."

"I hope that's true, Seymour." She slipped her arm through his as they started walking again. "You don't know how much I hope that's true."

Her words made his heart swell. During his time in Texas, he had grown very fond of Miss Magdalena Elena Louisa O'Ryan. She was smart and pretty and very sweet. She was devoted to her job of educating the town's youngsters—often whether they wanted to be educated or not—and Seymour found that quite admirable. Civilization brought education, and education brought progress of all sorts. The better educated people were, the less likely they would be to settle all their arguments and disputes with gunplay. Feuds such as the one between the Coltons and the Paxtons would cease to exist.

As if reading his mind, Maggie said, "You know, I'm sure there are people back East who are prone to violence, too."

Seymour shook his head. "Not like there are out here," he insisted. Continuing with the line of thought that had just been occupying his mind, he said, "Take the Coltons and the Paxtons. These are two of the leading families in the entire area. They own successful ranches. Their children are educated. They're not low-bred hooligans. And yet, if hostilities between them continue to escalate, there's a good chance that soon they'll be shooting at each other. Something like that would never happen back in New Jersey, where I come from. People are simply too civilized there to resort to such tactics."

"Maybe you're right, Seymour," Maggie said with a sigh. She didn't sound like she fully believed it.

Seymour did. No respectable Easterner would ever resort to violence to remove an obstacle from his path.

It just wasn't done.

In Trenton, New Jersey, Cornelius Standish sat behind the big desk in his office, in the building that housed the Standish Dry Goods Company, and intently regarded the three men who stood before him.

Warren Welch was a fresh-faced young man with curly brown hair and a friendly expression. You had to look at his cold, snakelike eyes to know what sort of man he really was. Daniel McCracken was a redheaded, belligerent Irishman. Standish didn't fully trust him, but he was said to be good at his job. Ed Stover was the tallest and the oldest of the three, a broad-shouldered man with a mostly bald head and a fringe of gray hair under his pushed-back derby.

All three men were associates of the late Wilford Grant, who had been hired by Standish to do a particular job—and who had failed miserably at that job. Grant and his cohort Spike Morelli had paid for that failure with their lives, but that didn't help Standish. He was still faced with the same problem he had sent Grant and Morelli to Texas to take care of for him.

McCracken pushed his jaw out and said in a surly voice, "I ain't sure I'm carin' for th' job ye've proposed, Mr. Standish. Who in his right mind is goin' t' believe that we're dry-goods salesmen?"

"No one will question it," Standish snapped, "because I'll be with you."

Stover scratched at his bald pate with a blunt finger. "That worries me a little, Mr. Standish," he said. "You comin' along with us, I mean. No offense, but we can handle this without havin' you lookin' over our shoulders."

Standish shook his head. "I made that mistake once already when I trusted Grant and Morelli. This time I'm going to make sure that nephew of mine is out of the way."

It was bad enough that Seymour owned half of the Standish Dry Goods Company, the company that had been built into a success by Cornelius and his brother, Seymour's late father. Half of the profits that should have belonged to Cornelius now went into Seymour's bank account, even though he was no longer here in New Jersey and had resigned his position as a salesman for the company.

The thing that was really goading Standish to take

action against Seymour was the way the company was increasing its ties to the criminal element in Trenton and elsewhere in New Jersey and New York. One way to increase business was to make it difficult for your competitors to be successful. If it took beating up deliverymen or artificially inflating freight rates for everyone else or even seeing to it that a fire "accidentally" broke out at a rival company's warehouse . . . well, that was just business. A smart man didn't draw the line at whatever tactics were necessary. The only "line" that mattered was the one that showed a profit or loss in a ledger.

But Seymour—soft, gullible, innocent Seymour— wouldn't understand that. If he ever found out about the way his uncle had the company branching out into legally questionable enterprises, he would cause a big stink and ruin everything. Cornelius Standish was sure of it.

Therefore, something had to be done about Seymour. Standish had thought that dispatching him to Sweet Apple, Texas, would take care of that. The place had a reputation for being one of the most dangerous settlements on the frontier. Standish had been certain that Seymour wouldn't last a week there before one of the local badmen gunned him down.

That had almost happened, in fact, but somehow Seymour had survived. Not only survived, but apparently he was thriving in Sweet Apple, as unbelievable as that might be. Those idiots had even made him the town marshal, and now he was regarded as some sort of hero.

That wouldn't last, Standish had vowed. He would see to that himself, with the help of the three men who now stood before him.

He continued. "Until I've had a chance to look the situation over and decide on the best plan of action, the three of you will pretend to be salesman who will be working the western part of Texas for the company. You shouldn't have to actually sell anything because I don't expect it to take very long to accomplish our real goal. Now, are all of you in . . . or not?"

Welch, McCracken, and Stover exchanged glances. They were brutal, uneducated men, but they were experienced enough and had enough natural cunning to know that if they backed out now, after Standish had revealed his plans to them, they would be putting their own lives in danger. Behind Cornelius Standish's smooth, prosperous veneer was a man who was every bit as ruthless as they were.

"We're in," Welch said as he jerked his head in a curt nod. The other two agreed.

"Very well," Standish said, keeping his face and voice expressionless so he wouldn't reveal how pleased he was by their decision. "We'll be leaving for Texas on the eleven o'clock train tomorrow morning."

With their business concluded, the three men left Standish's sanctum. When they were gone, Rebecca Jimmerson came in from the outer office. A beautiful young woman with sleek, honey-blond hair, Rebecca was Standish's secretary—and his mistress. She asked, "Did they agree?"

"Of course. They'll be well paid, and they know it. I'll need you to go down to the train station and purchase four tickets on the eleven o'clock westbound."

Rebecca came over to the desk and perched a trim hip on it so that she could lean closer to Standish. "Why don't I purchase five tickets," she suggested, "and make two of them for a sleeper?"

"*You* want to go?"

"I've never been to Texas," Rebecca said. "In fact, I've never seen anything west of New Jersey."

Standish shook his head. "From everything I've heard, Texas is a horrible place. You wouldn't like it."

"I was thinking that when your business was done there, we might go on to San Francisco for a week." She touched his cheek with soft fingertips and murmured, "Wouldn't you like to spend a week in San Francisco with me, Cornelius?"

She wasn't supposed to use his first name when they were in the office like this, but he couldn't bring himself to be angry with her. Not with the way her delicate scent filled his senses and the warmth of her breath brushed his face. Even though he tried not to, he couldn't help but think about San Francisco and all the things they could do there . . .

"I suppose it would be all right," he conceded. "The office can get along without both of us for a while."

"Of course it can." She leaned closer and nuzzled his ear. "Thank you, Cornelius."

He slipped an arm around her waist, pulled her onto his lap, and kissed her. After a moment, he drew back and said in a voice that was rough with desire, "Go lock the door."

"Of course."

It was dangerous, indulging their passion in the office like this, but Standish didn't care. He wanted her too badly to hesitate.

And his need was fueled by something else, too, something that filled him with power and made his fleshly appetites even stronger.

That something was the sure and certain knowledge that soon, very soon, his nephew Seymour would be dead.

Chapter 3

Jessica Colton knew she made an appealing picture as she rode along with the wind making her long red hair stream out behind her head. She wore trousers and a man's shirt and rode astride, even though she knew that scandalized her mother Carolyn. A sidesaddle was fine for cantering through a city park back East; Jessie had done that more than once. But for pure enjoyment there was nothing like galloping over the West Texas hills and plains, and that required some real riding.

She had ridden out today, the day after the dance in Sweet Apple, to meet Sandy Paxton at the creek that formed part of the boundary between the Double C and Pax ranches. Her father had tried to discourage her from spending so much time with Sandy, but Shad Colton knew better than to forbid his strong-willed daughter from doing anything. That would just make Jessie even more determined to do it.

She knew from things Sandy had told her that her father, Esau Paxton, was the same way. Esau didn't like the two of them being friends, but it was much too late to do anything about that now. Jessie and Sandy had been close companions ever since childhood. They had grown up together, more like sisters than second cousins, and gone away to school together. It was while they were back East that the rift had developed between their families. Neither young woman knew what had caused it, but whatever it was, they didn't see any reason why it should keep them from being friends.

Jessie came in sight of the creek, which ran roughly north and south, rising in the rugged hills and meandering some twenty miles before finally running into the Rio Grande. Pax lay to the east of the stream, Double C to the west. Both spreads extended on into the hills, past the spring where the creek bubbled to life, and up there the boundary was less well defined. That didn't matter much, because all the good graze was down here along the creek. The stream's banks were dotted with scrubby cottonwood and mesquite trees, as well as the occasional desert willow or oak.

Sandy hadn't gotten there yet, Jessie saw as she reined to a halt on the bank, in the shade of one of the cottonwoods. They had agreed to meet here this morning so they could talk about everything that had happened at the dance the night before.

Sandy would want to talk about Sam Two Wolves, Jessie thought with a smile. Sandy thought Sam was just about the handsomest man she had ever seen, and the fact that he was half-Cheyenne didn't bother her. It wasn't like he was Apache or Comanch'. That would have been different. The Cheyenne weren't longtime blood enemies of the pioneer families that had settled in West Texas.

Jessie had to admit that Sam was a good-looking man. But Matt Bodine was better looking, she thought.

She and Sandy had met Matt and Sam at the train station in Marfa when the young women were returning to Sweet Apple from school. There'd been some trouble there, and two hardcases who had been bothering Jessie and Sandy had made the mistake of drawing on the blood brothers when Matt and Sam intervened on their behalf. Those fools had wound up lying dead on the platform.

It might have turned out like that anyway, since both of the girls had been packing iron and knew how to shoot. That fancy Eastern school had taught them quite a bit, true enough, but it hadn't *changed* them, made them something they weren't. They were still West Texas gals, through and through.

They had enjoyed talking to Matt and Sam on the train after that, although Jessie figured that Mr. Matt Bodine was pretty full of himself. Sam was quieter and more modest.

But Sam didn't have the same sort of reckless, devil-may-care attitude about him that Matt did, and whether she wanted to or not, Jessie had to admit that she found that attitude mighty appealing in a man . . .

Not that she was any sort of expert on men or anything like that, she reminded herself as she felt a warm flush creeping over her face. It was best not to think too much about how handsome Matt Bodine was.

The drumming of hoofbeats made her look up. She spotted Sandy on the other side of the creek, riding toward her.

And something was wrong, too, Jessie realized as Sandy came closer. Her friend had a worried look on her face.

Sandy rode across the creek, the hooves of her horse

splashing the shallow water. She brought the animal to a halt. Like Jessie, she wore men's clothes and a broad-brimmed Stetson. Her blond hair was pulled into a thick braid that hung down her back.

"What's wrong, Sandy?" Jessie asked.

"Pa fired Jeff Riley this morning."

Jessie's mouth tightened. "Good riddance, I'd say. I know he was a good bronc-buster, but I never liked him. I saw the way he looked at you sometimes in town, when you didn't know he was watching you."

Sandy made a dismissive gesture. "I knew it. I just didn't let it bother me all that much. Hell, girl, men have been looking at both of us like that for quite a while now."

Jessie couldn't help but grin. "Yeah, I know. Sometimes I don't mind . . . depending on who's doin' the lookin'."

That brought a laugh from Sandy, relieving her grim demeanor for a few seconds. It came back quickly, though, as she said, "I don't trust Riley. He's liable to try to get even with Pa."

"Why'd your father fire him? Because of that ruckus in town last night?"

Sandy nodded. "That's right. Everybody had strict orders not to cause any trouble, no matter what."

"The same was true for the Double C riders," Jessie said. "My pa gave Tom Danks a good, old-fashioned chewing out this morning, since it was Tom that Riley almost drew on . . . but he didn't fire him."

"Riley cussed my father," Sandy went on. "I thought for a second Pa was going to have him horse-whipped and then thrown off the ranch. But Riley left on his own."

"I reckon he was pretty mad, all right. He got knocked out by Matt Bodine last night and then lost his job this morning."

"He'd better be glad he didn't try to draw on Matt or Sam," Sandy said. "If he had, he'd be dead now."

Jessie gave a solemn nod. She and Sandy had seen a first-hand demonstration of how well Matt Bodine and Sam Two Wolves handled their guns, right after they'd first met the two handsome, charming drifters.

They had figured Matt and Sam for no-account gunslingers at first, but Shad Colton and Esau Paxton both had heard of the vast ranches that the blood brothers owned in Montana and had set their daughters straight. Matt and Sam might look and act like saddle tramps at times, but that was hardly what they were.

"Well, there's nothing we can do about Riley," Jessie said, "and anyway, your pa can take care of himself. Besides, there's something else that's bothering me."

"What's that?"

"How come that blasted Matt Bodine and Sam Two Wolves didn't ask us to dance last night? What's wrong with them?"

Sandy laughed. "Some girls would be asking what was wrong with *themselves* if a couple of boys they liked didn't ask them to dance."

Jessie gave a defiant toss of her head. "There's nothing wrong with us, and you know it."

"I reckon they must've thought they shouldn't be dancing, since they were there to help the marshal."

"Marshal Standish danced with that little schoolmarm. I saw him."

"Yeah, but Matt and Sam didn't dance with anybody," Sandy pointed out. "At least not that I saw."

"Well, Matt Bodine just missed his chance, that's all I've got to say."

"Yeah, sure," Sandy said with a smile. "If he asks you next time there's a social, you'll fall all over yourself saying yes, Jessie."

"I will not! Why, Matt Bodine can go climb a stump as far as I care—"

The swift rataplan of more hoofbeats silenced her and made both young women turn in their saddles to look in the direction of the sound, which was back toward the headquarters of the Double C. Half-a-dozen riders were coming toward them, trailed by a wagon carrying posts, rolls of wire, and several more cowboys.

"Oh, Lord," Jessie breathed as she recognized the big figure leading the party. "What's Pa up to now?"

Shadrach Colton was the source of the red hair that Jessie and her younger brothers and sisters had inherited, although Colton's still-thick and shaggy mane was shot through with gray. He had the burly build and rugged face of a man who had worked outdoors and worked hard most of his life. As he and the other riders came up to the creek, he reined in and looked at his daughter and Sandy with hard, pale blue eyes.

"Miss Paxton," he said as he gave Sandy a polite nod.

"Hello, Uncle Shad," she replied. Even though Colton wasn't really her uncle, as a child she had referred to him that way, just as Jessie had called Sandy's father Uncle Esau.

"You'd better ride on back home now," Colton told her.

"Sandy doesn't have to go if she doesn't want to!" Jessie flared.

"It's all right," Sandy said. "I'm on Double C range on this side of the creek, after all."

With gruff courtesy, Colton said, "It ain't that, Sandy. You're welcome over here any time. You know that. So's your ma."

"What about Royce and Dave?" Sandy asked, referring to her twin brothers who were two years younger than her.

Colton's mouth tightened. "They stand with your pa, I reckon. Couldn't be any other way, with Esau raisin' 'em."

"What are you going to do?" Jessie demanded. "What are all those posts and wire for?"

"Don't you worry about that," her father said. "Get on back home now."

"Not until you tell me what this is all about," Jessie shot back. Her jaw was tight, too, and her green eyes blazed with defiance. She was her father's daughter, no doubt about that. She jerked a hand toward the wagon and went on. "You always said you'd never have any truck with that . . . that devil wire, you called it. This is open-range country. Always has been and always will be."

Colton sat stiffly in his saddle for a moment, then spit and wiped the back of his hand across his mouth as if he were trying to get rid of a bad taste. "I wish it was still that way," he said, "but the time's come to put up a fence."

"Where? The creek's always been the boundary line between the two ranches."

Colton shook his head. "Nope. Accordin' to the papers filed at the county seat, the boundary is the east bank of the creek, and then a line due north from the spring where it rises."

Sandy's eyes widened with surprise as his meaning

sunk in. "You're going to put a fence on the *other* side of the creek? On my father's land?"

"Pax range stops where the creek starts. That's where the fence is gonna go."

"But . . . but then our cattle can't get to it!" Sandy protested. "What'll they do for water?"

"You got a creek on your range," Colton said with a nod in that direction.

"But it dries up half the year! It's almost dry now! Our stock has always used *this* creek!"

Colton shook his head. "Not any more."

Jessie spoke up again, saying hotly, "Pa, this ain't right—"

"Good Lord, gal!" her father exploded. "What kind o' talk is that? Didn't I send you to school so you could learn how to talk like a proper lady?"

"All right then," Jessie said through gritted teeth. "Father, this isn't right. It isn't proper behavior. And it certainly isn't fair to Mr. Paxton." She took a deep breath. "It's a bunch o' damn bullshit, that's what it is!"

Colton flung a hand toward the Double C headquarters, several miles to the west. "Git!" he shouted at Jessie. "Go on home before I forget that you're damned near growed and paddle you like the spoiled brat you're actin' like!"

Jessie folded her arms across her chest and glared coldly at him. "I'd like to see you try it," she grated.

Father and daughter glowered at each other for a moment before Colton turned and bellowed at the hands who had accompanied him, "Get to work! I want a good stretch o' that fence up before sundown today!" He swung his horse toward Sandy again and went on. "Sandy, gal, you got to go now. I'm sorry."

"I'm going, Uncle Shad," she said, "but I don't believe you're really sorry, or you wouldn't be doing this. I'm going to see what my pa has to say about it. I can't believe he'd ever agree to this!"

She heeled her horse into motion and splashed back across the creek. "So long, Sandy!" Jessie called after her, but Sandy didn't acknowledge the farewell.

The Double C hands who had ridden out on the wagon hopped down, and the ones on horseback dismounted. They showed an obvious reluctance for working with the newfangled barbed wire, which had been introduced several years earlier but was still quite unpopular in Texas. The fact that Shad Colton would resort to using the devil wire was a sign of just how deep his ill feelings toward Esau Paxton really ran.

Jessie watched in dismay as the cowboys began sinking posts along the far bank of the creek and stringing wire between them. Shad Colton dismounted and worked alongside them. He had never been the sort of hombre to ask his men to do anything he wouldn't do himself, which was one reason they felt such fierce loyalty to him.

The work was slow and hard, and it hadn't progressed very far by late morning. That was when Jessie spotted the dust cloud in the distance to the east, on Pax range, and unbent from her anger long enough to say, "Riders comin', Pa."

Colton lowered the fence post he was holding and looked where Jessie was pointing. He grunted and took off the work gloves he had donned earlier. Then he came over to where Jessie still sat on her horse under the cottonwoods and put a hand on the animal's shoulder.

"Jessie, I mean it now," he said in a soft but urgent

voice. "I want you to go home. There's liable to be some trouble, and I don't want you anywhere around here."

"Gun trouble, you mean," Jessie said, trying to keep her voice from trembling with the nervousness she felt. That tension had been growing ever since Sandy rode off. Jessie knew Esau Paxton well enough to be certain that he wouldn't sit still for having his cattle fenced off from water. He would ride out here with some of his men to see for himself what was going on . . . and they would come armed.

Colton shook his head. "I don't reckon it'll come to that—"

"You know better, Pa."

Stubbornly, Colton repeated, "I don't reckon it'll come to that, but if it does, I want you safe, girl."

Jessie reached for the butt of the Winchester that stuck up from the sheath strapped to her saddle. She never went riding without a rifle. She would have felt naked out on the range without a gun.

"I'm a Colton, too," she said as she drew the Winchester. A simple statement, but it spoke volumes.

"Jessie, Jessie," Colton said, shaking his head. "What if Sandy's with them?"

Jessie's blood seemed to turn to ice water in her veins.

But it was too late to ponder what her father had said. With a rattle of hooves, the riders swept up on the other side of the creek and reined in. The air was thick with dust and a sense that all hell was about to break loose.

Chapter 4

During Sandy Paxton's ride back to the headquarters of her father's ranch, she had pondered long and hard about whether or not she ought to tell him about what was going on at the creek. If she did, he was liable to fly off the handle, and then there was no telling what might happen . . . but chances were, it wouldn't be anything good.

When she reached Pax, she spotted her father walking out of one of the barns with a couple of ranch hands, including Gil Cochran, the foreman. A few yards away, Sandy's brothers Royce and Dave perched on the top rail of a corral fence, watching as one of the cowboys tried to break a mustang. Pax would miss the services of Jeff Riley, who had been a top-notch bronc-buster despite the fact that he wasn't very pleasant to be around. Esau Paxton wouldn't abide a man who couldn't—or wouldn't—follow orders, though.

Sandy's mother Julia sat in the shade of the porch that wrapped all the way around the main house. She had her apron full of ears of corn from the vegetable garden and was shucking them, putting the roasting ears in a basket on the porch beside her and tossing the shucks to a pair of goats who stood in front of the porch, waiting for the bounty. Julia waved at her daughter, and for a second Sandy thought about riding over and talking to her first, asking her advice about what she should do.

But she was old enough to make up her own mind, she told herself, and she decided that her father needed to know about the problem at the creek as soon as possible. She turned her horse so that she could intercept him and his two companions.

Esau Paxton knew his oldest child well enough to realize that something was bothering her. "What's wrong, Sandy?" he asked as she drew her horse to a halt.

When you had bad news, it was best to just spit it out. That was what he'd always taught her. So she said, "Shad Colton's fixin' to fence off the creek."

Paxton looked confused. He took off his hat and ran his hand over his mostly bald head. "Fence off the . . . what creek? Not the one between his place and ours?"

Sandy nodded. "That's right."

"Dad-gum it, he can't do that! That creek belongs to both of us! We've always both used it, as long as the spreads have been split up!"

"I know, but he says it's his, and he's going to put up a fence along the east bank."

"You mean *barbed wire*?" Paxton's tone of voice made clear the loathing he felt for the very idea.

"Yeah. He's got a wagon full of posts and rolls of wire out there."

"Where exactly?"

"That spot between Rattlesnake Ridge and the prairie dog town, where Jessie and I always meet."

Paxton's head jerked in a nod. "I know the place.

We'll just see about that." He turned to Cochran, his foreman. "Gil, round up half a dozen of the boys. We're ridin' out."

Cochran looked almost as angry and upset as his employer. "Sure thing, Boss," he said. "Should I tell 'em to bring along plenty of ammunition?"

"Damned right you should."

Worry shot through Sandy. "Pa, Uncle Shad's got eight or ten men out there with him. If you go storming out there with a burr under your saddle, there's liable to be a fight."

"What do you expect me to do?" Paxton snapped. "Our cattle need that creek for water."

"I know, but maybe you should go to town and let your lawyer handle this. In school we learned that it's better to trust the legal system—"

"Back East maybe. Not out here." Paxton turned and stalked toward the house. "I'll get my rifle."

"Pa!" Sandy called after him, but he didn't stop or even slow down. When he reached the porch, he brushed past his wife, who had gotten up by now, setting the corn aside.

"Sandra, what's going on?" Julia asked when Sandy rode over to the house. "What's your father so upset about?"

Quickly, Sandy filled her mother in on what was happening out at the creek. Julia's face grew more and more worried as she listened.

Paxton came out of the house carrying a rifle. Julia turned to him and reached out to stop him with a hand on his arm.

"Esau, where do you think you're going?"

"To set that damned Shad Colton straight," he replied. "He can't get away with such high-handed behavior."

"Why not let the law handle—"

Paxton jerked away from her. "Lord, woman, you're as bad as your daughter!" Without looking back, he went down the steps and headed toward the barn, where several cowboys were already leading out saddled horses.

Sandy watched, her alarm growing, as her brothers hurried over to their father and spoke to him. Paxton jerked his head in a nod and gestured toward the horses.

"Oh, dear Lord," Julia breathed. "He's taking the boys with him!"

Sandy turned to her. "Can't you do anything to stop this, Ma?"

Julia bit her lip and shook her head. "When your father gets all het up like this, there's no stopping him. He won't listen to me or anybody else. He's always been that way."

As the two women watched, the men mounted up and galloped out of the ranch yard, heading west toward the creek. Dust hung in the air from their leave-taking.

Julia turned to Sandy and gripped her shoulders. "Can you ride to town?" she asked.

"Of course."

"Then get there as fast as you can and tell the marshal what's happening. Maybe he can do something about it."

Sandy wasn't sure about that. Seymour Standish had handled himself all right during that showdown with the outlaws and the Mexican bandits, but she wasn't confident in his ability to head off this trouble. Besides, he was the town marshal. His jurisdiction ended at the edge of Sweet Apple.

But there were two men in the settlement who might be

willing to take a hand, and they had a lot more experience with trouble than Marshal Standish did.

Sandy flung herself back in the saddle and galloped hell-for-leather toward Sweet Apple, hoping against hope that she could find Matt Bodine and Sam Two Wolves.

Sandy wasn't with the group from Pax, Jessie saw to her great relief. But Sandy's father Esau was there, along with the twins, Royce and Dave. All of them looked tense and angry, as did the seven cowboys who were with them. The odds were just about even between the two bunches.

Esau Paxton broke the taut silence by demanding, "What the hell do you think you're doing, Colton?"

With a defiant jut of his jaw, the redheaded rancher answered, "Only what I have a legal right to do. I'm fencing the boundary between your land and mine, Paxton."

"The creek is the boundary!"

Colton shook his head. "Not accordin' to the deeds that were drawn up when the CP was divided." The ranch that had been jointly owned by both men had been called the CP, for Colton and Paxton. "The deeds say that the boundary line is the east bank of the creek. You can go to the county seat and look 'em up if you don't believe me."

Paxton glared for a long moment, then shook his head. "That can't be. I looked that paperwork over before I signed the agreements. That's not what it said."

"Go see for yourself."

Jessie thought she detected a little uncertainty on

Paxton's face, as if he thought there was a slim chance that her father's seemingly outrageous claim might be right. The breakup of the CP had been a trying time for everyone involved. It was just possible that Paxton could have overlooked a small detail like that. He could have glanced over the deeds, seen the creek mentioned in conjunction with the boundary line, and assumed that the stream itself formed the boundary and not the eastern bank.

And in the years since then he wouldn't have had any reason to think otherwise, because the Pax cattle used the creek for water just as the Double C stock did. That unopposed access to the creek would have reinforced Paxton's belief that the creek belonged equally to both ranches.

"It . . . it doesn't matter!" Paxton sputtered, so angry that he could barely force the words out. "This is Texas, for God's sake! Nobody fences off cattle from water, no matter what it says on some damned pieces of paper!" He glanced at the young redheaded woman on the other side of the creek and added in a growl, "Sorry, Jessie."

She didn't acknowledge the apology. She didn't care about cussing at the moment.

Her father put his left hand on one of the fence posts and kept his right near the butt of the gun on his hip. "It's true that I've been generous and let your cows drink from this creek, Paxton. But it's *my* creek, and I've decided that I need all the water from it. This is the only dependable water supply on the Double C after all."

"It's the only dependable water supply on Pax, too."

Colton shook his head. "You've got another creek."

"One that's not worth a damn!" Paxton didn't bother apologizing for his language this time.

"That's not my problem," Colton said.

Paxton's eyes narrowed. "It will be when my men tear that fence down."

Colton returned the intense, dangerous stare. "The first Pax man who lays a hand on this fence will get a bullet in his mangy hide."

Paxton didn't say anything to that. After a second, he turned and snapped at his sons, "You boys get on back to the ranch."

"But, Pa—" one of them started to protest. Jessie didn't know which. She'd never been able to tell Royce and Dave apart.

"Do what I tell you, blast it! You shouldn't have come out here in the first place."

While Paxton was trying to order his sons away, Colton made another attempt with his daughter. "Jessie, please ride on back home now."

"And what do I tell Mama when she asks me where you are?" Jessie demanded. "That you're out here getting yourself shot full of holes over a damned fence?"

"Jessie . . . I warn you, gal, I'm not gonna take much more talk like that from you."

Colton stalked across the creek, water splashing up around his boots. Taking Jessie by surprise, he grabbed the reins of her horse from her and hauled the animal's head around.

"Pa, what are you—"

Before she could finish the question, Colton snatched his hat off his head with his other hand and slapped it hard against the horse's rump. *"Hyaaah!"* he shouted.

The horse leaped into a wild gallop, heading away from the creek.

The reins were trailing, and when Jessie lunged to

grab them, she missed on the first couple of tries. After that, it was all she could do to stay in the saddle atop the bolting horse. Over the pounding of its hooves, she thought she heard angry yells.

Then she definitely heard shots as guns began to roar behind her.

Matt and Sam had taken rooms in Sweet Apple's only boardinghouse, which was run by a hatchet-faced widow named Ferguson. Despite her intimidating appearance, she was really a friendly, kindly woman, and her biscuits were just about the best between San Antonio and El Paso. The blood brothers were just about to sit down to lunch in the house's dining room along with some of the other boarders when Sandy Paxton hurried in with a worried expression on her pretty face. Seymour came in behind her, looking a mite worried himself.

"Thank goodness!" Sandy said when she saw Matt and Sam. "Marshal Standish . . . told me . . . I'd probably find you here."

"What's wrong, Sandy?" Sam asked.

She was a little out of breath, probably from a hard ride into town, so it took her a minute to get the answer out. "My father . . . and Jessie's father . . . trouble at the creek between our ranches . . ."

Seymour put in, "Miss Paxton seems to think that there may be shooting."

"Uncle Shad's trying to . . . fence off the creek," Sandy managed to say.

Matt and Sam exchanged a glance as their eyebrows rose in surprise. "Devil wire?" Matt asked.

Sandy nodded.

On nearly all of the vast ranches that filled the frontier from Montana to Texas, from the Milk River to the Rio Grande, open range was the rule. True cattlemen hated barbed wire with an unmatched passion. For Shad Colton to stoop to using the stuff, the rift between Double C and Pax had to be even deeper and more bitter than anyone had realized. Sandy was right—to deny water to thirsty cattle, and to do it by using devil wire, was a surefire recipe for gunplay.

She gasped out directions to the place where the confrontation was going to take place. Then Seymour stepped forward.

"Miss Paxton thought you two might be able to do something to stop her father and Mr. Colton from killing each other," he said. "I'll come with you."

Matt and Sam shook their heads at the same time. "No offense, Seymour," Sam said, "but you don't have any authority out there."

"Neither do you," Seymour pointed out.

"Yeah, but we don't have a marshal's job to lose," Matt said. "We're just a couple of saddle tramps, remember?" He jerked his head at Sam. "Let's ride."

There was no hesitation on the part of either blood brother. They liked Jessie Colton and Sandy Paxton, and they didn't want either of the young women having to mourn a dead father. They felt some respect for Shad Colton and Esau Paxton as well. Both ranchers were the sort of rock-solid pioneers who were helping to settle the West. Other than their hatred for each other, each was as fine an hombre as you could find.

"Thank you," Sandy called after Matt and Sam. She swayed, suddenly a little unsteady on her feet, and put a hand on one of the chairs next to the dining table to brace herself.

Quickly, Mrs. Ferguson came up to her, put an arm around her shoulders, and urged her to sit down and get off her feet for a spell. "Land's sakes, child, you're plumb worn out! You must've just about rode your horse into the ground gettin' here so fast."

Seymour followed Matt and Sam outside as they went to the stable behind the boardinghouse where their horses were. As they saddled up, Seymour said again, "I can come with you."

"You've got a job to do here in town," Sam said. "The citizens of Sweet Apple are counting on you to keep the peace."

"Besides," Matt added, "it'll be better if you don't take sides in this fight. Men from Pax and the Double C ride into the settlement all the time, and it's best that none of them think you're one of the enemy. They'll be more likely to behave themselves that way."

"Well, yes, I suppose I can see that," Seymour admitted. "And I doubt that my presence would be that helpful anyway. What sort of trouble could I handle that Matt Bodine and Sam Two Wolves couldn't?"

Seymour needed to stop downgrading himself that way, Matt thought, but that conversation could wait until another time. Right now, he and Sam needed to get out to the creek between Pax and the Double C as fast as they could, so that maybe those two old he-wolves wouldn't shoot each other full of holes.

They swung up into their saddles and put the horses into a hard run out of town. During the weeks they had been around Sweet Apple, they had ridden over the surrounding range several times, familiarizing themselves with the landscape. That was just habit. The more you knew about a place, the better, because you never knew when you might need to get from one spot to another in a hurry. And both of the blood brothers had a frontiersman's eye. Once they had ridden over a trail, they would never forget it.

Because of that, they were able to make good time, but still, it was a good five miles from the settlement to the creek and it took a while to get there. With every minute that passed, Matt and Sam worried that a gun battle might have already broken out.

They were still half a mile from the creek, Matt reckoned, when he heard a faint popping over the drumming of hoofbeats. He glanced over at Sam and saw that his blood brother had heard the same thing. Those were gunshots, no doubt about it.

And it meant they were too late to stop this range war before it started.

Chapter 5

A couple of minutes later, Matt and Sam came in sight of the line of trees that marked the course of the creek. They were on the western side of the stream, so they couldn't see very well what was going on to the east. The cottonwoods and mesquite screened off that part of the view.

But it was obvious that the continuing gunfire came from over there. Clouds of smoke rose into the air, indicating that a lot of powder was being burned. Of course, Matt and Sam already knew that from the constant crashing of shots.

Movement on this side of the creek caught their attention. A rider careened at top speed across the flats. The long red hair blowing in the wind told Matt that the person in the saddle of that madly galloping horse was Jessie Colton.

"That horse is a runaway!" Sam called.

"I know!" Matt replied as he swung his mount into a course that would intercept the horse carrying Jessie. She seemed to have her hands full just hanging on. Matt figured she was a good rider, but even an excellent horsewoman would have trouble bringing a horse under control once it had lost its head.

He knew he was leaving Sam to deal with the fight between the forces from the Colton and Paxton ranches, at least for the time being, but he couldn't help it. If that runaway horse stepped in a hole and tripped, or didn't see a gully in time to avoid it, Jessie's life would be in definite danger. Matt had to help her if he could.

His horse stretched out underneath him, running for all it was worth. Matt had been riding the rangy gray stallion for several years and knew the animal had plenty of strength, speed, and stamina, despite its mean-eyed, unprepossessing appearance. They swept over the plains now like a centaur, man and horse working together as one.

As they closed in on Jessie Colton and the runaway horse, Matt could see the fear on the young woman's face. Jessie hadn't given up, though. She was still trying to get hold of the trailing reins. It appeared that she couldn't quite reach them.

Matt turned his horse more, so that he was riding in the same direction as Jessie. Leaning forward over the stallion's neck, he urged the gray on. Gradually, the distance between Matt and Jessie began to shrink. He drew alongside her and reached over, balancing precariously in his saddle and trusting to his mount to maintain a steady pace. His fingers brushed the dangling reins. Matt strained forward and closed his hands around the lines. He straightened in the saddle and hauled back on them.

Jessie's horse settled down as soon as it felt a strong hand on the reins. Matt slowed both animals to a walk and then brought them to a stop. He held out the reins to Jessie and said, "Here you go."

She was trembling and holding tightly to the saddle horn. But with a flare of defiance in her eyes, she let go of the horn with one hand and took the reins from Matt.

"Thanks. I could have gotten him under control, but I appreciate you giving me a hand."

Matt was about to grin at this display of stubborn pride on Jessie's part, but a fresh spurt of gunfire from the creek made both of them turn in their saddles and stare back in that direction.

"You've got to stop them before they all kill each other!" Jessie cried.

"I reckon Sam's working on that already," Matt said. He couldn't resist adding, "But I'll go see if I can give *him* a hand, too."

When Matt had peeled off to go to Jessie's rescue, Sam had continued on toward the creek. Not at the breakneck gallop Matt was using. Sam proceeded more cautiously, because he didn't know exactly what he was getting into and lead was flying over there.

He got proof of that when he heard the wind-rip of a bullet passing uncomfortably close to his head. He rode into the trees along the western bank of the stream and swung down from the saddle, pulling his Winchester from the saddle boot as he did so. The cottonwoods and mesquites weren't very tall and had slender trunks, but they were better than nothing as far as cover was concerned. Sam pressed his back against a cottonwood trunk and edged his head around for a look-see.

Close to a dozen men were sprawled on their bellies along the eastern bank, firing at a low hummock of ground about a hundred yards away. The slight rise was forty or fifty feet long. Puffs of gun smoke rose from the grassy crest.

Sam spotted the burly figure of Shad Colton among the men lying along the creek bank. It was pretty easy to figure out what had happened. When the battle had broken out, Colton and his men had dug in here, using the bank for cover, while Paxton and *his* men had retreated and taken shelter behind that hummock. Neither force was in a particularly good position, and judging from the smoke Sam saw along the rise, they were about equal in numbers. It was a standoff. They could keep this up as long as they didn't run out of ammunition.

Although Sam saw a few bright splashes of blood on the clothes of the Double C men, none of them seemed to be badly wounded. They were all still in the fight. He hoped the same was true of Esau Paxton and the Pax riders.

But even if it was, things wouldn't stay that way. Somebody was bound to be killed if this kept up. Sam didn't want that.

So he did the only thing he could to break up this stalemate. He drew a bead with his Winchester and blew Shad Colton's hat right off his head, drilling it neatly through the crown.

By the time Colton's hat flew in the air and the red-headed rancher let out a yell of surprise, Sam had worked the rifle's lever and was ready to fire again. As Colton started to roll over, Sam bellowed, "Hold your fire! Don't move! Hold your fire, or I'll drill your boss next time, not his hat!"

He wasn't going to shoot Colton, but the rest of the men didn't have to know that. As the gunfire died away, Sam heard hoofbeats coming closer. He risked a glance and saw Matt approaching at a gallop. That had to mean Jessie was all right.

"Matt!" Sam called. "Bring in the Paxton bunch!" He waved a hand toward the hummock to indicate where they were located, while keeping the Winchester pointing at Colton with the other hand.

Matt waved to show that he understood, and turned his horse to circle around the spot where Sam had taken Colton's men prisoner. The guns along the crest of the rise had fallen silent, too, in response to the Double C ceasing fire.

It was a precarious truce, though. One of Colton's men yelled, "Damn it! There's only one man back there in the trees! I don't care if he does have the drop on us, we can blast him to hell!"

An older man with a ruggedly powerful face said, "I recognize that hombre. He's Sam Two Wolves. If you want to get a hole blowed through you, you just try to gun him, Sloan!"

The loudmouth didn't seem to care much for that idea. He didn't say anything else. But Sam knew that he was still facing nearly a dozen armed, angry men, and even though he had them at a slight disadvantage right now, that might not last very long.

"What do you want, Two Wolves?" Shad Colton demanded.

"For you to show a little sense, Colton," Sam snapped. "Going to war against Paxton's not going to solve anything."

"Tell that to Paxton. He's the one who started the ball, damn it! One of his men fired the first shot!"

Sam didn't know if that was true or not, since he hadn't been here when it happened. It didn't surprise him that Colton made such a claim. Men who were mixed up in a feud always felt like they were in the right and the other side was in the wrong.

Meanwhile, Matt pulled out his bandanna and tied it to the end of his rifle barrel. The bandanna was red, not white, but he hoped it would serve as a flag of truce anyway. Either that, or it would be like waving a red flag in front of a bull, he thought with a grim smile as he rode toward them with the rifle barrel upraised. He saw one of Paxton's cowboys holding their horses, about two hundred yards behind the hummock.

Paxton and his men had stopped shooting, and they held their fire as Matt approached. They turned so that they could cover him, though, and he felt distinctly uncomfortable with nearly a dozen rifles and six-guns pointing at him. Several of the men had bloodstains on their clothing, but none of them seemed to be hurt badly. In the dime novels, everybody was a great shot, but in reality, a gunfight was a confusing, terrifying blur to most men. Sometimes hundreds of shots were fired without doing any serious damage. That appeared to be the case here, at least on the Paxton side. Matt couldn't say yet about Colton and his men.

"Bodine!" Esau Paxton said as Matt reined to a halt a few yards away. "What are you doing here?"

"Tryin' to keep you idiots from killin' each other," Matt said, not bothering to be diplomatic about it. Diplomacy had never been his strong suit anyway. "Your daughter rode into Sweet Apple and told us what was goin' on out here."

Paxton glared at him. "You've got no authority except in the settlement, and you're not even real deputies there. What the hell makes you think you can tell us what to do?"

Matt had lowered the Winchester as he reined in, and he smiled thinly as he said, "The fact that I've got this rifle pointed at you, Paxton. That's why I think I can tell you what to do."

Paxton paled a little, but he didn't lose any of his belligerence. "You pull that trigger and you'll be full of lead a second later," he threatened.

"More than likely," Matt agreed. "But you'll be dead before me."

Their gazes dueled for a second, Paxton's hot rage doing battle with Matt's icy-nerved calm. Matt won out, as Paxton growled at his men, "Hold your fire. Put your guns down." He turned back to Matt. "What do you want from us?"

"Go on back over to the creek and talk to Colton," Matt said. "Just you. Your men stay here."

Paxton gave a snort of disgust. "That bastard's liable to shoot me. He already tried to. He and his men started this fight, not us."

"I don't care who started it. And Colton's not gonna shoot anybody, because my blood brother Sam Two Wolves is holding a gun on him right now. Get it through your head, Paxton—this fight's over."

Paxton didn't look like he believed that for a second. He said, "Have Colton come out of the trees and meet me halfway. Then maybe I'll talk to him. Although it's not going to do a damned bit of good. That hardheaded son of a bitch won't listen to reason. He never would."

Matt thought about it for a second and then nodded. "Sam!" he called. "Send Colton out! Paxton's gonna come talk to him—alone!"

Matt didn't know if Colton would agree to that, but a moment later the redheaded rancher appeared, stalking forward. With a jerk of the rifle barrel, Matt indicated that Paxton should go out and meet him. Paxton walked over the top of the hummock and started toward Colton. A muscle in his jaw was jumping from the strain of how hard his teeth were clamped together.

Matt followed Paxton on horseback. He hated turning his back on Paxton's men, but he didn't figure any of them would take a chance on shooting him out of the saddle, not with his Winchester still trained on their boss. They had no way of knowing how sensitive the rifle's trigger was.

Colton and Paxton stopped when about ten feet still separated them. "I don't know why these two crazy hellions wanted us to talk to each other," Colton said. "I don't have anything to say to you, Paxton."

"And I wouldn't want to listen to it if you did," Paxton snapped in reply.

"Then talk to *me*," Matt suggested from his position behind Paxton. "What in blazes is this ruckus all about?"

Paxton turned his head to look at Matt. "This bastard plans to fence off my cattle from that creek!"

"It's *my* creek!" Colton insisted. "I got every right to put up a fence if I want to."

"The creek belongs to both of us! That's the way we split it up!"

"Not accordin' to the paperwork at the county seat," Colton said. "The boundary line is on *this* side of the creek. That means all the water belongs to me."

Keeping his own voice calm and reasonable, Matt said, "Out here on the frontier, folks share water when they can. That's just the way things are done."

"My cows need it," Colton snapped.

"So do mine," Paxton said. "And no legal shenanigans are going to keep them from it!"

Colton's hands clenched into fists. "Are you accusin' me of bein' crooked?"

"You must be trying to pull a fast one with those papers you keep talking about. I never would've signed over full ownership of that creek to you, and you know it!"

Matt frowned in thought. "What do those documents at the county seat say exactly?"

"They say that the boundaries o' the Pax ranch run from Big Turtle Draw on the east to Garford Creek on the west." Colton pointed to the tree-lined stream. "That's Garford Creek, although folks don't hardly ever use the name."

"That the way you remember it, Paxton?" Matt asked.

"Yeah, but . . . but that doesn't say that my range ends on this side of the creek. It says it runs all the way to the creek."

"All the way *to* the creek," Colton repeated with a note of triumph. "Not to the midpoint of the creek. *To* the creek."

"Will you stop saying that?" Paxton shouted. He pointed a shaking finger at Colton. "You know damned well what it means! It means we both own the creek!"

Colton shook his head. "That ain't what it says, so that ain't what it means."

"I've been watering my cows there for years! You never claimed I didn't have any right to the water!"

"Didn't care until now," Colton said with a shrug. "Now I do."

"You . . . you son of a . . . I never thought you'd stoop so low . . . you snake-blooded bastard!"

"Bluster all you want," Colton sneered. "It don't change nothin'."

"Listen to me, Paxton," Matt said. "It sounds like Colton's got the law on his side. Maybe that wasn't the way you intended for the deeds to read, and maybe nobody ever even thought about the way they could be applied, but Colton's within his legal rights."

Stubbornly, Paxton shook his head. "You're not a lawyer, Bodine. You're just a damned gunslinger!"

"If you want to fight Colton's claim in court, you go right ahead," Matt told him. "I don't give a damn one way or the other about that, just like I don't care who owns that creek." His voice hardened. "But your daughters don't want you two old pelicans fillin' each other with lead, and I like to oblige the ladies whenever I can. So for today, both of you turn around and go home."

"I got a fence to put up," Colton protested.

Matt shook his head. "Not today. Let it go. Go home and cool off. See that whatever bullet creases your men got in this little dustup get taken care of. And for the rest of the day, damn it, try not to kill each other!"

The two cattlemen glared at each other for a long moment. Finally Paxton said, "I'll sue you."

"Go ahead," Colton snapped. "See if that keeps me from puttin' up my fence."

"Oh, it will. It will. You can't win, Colton. You can't deny water to thirsty cows and get away with it."

Paxton might have a point there, Matt thought. Even though Colton might have the letter of the law on his side, a jury made up of Westerners might well agree with Paxton. In this country, the needs of cattle came before everything else, even legal technicalities.

That was probably the way it should be, too. Lawyers

could always twist everything around beyond all sense of reason.

The important thing was to keep these two from shooting at each other until they calmed down. The rest of it could be hashed out later. Matt prodded them. "Well, are you leavin'?"

"What if we don't?" Colton asked.

"Then you'll have to fight me and Sam."

Paxton snorted. "Two men against twenty!"

"Oh, you mean you'd join forces?" Matt asked with a faint smile.

"Hell, no!" Colton burst out. "I mean . . . Hell, I don't know *what* I mean!" He glared at Paxton. "I'll be back tomorrow to put up that fence."

"And I'll be in court this afternoon to stop you!" Paxton shot back.

"If you're goin' to court, then I can go to court, too, damn you!"

"I reckon I'll see you there then." Paxton turned on his heel and stalked off, heading back to his men.

Colton did the same.

Matt heaved a sigh of relief.

Sam rode out to join him as both groups mounted up and got ready to ride out. Colton's men left the posts they had already put up in place, but the wagon carrying the rest of the posts and the rolls of barbed wire rolled along after the riders as they headed for Double C headquarters. Paxton and his men rode east, toward the Pax ranch house.

"Well, that was mighty damned close to being a massacre," Sam said as he reined in.

"Them or us?" Matt asked with a grin.

"I'm not sure. Wouldn't want it either way. I heard

Colton telling his men that Paxton is going to take him to court."

"Yep. From what I heard, Colton's got the law on his side, but that doesn't always mean much."

"At least they're not shooting at each other. That's something to be thankful for." Sam pointed. "Here comes Jessie."

Matt had already seen the young woman riding toward them. She reined in beside them and said, "I'm not sure how you did it, but thank you, Matt, and you, too, Sam. I thought for sure they were all going to kill each other."

"It could happen yet," Matt warned her. "I hate to say it, but I'm afraid this war between your pa and Esau Paxton isn't over yet. Not by a long shot."

Chapter 6

There were no lawyers practicing in Sweet Apple, since there was no court there. All legal business was conducted in Marfa, the county seat located some twenty miles to the east of Sweet Apple. So for several days Shadrach Colton and Esau Paxton were kept busy traveling back and forth between the settlements. Each man engaged the services of an attorney, and Paxton made good on his threat to file suit against his cousin and former partner.

Matt and Sam didn't really care how that played out. What was important was that the two sides weren't shooting at each other, and peace reigned in Sweet Apple.

Neither of the blood brothers expected that to last, however—and as usual, they were right.

As town marshal, Seymour made a habit of being at the railroad station whenever a train rolled in, either Eastbound or westbound. He considered it part of his duties to check out the passengers who got off in Sweet Apple. So he was standing on the platform, talking through the barred opening of the ticket window with the clerk, Harvey Bramlett, when the two o'clock westbound arrived. It was 2:18, according to the clock inside Harvey's little office, so the train was a little late, but not too much.

With a clatter of wheels, screech of brakes, and hiss of steam, the train came to a stop with the passenger cars lined up next to the platform. Smoke from the diamond-shaped stack atop the big Baldwin locomotive drifted back along the train's length. Seymour turned from the ticket window and watched as the conductor appeared in the vestibule at the front of the first passenger car. The conductor lowered a set of portable steps to the platform, then went down them and turned to call, "Sweet Apple! Sweet Apple, Texas!"

The first passenger off the train was a white-haired man in late middle age who held himself stiffly and wore an expensive suit and hat. He carried a black, silver-headed walking stick in his left hand. When he reached the platform, he turned and extended his right hand to grasp the hand of the young woman who followed him down the steps. A whistle of admiration came from the ticket window as the clerk stared at the honey blonde in an elegant traveling outfit.

"That's a mighty nice-lookin' gal," Bramlett said. "Wonder what she's doin' in Sweet Apple. And is that her pa with her, you reckon, Marshal?"

Seymour swallowed hard. His pulse pounded hard inside his head in pure surprise. Never in a million years would he have expected to see these two people in Sweet Apple.

"No, he's not her father," Seymour said in a voice that sounded hollow to his ears. "But he *is* my uncle."

"Your uncle?"

If Bramlett said anything else, Seymour didn't hear it, because he was already striding across the platform toward the train. The newcomers turned, saw him coming, and stopped in their tracks. They looked a little shocked, too.

"Hello, Uncle Cornelius," Seymour said. He raised his hand to the brim of his hat and tugged on it politely. "Miss Jimmerson."

He supposed his appearance had changed considerably since the last time they had seen him. Instead of the sober suit he had worn when he was a salesman for the Standish Dry Goods Company, he was now clad in black whipcord trousers, a white shirt, and a black vest. A wide-brimmed, flat-crowned black Stetson rested on his head instead of a derby.

And he certainly hadn't had a gunbelt strapped around his waist with the butt of a Colt revolver sticking up from the holster. The only thing still the same about him was the spectacles he wore. Even his face had started to lose its pasty hue and was taking on a bit of a tan.

Cornelius Standish recovered from his shock enough to extend a hand. "Hello, Seymour," he said as he shook hands with his nephew. "I don't mean to stare. It's just that—"

"You look like a character out of a dime novel!" Rebecca Jimmerson broke in. She looked around the platform. "All these people do."

It was true, at least to a certain extent. The other passengers who had gotten off the train so far were people who lived in Sweet Apple or the vicinity of the settlement. They were Westerners, and looked it. The illustrations in the dime novels published back East were exaggerated, of course, but had a core of reality to them. Men in Texas wore big hats and packed iron. That's just the way it was.

Seymour let go of his uncle's hand and turned to Rebecca. She wore stylish gloves, of course. He grasped her hand and shook it as well. The relationship between them had always been polite and friendly, nothing more. Seymour had been quite impressed by her beauty, but he wasn't the sort of man to press his attentions on a young woman. In fact, Rebecca had always made him nervous and tongue-tied whenever he was around her.

It was wonderful for Seymour to discover that that was no longer the case. He was able to smile at her and say, "You look stunning, Miss Jimmerson, despite what must have been an arduous journey out here." Seymour turned back to Standish and went on. "What *are* you doing here, Uncle Cornelius?"

"I'm here because of you," Standish snapped.

Seymour's eyes widened again. "Me?" he repeated.

"That's right. I received the telegram you sent resigning your position with the company as a salesman. I must say that I was disappointed you would abandon your responsibilities like that, Seymour. I believe your late father, rest his soul, would have been disappointed, too."

"I . . . I . . ." Seymour felt his newfound confidence evaporating rapidly in the face of his uncle's disapproval. Finally, he managed to say, "I'm sorry, Uncle Cornelius. I just discovered that I . . . I'm not suited to be a dry-goods salesman."

"That's all you ever were, until you took on this ridiculous job." Standish gestured toward the badge pinned to Seymour's vest. "I suppose you're suited to be a Wild West lawman."

The scorn and disbelief in his uncle's voice sparked a surge of defiance in Seymour. "As a matter of fact," he said, "I've done all right so far."

"The newspapers call you The Most Cowardly Man in the West."

Seymour shook his head. "Not any more. Not since the battle with Deuce Mallory's gang and the raid by Diego Alcazarrio and his bandits." He paused. "Mallory's dead, by the way, and Alcazarrio was sent limping back across the border into Mexico."

Standish waved a hand as if to dismiss those accomplishments, but Rebecca was looking at Seymour with a mixture of respect and interest, two things she had never seemed to feel for him before, Seymour thought.

"It doesn't matter now," Standish said. "What's important is that the company has been left high and dry by your rash actions, Seymour, and I've been forced to come out here myself to set things right."

"You want me to come back to work for you?" Seymour was prepared to argue vehemently against that idea.

"Hardly," Standish said in a cool voice. "You've made your choice, and I suppose I have to accept that. No, I've brought someone to take your place. Three men, in fact, since Texas is such a vast territory."

He half-turned and held out a hand, motioning forward three men who had climbed down from the train after him and Rebecca. They wore Eastern suits, too, although not as expensive and stylish as the one Standish sported.

"These are my new salesmen," Standish went on. "Warren Welch, Daniel McCracken, and Ed Stover."

Welch was a very clean-cut young man with a

friendly smile, but as Seymour shook hands with him, he thought there was something wrong with Welch's eyes. It took a moment for him to realize that they reminded him of a lizard's eyes. Well, perhaps not a lizard exactly, but something similar.

Daniel McCracken made no pretense of being friendly. He barely shook Seymour's hand and gave him a curt, sullen nod.

The bearlike Stover wasn't very effusive either. Seymour supposed that his uncle knew what he was doing—Cornelius Standish had helped Seymour's father build the dry-goods company into a very successful business—but it didn't seem to him that these three men would make very good sales representatives, not even Warren Welch.

Seymour no longer considered that any of his business, even though he still owned half the company. He was content to let his uncle run things as always, and Seymour would just collect his share of the profits. His real work now was keeping the peace here in Sweet Apple.

"I wish you luck," he told his uncle, then nodded to the three salesmen. "All of you. If there's anything I can do to help you, I'd be glad to. I can introduce you to the merchants here in town. I know all of them now."

"That would be fine," Standish said. "But later. We've all had a long journey, and we're tired." He looked around. "I assume there's a hotel in this . . . town?"

He said it as if he thought that Sweet Apple didn't really deserve to be called a town.

"Certainly, there is. Of course, it's not what you'd call fancy. You'd have to go all the way to El Paso for that."

"Take us there," Standish said, falling right back into the old pattern of snapping orders at his nephew.

Seymour let that pass. He knew from experience that it wouldn't do any good to argue with his uncle.

He told one of the porters who worked at the station to gather the bags belonging to Standish, Rebecca, and the three salesmen and have them taken down to the hotel. Then, as he ushered them off the platform and through the lobby of the depot, Rebecca surprised him by slipping her arm through his. Nothing like that had ever happened before, and as Seymour's pulse began to pound again, he felt the pressure of the soft curve of her breast against his arm. His mouth was suddenly dry.

And as they left the station, he found himself thankful that their route wouldn't take them past the school. He wouldn't want Maggie O'Ryan to look out the window and see him walking along arm in arm with the beautiful, smugly smiling Rebecca Jimmerson!

"Why were you playing up to that young fool?" Standish snapped after he had come into Rebecca's hotel room without knocking. Of course, considering their relationship, propriety was hardly required. Still, he could have been more discreet, she thought.

"I wasn't playing up to him," Rebecca said. "I was just being polite."

Standish grunted. "That's not what it looked like to me."

Rebecca smiled and said, "What, are you jealous of your own nephew, Cornelius?"

He snarled as he stepped over to her and grabbed her arms, taking her by surprise. His grip was tight enough to be a little painful, but she didn't let that show on her face.

She had long since mastered the art of not letting *anything* show on her face unless she wanted it to.

"I have no reason to be jealous, do I?" he demanded.

Rebecca shook her head. "None at all."

That wasn't strictly true. Although she would never admit it to Cornelius, and Seymour himself seemed to have no idea, Rebecca felt a certain affection for the young man. That was what had led her to visit his rooming house in Trenton before he left for Texas and give him a gun to take with him. She had known even then that Seymour's uncle intended for the trip to be a fatal one. Standish had counted on the lawless element in Sweet Apple to do the job of getting rid of Seymour for him. Rebecca had been very much afraid that was exactly what was going to happen. She didn't think the gun would really be of much help to Seymour, but she couldn't stand the thought of him coming out here to the Wild West completely defenseless.

Somehow, Seymour had survived. More than that, he had carved out a new life for himself and become the town marshal, which was even more unlikely than his simple survival.

And now that she had seen him in this new persona, Rebecca found herself more drawn to him than ever before.

But she couldn't admit that to Standish. She barely wanted to admit it to herself. There was no point in having any real feelings for Seymour, because with three hired killers now stalking him, his days were numbered. Rebecca knew she couldn't do anything to forestall Standish's plans.

Cornelius Standish always got what he wanted, sooner or later.

Rebecca was living proof of that. She suppressed a shudder of revulsion as his grip on her arms turned into a caress . . .

Seymour was still thinking about the unexpected appearance in Sweet Apple of his uncle, Rebecca, and the three new dry-goods salesmen as he went up the walk to the little house where Maggie lived. She had asked him to supper tonight, but he had suggested that they eat at the café instead, since it wouldn't really be proper for them to be alone together at her house. Seymour didn't want to do anything that might jeopardize Maggie's reputation.

He had put on a black jacket and a string tie to make his outfit more appropriate for an evening out. He still wore his Stetson, though, and the gunbelt. As marshal, he had to be armed, even when he was just enjoying a meal with a young lady. He was sure Maggie would understand. Having grown up around here, she knew more about such things than he did.

He knocked on the door of the neat little adobe house and then took his hat off, holding it in both hands in front of him. Maggie didn't answer right away, as she usually did. Seymour frowned, and was wondering if he ought to knock again when the door opened.

Maggie stood there, wearing a nice dark blue dress with tiny yellow flowers on it. She always smiled prettily when she greeted him, but not this time. She gave him an intense look that Seymour, if he hadn't known better, would have sworn was suspicious and maybe even a little angry.

But she couldn't be angry with him, he told himself,

because he hadn't done anything. Something else must have happened to upset her, he decided. Hoping that she would confide in him, he said, "Good evening, Maggie. How are you?"

"I'm fine," she said. Her voice was cool. "What are you doing here, Seymour?"

He was taken aback by the question. After a moment, he said, "Why . . . we're supposed to have dinner together this evening. Have you forgotten? Or . . . do I have the wrong night?" That had to be it, he thought. Stupid fool that he was, he had gotten mixed up and called for her on the wrong night.

"No, we had a dinner engagement, but I assumed that you'd need to cancel it."

Seymour was getting more confused by the second. "Why would I need to do that?" he asked.

"You have visitors in town. Your uncle . . . and a very attractive young woman."

A common word that Seymour often heard uttered in disgust by cowboys who frequented the Black Bull and the other saloons in Sweet Apple crossed his mind, although of course he couldn't actually say it in front of Maggie. He wasn't sure he could have allowed such a coarse exclamation to cross his lips whether she was there or not.

But he certainly thought it as he realized that someone had told Maggie about him walking arm in arm from the train station to the hotel with Rebecca Jimmerson, with her pressed so intimately against him. Plenty of people in the street had seen them, so there was no telling who had carried the tale to Maggie—or why, other than as sheer gossip.

But surely Maggie would understand and not be

angry once he explained the situation. "It's true that my uncle is in town," he said quickly. "The, ah, young lady is his secretary, Miss Jimmerson. That's all. She and I aren't friends."

Maggie sniffed. "That's not the way I heard it. Mr. Delacroix told me that the two of you seemed *quite* friendly when you walked past the Black Bull with her this afternoon."

So that was who had spilled the beans to Maggie, Seymour thought. Pierre Delacroix owned the Black Bull Saloon; his son Oliver was one of Maggie's students. Seymour knew that Delacroix was friendly with Maggie. He had even wondered if the gambler and saloon keeper had some romantic feelings for her, even though the dapper Cajun probably wouldn't admit it. If that were the case, it would be to Delacroix's benefit to make Maggie jealous of Rebecca. Nothing drove a wedge between people faster than jealousy.

"Mr. Delacroix was incorrect," Seymour stated firmly. "Miss Jimmerson took my arm, but only because she was a bit nervous about being in a frontier town, especially one with a lawless reputation such as Sweet Apple enjoys. I explained to her that there's law and order here now—"

"Provided by you, the heroic marshal." Maggie crossed her arms over her bosom. "I'm sure you told her all about that, too."

"As a matter of fact, I didn't even mention—" Seymour stopped short as he recalled that he *had* brought up the topic of the battle with Mallory's outlaw gang and Alcazarrio's so-called revolutionaries. "I never referred to myself as a hero," he finished, knowing the claim sounded a bit limp.

"Your Miss Jimmerson probably read about you in the newspapers."

"She's not *my* Miss Jimmerson," Seymour insisted. Frustration with the situation and with Maggie's intractable attitude made him add, "If anything, she's my uncle's Miss Jimmerson."

He caught his breath as he realized that was the first time he had ever put into words his long-held suspicion that there was something unseemly going on between Cornelius Standish and the young woman who worked as his secretary. It was scandalous enough that a businessman even had a woman as a secretary. Nearly all of those jobs were held by men. Seymour had always preferred not to even think about what *other* duties Rebecca might be required to perform for his uncle.

"You believe me, don't you, Maggie?" he asked, a note of desperation creeping into his voice. He didn't like hearing it there—he had enjoyed his newfound self-confidence—but there was nothing he could do about it. Even he was surprised by how important it was to him that Maggie not think anything bad about him.

After a moment, her expression softened, but only slightly. "I suppose so," she said. "You've always struck me as a very truthful man, Seymour."

"I certainly try to be," he said. "Does this mean we can go ahead and have dinner like we planned?"

"No, I'm sorry. I'm afraid I've worried myself into a headache, and I don't feel like it. But . . . another time perhaps."

"Of course," Seymour agreed without hesitation. Even with his relative lack of experience, he knew that when a woman said no and extended the hope that she might say yes another time, it didn't really mean anything, but what else could he do besides accept her decision? He went on. "I hope you get to feeling better."

"I'm sure I will . . . now."

Now that he had promised her there was nothing going on between him and Rebecca, that was what she meant, he thought as he put his hat on and turned away. Maggie eased the door closed behind him. He sighed and started down the walk toward the street. Night had fallen while he was talking to Maggie, and the shadows were thick.

But not so thick that he didn't see the indistinct movement nearby—and a second later the gloom in that direction was sundered by a sudden gout of flame from the muzzle of a gun.

Chapter 7

Matt Bodine felt some familiar stirrings inside him. He and Sam had been in Sweet Apple for several weeks now. Most of the time in their travels, they stayed in a town for only a few days, a week at most. Their only lengthy sojourns had been when they returned to Montana to visit their families. Other than that, they had stayed on the move more often than not.

So when Matt felt the wanderlust growing within him, he knew what it was. As he sat behind the marshal's desk in Seymour's office and tipped his chair back, rocking it a little with a booted foot against the desk, he looked across the room at Sam and said, "I've been thinkin' . . ."

Sam was cleaning his Winchester. Without looking up from the task, he said, "We can't leave."

"I didn't say we should."

"No, but when you get to thinking, that's usually what it's about. Either that or some pretty girl."

Matt grinned. "I *do* have an eye for the ladies," he said. "But you're right, that's not what I was thinkin' about."

"Do you really believe that Seymour is capable of handling things here by himself?"

Matt let the chair down. "We didn't sign on to be permanent wet nurses. Besides, he stood up for himself just fine in that big fight with those owlhoots."

"With our help," Sam pointed out. "And now he has to worry about a full-scale war breaking out between Double C and Pax."

"Aw, Jessie and Sandy's daddies will settle all that in court," Matt said with a dismissive wave of his hand.

"Do you really believe that?"

"I'd *like* to believe it."

"So would I," Sam said, "but I don't."

Matt sighed. "No, neither do I, if you come right down to it. Those two old pelicans are too used to getting their own way. Neither one of them will back down, no matter what some judges or lawyers say."

Sam worked the lever of the unloaded gun and nodded in satisfaction at the smoothness of the action. He took cartridges from an open box on the table beside him and began thumbing them through the Winchester's loading gate.

"That's what I think, too," he agreed. "So I don't believe it would be a good idea for us to leave right now."

"So what do we do? We have to leave sometime."

"Maybe we should tell Seymour to start looking around for some permanent, full-time deputies," Sam suggested. "If he could find a couple of good men who actually wanted the job, and if the town council would agree to pay their wages . . ."

"Now you're talkin'," Matt said as he stood up and reached for his hat, which he had dropped on the desk earlier. "I don't really want to go off and leave Seymour in a bad spot, but I've started to get a hankerin' to ride out to California."

"California?" Sam repeated. "What's in California?"

"We won't know till we get there, will we?" Matt asked with a smile as he settled his hat on his head. "That's sort of the whole point, ain't it?"

Sam chuckled. "Where are you going?"

"Thought I'd go get some supper. Want to come along?"

"No, I'll hold down the fort here until you or Seymour gets back."

"Don't hold your breath waitin' for Seymour. He was havin' supper with that little schoolmarm of his. They'll probably go for a walk afterward, maybe do a little sparkin'. I don't expect him back until late."

"That's all right. More power to him."

"Yeah," Matt agreed with a nod. "More power to him."

He left the marshal's office and turned toward the café, still thinking about California. He and Sam had been there before, and had even gotten mixed up in a ruckus or two while they were visiting the so-called Golden State—no surprise there, they generally found the nearest ruckus wherever they were—but it had been a while. He wouldn't mind seeing the ocean again, Matt thought.

Those musings were going through his mind when he heard the sudden roar of a gunshot from somewhere along the street.

One shot didn't necessarily mean anything bad, but a whole flurry of them did, especially when they came from different guns. Matt broke into a run toward the sounds of battle, drawing his Colt as he did so.

He saw spurts of orange flame in the gloom up

ahead. One of the combatants was to his left, two more to his right behind a parked wagon. The man to Matt's left was lying on the ground. Matt suspected that he'd been bushwhacked by the two men behind the wagon. That was how setups like this usually played out. His sympathy naturally went to the fella who was outnumbered, but as he approached, he warned himself that he didn't really know what was going on here.

Then, with a shock of recognition, he realized that the house behind the little yard where the lone man lay belonged to Maggie O'Ryan. Seymour had been headed here earlier. Was he the one who had been ambushed?

That guess was confirmed a second later when the door of the house opened, spilling light from inside. The man in the yard saw it and twisted around, shouting, "Maggie, no! Get back inside!"

Matt recognized Seymour's voice. Another pair of shots rang out from the men behind the wagon, and Seymour grunted as if in pain. He must have been hit, Matt thought.

That cinched it. Matt knew who the bad hombres were here, and veered to the right so that he could get a shot at the men using the wagon for cover.

They must have heard his boots slapping against the dusty street, because one of them suddenly whirled and blazed away at him. Something slammed against Matt's right foot and knocked that leg out from under him as he ran. Thrown off balance, he tumbled to the ground and rolled over a couple of times. Slugs smacked into the dirt near him.

He came to a stop on his belly with the revolver still in his hand. Tipping up the barrel, he triggered twice. One of the bullets ricocheted off a metal fitting on the

wagon. Matt didn't know where the other one went—
but he hoped it was right into the mangy hide of one of
those bushwhackers.

Seymour was still firing from Maggie's yard. Facing
threats from two different directions now, the would-be
killers broke and ran. Matt sent two more shots whistling
after them as they sprinted for the mouth of a nearby
alley, but since neither man broke stride, he figured his
bullets missed.

The men disappeared into the stygian darkness of the
alley. As Matt pushed himself to his feet, he heard their
swift footsteps fading away. They weren't doubling back
to try again. They had given up on killing Seymour and
were taking off for the tall and uncut instead.

Matt's right foot was numb. He didn't know if he was
hit or not, but when he tried to take a step he almost fell,
barely catching himself before he sprawled in the dirt
again. He didn't feel any blood leaking into his boot. He
limped over to the wagon, which was the closest thing
he could grab onto and use to steady himself. When he
lifted his right foot and examined the boot, he saw that
the heel had been shot away. His foot was numb from
the impact of the bullet, but otherwise unharmed.

He couldn't move very fast with his boots uneven like
that, so he holstered his gun and yanked both boots off
his feet, tossing them into the back of the wagon. Then he
drew the Colt again and hurried across the street to
Maggie O'Ryan's front yard. The feeling was starting to
come back into his foot, so his stride wasn't too awkward.

"Seymour!" Matt called. "Seymour, are you all right?"

The door burst open again and this time Maggie wasn't
going to be sent back inside. Now that the shooting was

over, she rushed out, crying, "Seymour! Seymour, are you hurt? Oh, Dear Lord, you can't be dead!"

"I'm not," Seymour replied in a strained voice as he struggled up into a sitting position. Matt and Maggie reached him at the same time and knelt on either side of him.

"Where are you hit?" Matt asked.

"I . . . I don't believe I am."

"Way you grunted, I thought one of 'em had winged you."

"No, a bullet hit the ground quite near my face and threw dirt in my eyes." Seymour wiped at his eyes with his free hand. "It was rather painful, and for a moment I couldn't see anything. But it's getting better now."

Maggie threw her arms around him and hugged him tightly. "Thank God you're all right!"

Matt heard more running footsteps and straightened, thinking that the bushwhackers might be coming back after all. But even in the shadows of evening, he recognized the tall, broad-shouldered figure hurrying toward them.

"Over here, Sam," Matt called.

Sam trotted up, hatless and carrying the Winchester he had been cleaning earlier. "What happened?" he asked. "Is everybody all right?"

"A couple of varmints bushwhacked Seymour," Matt explained. As he turned back toward the marshal, he saw that Maggie had helped Seymour to his feet and was still standing there close beside him, with one arm around him. "You sure you're not hurt, Seymour?"

"I'm fine," he insisted.

"Tell us exactly what happened," Sam urged.

Matt said, "I can tell you that. Those no-good bushwhackers were hidin' behind that wagon over there, and they threw down on Seymour when he came out of Miss O'Ryan's place."

It seemed awfully early to Matt for Seymour and Maggie to be getting back from their supper, but he didn't bring that up. Seymour could explain that part of it if he wanted to.

"Well, it wasn't *exactly* that way," Seymour said, causing Matt to look at him in surprise.

"How was it then?" Sam asked.

"Those men were lying in wait for me when I came back down the walk, true, but they weren't behind the wagon. They walked toward me bold as brass and started to shoot."

"How come you're not ventilated?" Matt wanted to know.

"When I saw them in the shadows, some . . . instinct, I suppose you'd say, warned me. I crouched down and leaped to the side just as they opened fire. Then I lay down on the ground, pulled my gun, and returned their fire."

In the light that came through the open door of Maggie's house, Matt and Sam exchanged a glance. What Seymour had just described was a pretty slick job of reacting to danger. They were a little surprised he had it in him. It was starting to look like he had a gunfighter's instincts. A fella with his talent had been wasted as a dry-goods salesman.

He proved that again by saying, "Perhaps we should go inside. I don't think those scoundrels will be back, but if they were to return, we make awfully tempting targets out here in the light."

Matt clapped a hand on his shoulder. "You're right as

rain, Seymour." He looked at Maggie. "That is, if it's all right with Miss O'Ryan."

"Of course, of course," she said. "Come in. Seymour, you're sure you're all right?"

"Indeed I am." He paused to look around and find his hat, which had flown off his head when he dived to the ground to avoid the bushwhackers' bullets. As he picked the hat up and looked at it, he suddenly swallowed hard and said, "Oh, my."

"What is it?" Sam asked.

"Look," Seymour said. He held up his hat with one hand inside it. A finger poked out through a hole in the crown. "Is that . . ."

"Yep," Matt said. "That's a bullet hole. You may not've got elected, Seymour, but you came damn close to bein' nominated."

Matt waited for Seymour to faint at the realization of how close he had come to dying, but after a moment Seymour just sighed and clapped the Stetson on his head. "I'll have to get a new hat, I suppose," he said.

Matt and Sam both chuckled. They couldn't help it. Seymour the Lily-Livered, he'd been called when he first came to Sweet Apple. Seymour the Icy-Nerved was more like it now.

Once they were all inside Maggie's house with the door closed and the curtains pulled, Seymour continued his story.

"I suppose they thought they could just walk up and shoot me. They weren't expecting me to fight back, or at least they didn't act as if they were expecting it. Once I'd fired a couple of rounds, they turned and ran behind that wagon to continue their assault. Luckily, the light was poor, and I suppose that threw their aim off."

"The fact that you was throwin' lead right back at 'em might've had something to do with it, too," Matt suggested.

"Did you get a good look at them?" Sam asked.

Seymour shook his head. "Not at all. They were never anything but two shadowy figures. I couldn't tell you how tall they were or how they were dressed or anything of that sort."

"Who'd want to kill you?"

"I have no idea. I don't have any real enemies that I know of in Sweet Apple." Seymour frowned in thought. "I had several encounters with various gunmen right after I came to town . . . Cole Halliday, Jack Keller, and Ned Akin all threatened to shoot me at one time or another . . . but those disputes have all been put behind us. If you recall, they fought side by side with us against Mallory and Alcazarrio."

Matt nodded. "I remember. It's not likely any of those three would try to ambush you like that. If they decided they wanted to kill you, they'd do it out in the open, where it would help their reputation as gunslingers."

A surprised smile lit up Seymour's face for a second. "Really? You really think it would help their reputation as gunslingers to kill me?"

"Well, I didn't really mean it like that," Matt said hastily.

"When I first came to Sweet Apple, the only reason they *didn't* shoot me was because they worried that it might harm their reputations. I'd say I've come up in the world."

"Land's sakes, Seymour," Maggie said, "you sound like you *want* those men gunning for you."

"No, no, not at all. It's just nice to think that I'm not completely an object of scorn and ridicule anymore."

"I don't think you have to worry about that," Sam told him. "Let's get back to those hombres who ambushed you."

"I'm sorry," Seymour said with a shrug. "It's a total mystery to me."

"Yeah, me, too," Matt agreed. "But we'll probably have another chance to figure it out."

"What do you mean?"

"Those fellas wanted you dead. Since you're still drawin' breath . . . there's a pretty good chance that sooner or later they're gonna try again to kill you."

Rebecca Jimmerson, wrapped in a silk dressing gown, poured cognac from a crystal decanter into a snifter. On the other side of the hotel room, Cornelius Standish sat in a wing chair smoking a cigar and reading the latest edition of the Sweet Apple *Gazette.* He rattled the newspaper, snorted in disgust, and said, "What a pitiful excuse for journalism. But then, what else can you expect in a frontier backwater like this?"

Rebecca took a sip of the cognac and said, "Sweet Apple has its advantages. No one knows us out here except Seymour, so you don't have to sneak around to see me. You don't have to act as if you're ashamed of me, the way you do back in New Jersey."

Standish's teeth clamped down on the cigar. "I don't do that," he said around it.

Rebecca just shrugged and didn't argue with him. She took another drink of the smooth yet fiery liquor.

A soft knock on the door made Standish turn his head

in that direction. "See who that is," he said. He sat forward expectantly. Rebecca had a pretty good idea what he was thinking.

The three killers who had accompanied them to Texas had done their job already.

Seymour was dead.

And Rebecca felt a sharp pang deep inside as that thought crossed her mind.

She tossed back the rest of the cognac and crossed to the door. When she opened it, she saw the smooth-faced, reptilian-eyed Warren Welch standing there, holding his hat in one hand in front of him. McCracken and Stover weren't with him. Without waiting for Welch to say anything, Rebecca stepped back and motioned for him to come in. For appearances' sake, Standish had his own room across the hall—but it was here to Rebecca's room that Welch had come looking for him.

Everyone knew what she was, Rebecca thought. Even this cold-blooded killer.

Standish came to his feet. "Well?" he snapped.

"McCracken has a bullet hole in his arm," Welch reported. "Stover's patching it up now. We didn't figure it would be a good idea to go to the local doctor, if there even is one in this godforsaken place, with a bullet wound."

Standish nodded. "That was smart thinking. I suppose McCracken must have been shot by accident while you were taking care of Seymour."

"No, he was wounded by that gunslinging nephew of yours."

Standish's forehead creased in a puzzled frown. "What the devil are you talking about?"

"I thought he was supposed to be an incompetent fool. That's the way you described him to us."

"That's the way he's always been," Standish insisted. "He can barely keep from falling over his own feet, and he's frightened of his own shadow."

"He's changed since he came out here, remember?" Rebecca said.

Standish shot an irritated glance at her. She knew he was annoyed not only by what she'd said, but also by the very fact that she had butted into the conversation.

"I don't believe half of what I read in the newspapers about Seymour," Standish said. "Reporters make those things up just to sell papers."

"Well, I'm not making this up," Welch said. "McCracken and I followed your nephew this evening, as planned, and ambushed him when he was leaving a house on the edge of town. It should have been a simple job. But he spotted us and moved like greased lightning. We missed with our first shots, and he returned our fire."

"*Seymour* did that?" Standish sounded like he couldn't believe it.

Welch jerked his head in a curt nod. "That's right. We had to take cover behind a wagon that was parked nearby. McCracken was hit while we were doing that. Then, before we could take care of your nephew, somebody else came running up and started shooting at us."

"Who?" Standish choked out. His face was flushed now from the anger and frustration he felt at the news that Seymour had escaped.

Welch shook his head. "I don't know. Some cowboy. One of Seymour's newfound friends, I suppose. Or just somebody who couldn't resist a fight."

"Where was Stover while this was going on?"

"He was close by. He was going to circle around and try to get a shot at your nephew from behind. But once that other gunman showed up, we decided it would be better to withdraw and try again at another time."

Standish smacked a fist into the palm of his other hand. "So all you really succeeded in doing was to warn Seymour that someone is after him!"

"If you had given us an accurate picture of what we were facing, we would have handled the job differently," Welch said. "This is going to take more planning. Seymour is a dangerous man, and he has friends. But we'll get him, don't you worry about that."

"Seymour? A dangerous man?" Standish sputtered a little as he spoke, as if the words were the most outlandish thing he had ever heard.

For her part, Rebecca found herself both surprised and thrilled to hear that Seymour was still alive. And he hadn't just survived the ambush attempt by his uncle's hired killers. He had fought back and wounded one of them. Rebecca never would have dreamed that such a thing was possible.

Why, if Seymour Standish could actually grow a backbone and demonstrate some skill with a gun, then anything was possible!

Even, perhaps, Rebecca turning her back on the money and all the other creature comforts that her relationship with Cornelius Standish provided?

It was something to think about, she told herself as she poured another drink.

Chapter 8

The little farming village some miles south of the border dozed in the predawn hours. Soon, the women would rise and begin preparing breakfast. In most of the huts, the meal would be a meager one, for this was a poor village. The soil in the foothills of the mountains that loomed over the community was rocky, and crops grew there only grudgingly. The men would stumble from their bunks and eat, then trudge to the fields with a step that was already weary, because men who lived this life were never truly rested.

Yet for all its hardships, life still held a few joys. A golden sky at sunset, a breeze to cool the heat of the day, the laugh of a child, the warmth of a woman's body, an occasional nip from a jug of pulque or tequila . . . these things allowed a man to tolerate all the less-than-pleasant aspects of life.

So their continued existence was precious to the men of the village, and because of that, they did as they were told when the riders came thundering down out of the mountains, galloping into the village with torches blazing in their hands. Guns blasted into the air, and sleepy-eyed men, women, and children hurried out of their homes, only to be herded together and forced to the village plaza by men who appeared to be giants when they were mounted on tall horses. The strangers wore broad-brimmed, steeple-crowned sombreros and carried weapons that gleamed in the flickering torchlight. In the entire village there were only a handful of firearms, most of them ancient shotguns that might not even shoot anymore. The men were farmers, not fighters. Their hands were curved to fit hoes and shovels, not gun butts.

The leader of the invaders was a big, barrel-chested man with a black beard. Just behind him rode a lean, hawk-faced man with a thread of mustache on his thin upper lip. The people of the village recognized both men. The leader was Diego Alcazarrio, the famous revolutionary whose goal was to overthrow the dictatorship of the evil Presidente Diaz. His whippetlike companion was Florio Cruz, Alcazarrio's second in command.

Of course, everyone in the village also knew that "revolutionary" was really just another word for *bandido,* and the struggle against El Presidente's rule was merely an excuse for Alcazarrio and his men to do whatever they pleased and take whatever they wanted. But no one was going to come right out and say that, especially not with Alcazarrio right there to punish anyone unwise enough to do such a foolish thing. Instead, when prodded, they would shout weakly, *"Viva Alcazarrio! Viva la revolución!"*

Life, with all its hardships, was still better than death, after all. Much better than the sort of slow, agonizing death that Alcazarrio could provide for his enemies if he chose to do so.

For a time, little had been seen or heard of the revolutionaries. It was said that they had ventured across the border into Texas on some sort of quest for modern repeating rifles. If so, they had failed. They had returned to Mexico bloodied and beaten. Even Diego Alcazarrio himself had suffered serious wounds at the hands of the hated gringos. There was talk that he might die.

But obviously, he had not, because here he was, as big and strong as ever, and as the citizens of the village huddled together in the plaza and waited to see what he wanted, Alcazarrio rode his big, beautiful horse back and forth in the torchlight in front of them and bellowed, "Amigos! I have come to help you!"

No one from the village could recall ever asking Diego Alcazarrio for his help, but none of them brought that up.

"In my generosity, I bring you an opportunity for greatness!" Alcazarrio continued. "Join me, and together we will strike a blow for freedom and justice! Join me, and we will throw off the yoke of the oppressor! We will bring fear to the hearts of the wicked gringos, and when that evil bastard Diaz hears of our exploits, he will tremble and take to his bed in Mexico City! Join me in seeking vengeance on all who have wronged us!"

Odd, but the farmers and their wives and children could not recall being wronged by anyone except Alcazarrio and others of his ilk, who in the past had taken their crops and their food and at times even some of the young women of the village . . . but again, no one was going to point that out to Alcazarrio, especially when it began to soak in on them what he really wanted.

He was looking for men to join his band of revolutionaries. His gang of *bandidos*.

The great Diego Alcazarrio had fallen on hard times indeed.

Now that the people of the village thought about it, the number of riders with Alcazarrio was less than half of what it had been before his foray across the border. Clearly, his losses had indeed been heavy.

"I have guns and horses," Alcazarrio went on. "I need men to use them, to help in the great struggle against those who would oppress us! Join me in this noble cause, my friends!"

Several of the younger men from the village stepped forward.

That brought wails of dismay from the heavy-set older women who were the mothers of these volunteers. Some of them ran after their sons and clutched at their arms. The young men shook off their mothers. A couple of the women dropped to their knees in the dust and sobbed.

Riderless horses were led forward for the new recruits. They were given rifles—old, single-shot weapons for the most part. They could arm themselves better from the loot of the next raid. Building and equipping an army was a slow process.

Alcazarrio harangued the crowd some more, but the rest of the men shuffled their feet awkwardly and looked down at the ground. Alcazarrio and Florio Cruz exchanged a glance. They could force some of the other men to come with them, but Alcazarrio preferred volunteers. Men fought better when they truly wanted to follow their leaders. General Santa Anna had discovered that when his army of conscripts had allowed those damned Texans to hold them at bay for thirteen days inside the Alamo, and then later when mere hundreds had defeated thousands at San Jacinto. A man had to be fighting *for* something to be truly effective, even if it was only lust and greed.

With a curt motion of his hand, Alcazarrio signaled for the riders to turn and head back up into the hills. They thundered away, torches bobbing in the predawn gloom, and the villagers who remained behind heaved a sigh of relief, other than the women who were still crying at the loss of their sons.

The *bandidos* were gone—this time. But they would be back. The villagers were certain of that.

Sooner or later, evil always came back.

The next morning after the bushwhack attempt on Seymour's life, Matt and Sam walked around the street opposite Maggie O'Ryan's house, intently studying the ground as they searched for any sign that might identify the men who had tried to kill the marshal.

It was no use, though. There had been too much traffic, too many men and horses and wagons that had passed by there. The blood brothers couldn't pick out any footprints that they knew belonged to the bushwhackers.

When they reported as much to Seymour, he shook his head and said, "I simply can't figure out for the life of me why anyone would do such a thing."

"For the life of you is just about right," Matt said. "Next time, they might not miss."

With his face set in grim lines, Seymour nodded. "I know." He stood up and reached for his hat. "Well, I have to go over to the hotel and see my uncle. He'll soon be sending out those new salesmen of his, and I owe it to him to give them as many tips as I can on covering the territory."

"Your uncle?" Sam repeated. "Your uncle's here in Sweet Apple?"

"With new salesmen?" Matt added.

Seymour's face brightened. "That's right. Didn't I mention that to you? Uncle Cornelius arrived on the train yesterday afternoon, along with his secretary and three men who'll be taking over as representatives of the Standish Dry Goods Company here in West Texas."

Matt smiled. "So it takes three men to replace you, eh, Seymour?"

"Well, I wouldn't go so far as to actually say *that*. I didn't set up all that many accounts before I resigned from the company to take the job of marshal. But West Texas is a big sales territory."

"It's just big, period," Sam said.

"So I'm not surprised that Uncle Cornelius has expanded his sales force. What *is* a little surprising is that he came out here to supervise them himself. He's not really the sort of man to be comfortable on the frontier."

"Not like you, eh?" Matt drawled with a grin.

"Oh, I'll be the first to admit that I didn't fit in here at first." Seymour settled his hat on his head. "But this is my home now, and I intend to spend the rest of my life here."

"Well, keep your eyes open," Matt said, "and maybe that life will be a mite longer."

Seymour frowned. "Surely, no one will try to kill me in broad daylight."

"Probably not, but you never know," Sam said. "Just be careful, that's all."

"I intend to be, I promise you." Seymour nodded to them and left the marshal's office.

"We gonna follow him and keep an eye on him?" Matt asked.

"Give him a minute," Sam said. "We don't want him to think that we believe he can't take care of himself." Sam frowned in thought, tugging at his earlobe as he did so. "Does it seem a little funny to you that Seymour's uncle shows up yesterday afternoon, and then last night somebody tries to kill him?"

Matt stared at him for a second, then said, "Why in blazes would Seymour's own uncle want to kill him?"

"I don't know. Probably one thing doesn't have anything to do with the other. It was just an odd coincidence, that's all."

Matt grunted. "And I reckon that's all it was. Maybe those bushwhackers were planning on robbin' the bank or something like that, and they wanted to get the local law out of the way first."

"Maybe," Sam said. He inclined his head toward the door. "Let's go make sure Seymour gets to the hotel all right."

They stepped out of the marshal's office and looked toward the hotel. Seymour had almost reached the building. He nodded and smiled to the townspeople he passed. Several boys trailed along behind him, watching him with something akin to hero worship. That was a far cry from how things had been shortly after his arrival in Sweet Apple, when children had followed him only to jeer and taunt him with cries of "Seymour the Lily-Livered! Seymour the Lily-Livered!"

Seymour disappeared into the hotel. Matt and Sam

looked at each other and shrugged. As long as Seymour was in there, he ought to be safe.

With a friendly nod to the desk clerk, Seymour started up the stairs to the hotel's second floor, where his uncle's room was located, along with the rooms rented for Rebecca Jimmerson and the three salesmen. Only one of the men, Warren Welch, struck Seymour as being the right sort to be a successful salesman. Daniel Mc-Cracken was too sullen, and Ed Stover too big and bear-like and intimidating. But he supposed he could be wrong about them. The only true measure of success was results, and Seymour wished them all luck. He would do what he could to help them. He owed his uncle that much.

Reaching the second-floor landing, Seymour turned and started toward his uncle's room. The corridor was deserted. As he walked along it, he heard a door open behind him but didn't turn around, figuring that it was just another guest departing his or her room.

The next second, Seymour heard the faint scuff of shoe leather on the carpet runner, and this time the sound came from close behind him. He started to whirl around as alarm bells went off in his mind. The other attempt on his life was too recent for him to have forgotten it. His hand stabbed toward the butt of his gun.

"Oh!" Rebecca gasped as she stopped short and flinched backward. "Seymour! What's wrong?"

As she stared at him, he realized how foolish he must look, standing there in a half-crouch with his hand hovering closely over his gun, ready to hook and draw, as

Westerners put it. With a sheepish look on his face, he straightened and moved his hand away from the Colt.

"I'm sorry, Miss Jimmerson," he said. "I didn't mean to startle you."

"You did more than startle me," Rebecca said. "For a second there, I thought you were going to draw your gun and shoot me!"

"I would never do that! You have my sincerest apologies. It's just that . . . well, I'm sure you haven't heard about it, but last night some miscreants attempted to shoot me."

Rebecca put a hand to her mouth in shock. "No! What sort of terrible place is this, Seymour?"

"It's not terrible at all," he said. "It's just . . . different from New Jersey. Very different."

"Evidently." Rebecca composed herself. "Are you looking for your uncle?"

"That's right. I thought I would talk to him and those new salesmen. Perhaps I can give them some advice that might prove useful in expanding the business of Standish Dry Goods here in West Texas."

"That's very generous of you." She moved closer to him and put a hand on his arm. "But that can wait. I want you to come with me and tell me all about everything that's happened to you since you got here. From what I've heard, it's a very exciting tale."

"Oh, I don't know about that . . ."

She smiled and slipped her arm through his before he knew what she was doing, as she had the day before. "Don't be so modest, Seymour. Now come along and talk to me."

"Well, I suppose we could go downstairs and sit in the lobby—"

"We'll go to my room," Rebecca declared.

Seymour felt a surge of nervousness ripple through him. "I don't know. That wouldn't really be appropriate, would it, Miss Jimmerson?"

"Oh, for God's sake, Seymour," she scolded him. "We've known each other for years. You can call me Rebecca. And you don't have to worry about being alone with me in my hotel room." She laughed softly. "I won't attack you or anything."

Seymour felt his face growing warm. More than warm, it was downright hot. He thought about how upset Maggie O'Ryan had been simply because she'd heard about him walking past the Black Bull arm in arm with Rebecca. How would Maggie react if she found out that he had been alone with Rebecca in her hotel room?

Despite his nervousness, though, Seymour had never really been able to argue successfully with a woman, especially an attractive, assertive one like Rebecca. He found himself walking down the hotel corridor at her side and then entering her room with her. Only when they were inside did Rebecca relinquish her hold on his arm, and then only so that she could close the door behind them.

They were alone.

This reminded him of the visit she had paid to his boardinghouse before he left New Jersey, when she had brought him the gun that now rode in the holster on his hip. They had been alone then, too, but at least the door had been open, as the landlady insisted that it always be if one of her boarders had a caller of the opposite sex.

"You see, Seymour?" Rebecca said with a smile. "You're perfectly safe. After all, you're the marshal of Sweet Apple now. If I cause any trouble, you can always . . . arrest me. You could handcuff me and put me behind bars."

Seymour was having trouble getting his breath. He wanted to reach up and tug at the collar of his shirt, but he was afraid of how that would look. He settled for swallowing hard and forcing himself to drag in a big lungful of air.

"I could never do that, Miss Jimmerson . . . Rebecca," he said.

"I might not mind. I'm sure you wouldn't do anything to me that I didn't deserve."

How had she gotten so close to him? One second she was on the other side of the room, the next only a step away from him. So close that he could feel the warmth of her breath on his face. So close he would barely have to reach out to touch her.

Trying to keep the desperation he felt out of his voice, he said, "You . . . you wanted to hear about everything that's happened to me since I came to Sweet Apple."

"That's right. Tell me all about it, Seymour."

He did, leaving out some of the more gruesome details of the gun battles in which he'd been involved, but not sparing himself any of the humiliation he had experienced early on, when he had been known as Seymour the Lily-Livered and The Most Cowardly Man in the West.

What appeared to be genuine anger flashed in her eyes as she heard those stories. "How dare people treat you so badly?" she asked. "They had no right to say those things!"

"They had every right," Seymour said. "Respect has

to be earned, and I did nothing to earn it. Not until I met Matt and Sam."

"Matt and Sam?" Rebecca repeated with a slight frown.

"My deputies. Well, unofficial deputies. Matt Bodine and Sam Two Wolves." He told her about the blood brothers and how they had come to Sweet Apple on the trail of Deuce Mallory and the rest of the gang that had raided a town up in the Texas Panhandle while Matt and Sam were there. He also mentioned briefly some of the other dangerous exploits Matt and Sam had taken part in during their adventurous career. Being a newspaperman, J. Emerson Heathcote knew all about them and had been glad to fill Seymour in.

"They sound quite dashing," Rebecca commented.

"I'd be happy to introduce you to them," Seymour offered. He knew what would happen if he did. Rebecca would be instantly smitten with one or both of the blood brothers. Young, pretty women just naturally fell for Matt and Sam. The only one in town who *didn't* practically swoon when they walked past was Maggie. She seemed immune to their charms . . . which was one more reason Seymour thought she was so special.

So he was surprised when Rebecca shook her head and said, "No, that's all right. I'd be glad to meet them, but don't go out of your way to arrange an introduction, Seymour. The real reason I came out here with Mr. Standish was to see *you*."

That statement was even more of a shock to Seymour. "Me?" he said. "Why would you want to see me? I mean, I know we were cordial enough back in New Jersey, but—"

"Seymour." Suddenly she was standing even closer to

him. Both of her hands rested on his chest. "Seymour, don't you understand? Don't you know how I feel about you? How I've always felt about you, ever since we met?"

Seymour could only gulp and shake his head. He didn't understand anything. He didn't know anything. He was suddenly, totally lost, and it was the way Rebecca smelled and felt as she leaned against him that made him that way. His head had begun to spin.

It seemed to explode right off his shoulders as she came up on her toes and pressed her lips to his in a passionate kiss.

Chapter 9

Seymour's pulse hammered like a drum in his head as he finally managed to pull away from her. Kissing Rebecca was wrong, completely wrong, and he knew it.

And yet, her lips had been so soft and sweet and warm . . .

They curved now in a devilish smile. "What's wrong, Seymour? Haven't you ever been kissed before?"

"Of course I . . . I've been kissed. But not like . . . I mean . . ."

"Not like that, I'd wager." She sounded quite satisfied with herself.

He had to shake his head and say in a hollow voice, "No. Not like that."

"You just don't give yourself enough credit, Seymour. You never have. You don't see what a handsome, desirable man you really are."

Could she really be talking about him? It didn't seem possible to Seymour. Even now, after all the changes he had gone through since coming to Texas, he didn't think he was the sort of man who could possibly be attractive to a beautiful woman like Rebecca Jimmerson. She could have had the pick of any man she liked.

Why in the world would she pick him?

"Now that we're being truthful," she went on, "how do you feel about me, Seymour? Have I wasted my time coming out here to see you? Or is there a chance that there might be a reason . . . for me to stay when your uncle goes back East?"

He felt that he had been caught up in a rushing river, buffeted along swiftly by the current until he couldn't breathe and the world was spinning madly around him. He had nothing but instinct to guide him as he said, "I'm sorry, but . . . there's someone else."

Rebecca's eyes widened in surprise. "Someone else?" she repeated. She sounded as if she could hardly believe that idea—which went directly against what she had just been saying about him being handsome and desirable.

Seymour's brain was all in a muddle now. The only thing he could think of to do was to plunge straight ahead with the truth.

"Her name is Maggie," he said. "Miss Magdalena Elena Louisa O'Ryan, to be precise. She's the local schoolteacher. A wonderful young woman. You'd like her, you really would—"

"I'm sure," Rebecca interrupted, her tone cool now, the way her green eyes had become when she found out that Seymour was already romantically involved with someone else.

"So you see, it . . . it's really not appropriate for me to be here . . . with you . . . for more than one reason," he stumbled on.

"Well, I wouldn't want you to do anything inappropriate, Seymour," she grated between clenched teeth.

She put a hand against his chest and practically shoved him toward the door. "You should go ahead with the errand that brought you here. Go talk to your uncle."

He managed to bob his head. "All right. I . . . I'll do that. I'm sorry, Rebecca . . . Miss Jimmerson. It wasn't my intention to hurt your feelings—"

"Hurt my feelings?" Rebecca gave a brittle laugh. "What in heaven's name makes you think you've hurt my feelings? I was just trying to be polite to you, Seymour." Her lip curled. "You seem so awkward and out of place here. I thought your spirits could do with some lifting, that's all."

"Oh." He blinked at the sledgehammer quality of her words. "Well, I . . . I'm glad you're all right."

"I'm more than all right," Rebecca said with another laugh. "I'm fine, just fine."

"Good. I suppose I'll see you later."

She gave a noncommittal shrug of her shoulders, as if the question of whether or not they would see each other again meant nothing to her. Less than nothing, in fact.

Seymour reached behind him, fumbled for the doorknob, got it open after a second, and escaped out into the corridor. Rebecca swung the door shut behind him with what seemed to be a bit more force than necessary, but he told himself that he might have imagined that.

After taking a couple of deep breaths, Seymour removed his hat and sleeved sweat off his forehead. Never in a million years would he have expected the encounter with Rebecca to go like that. He thought that he would have been less surprised if she had hauled off and punched him, instead of kissing him.

Come to think of it, there at the end she *looked* like

she wanted to punch him. And maybe he would have deserved it, although for the life of him he couldn't think of anything he had done to lead her on or to make her think that he felt anything for her other than friendship.

There was no figuring out women, he thought. A man was wasting his time to even try. Seymour put his hat on and went across the hall to his uncle's room.

The bitter taste of defeat filled Rebecca's mouth. Rage seethed inside her. Some of it was directed at Seymour. How dare he reject her like that? Did he think she was really interested in hearing about his frumpy little schoolteacher? Was he really that foolish?

Part of her anger was directed at herself, though. She had thought that if she could establish a liaison with Seymour, she could double-cross Standish and tell Seymour all about what his uncle was really planning. Then Seymour would go back to New Jersey and take over the dry-goods company, and Rebecca could go with him, free at last from being in Standish's power. True, she was the one who had chosen to place herself in the position of being Cornelius Standish's mistress, but she was tired of his coldness and his brutality. She wanted to escape from his grip, but she didn't want to have to give up all the comforts to which she had grown accustomed in the process. Seymour had seemed to be the perfect way out.

Except for the fact that he didn't feel anything for her except some mild friendship. As unlikely as it seemed, he preferred another woman to her.

Well, if that was the way Seymour wanted it, then whatever happened from here on out was on his own head. Standish needed to know about those two drifting gunfighters who had befriended Seymour, because it was likely they would have to be disposed of, too, somewhere alone the way. Otherwise, they might protect Seymour from any more attempts on his life. At the very least, they had to be decoyed, distracted, gotten out of the way.

She would tell Standish all about it, Rebecca decided, as soon as Seymour got through talking to him. And in the meantime . . .

She stretched out on the hotel bed and cried bitter tears, tears that she would never admit to another living soul she had shed.

His Uncle Cornelius didn't seem particularly happy to see him, Seymour thought when Standish opened the door of the hotel room. Seymour thought that Welch, McCracken, and Stover might be here, but Standish seemed to be alone.

"Hello, Uncle Cornelius. How are you this morning?"

Standish grunted. "Is it always this hot out here? It was stifling last night. There wasn't even a breath of fresh air."

"I don't really know. I haven't been out here long enough to become familiar with the climate. But I suspect it is rather warm most of the time."

Standish stepped back and motioned for Seymour to come in. "What do you want?" he asked.

"I thought I'd come talk to you about establishing a sales territory here in West Texas. I might be able to give some pointers to your new salesmen."

Standish shook his head. "That's not necessary. They

have plenty of experience at what they do. I'm sure they'll be fine."

"Really, I wouldn't mind—"

"Forget it, Seymour." Standish's voice was cold and sharp. "You made your decision. You have your job as marshal to take care of. You should concentrate on that."

Seymour was surprised that his uncle seemed genuinely offended that he'd resigned from his position. He had always gotten the feeling that Uncle Cornelius didn't like him very much, especially after Seymour's father had died and the two of them inherited the company jointly. Perhaps he had misjudged his uncle. Perhaps Cornelius did feel some honest affection for him.

"I'm sorry if you were disappointed by my resignation," Seymour said. "This new life of mine . . . it's just something that I have to do."

"Fine, fine. Now, if you don't mind, I have some work to do . . ."

Seymour nodded. "Of course. But if anything comes up that I can help with—"

"I'll be sure to let you know." Standish opened the door. "Good day, Seymour."

Seymour nodded, tried and failed to smile convincingly, and left the hotel room. The door shut solidly behind him. That seemed to have become a pattern. He felt like he had been thrown out of both hotel rooms he had visited this morning.

But he couldn't let that bother him, he told himself. As he had mentioned to his uncle, he had a whole new life here in Sweet Apple. For the time being, at least, that was what he was going to concentrate on.

Anyway, there remained the question of who had tried to kill him—and would they try again? And there were the ongoing problems between the Double C and Pax ranches to be worried about, too. Even though that conflict seemed to be at a stalemate for the time being, there was no telling when it would boil over again, and the next time the violence might spread here to the settlement. Seymour would have to be ready in case that happened.

He left the hotel with a great deal on his mind.

"What do you want?"

Standish didn't seem too happy to see her, Rebecca thought as she stood in the hotel's second-floor corridor.

"Aren't you going to ask me in?" she demanded. Her tone was just as brusque as his was.

Standish grunted and stepped back so that she could enter the room. As he closed the door behind her—no worries about propriety here, she thought—she went on. "Seymour came to see me a little while ago." That wasn't exactly the truth, since she'd had to practically drag him into her room, but Standish didn't have to know that.

Standish sounded surprised as he said, "He just left here. What did he want with you?"

"He was telling me all about his life here. Have you heard of Matt Bodine and Sam Two Wolves?"

Standish frowned in thought. After a moment, he said, "The names sound familiar for some reason—"

"They were probably mentioned in those newspaper stories about Seymour. They're gunmen. Adventurers who drift around the West looking for trouble."

Standish nodded as he remembered. "That's right. Seymour's deputies."

"Not officially. The town isn't paying them anything, and they don't wear badges. But they've befriended him, and they're helping him keep law and order here."

"It must have been one of them who ran up and interrupted Welch and McCracken yesterday evening."

Rebecca nodded. "That's what I thought, too. It's going to be difficult to get rid of Seymour as long as those two are around, Cornelius." It was difficult for her to frame the words, because she had hoped that somehow Seymour's death could be avoided. Even now, after his rejection of her, a part of her still didn't want him to die. But there was nothing she could do to help him without betraying her own involvement with Standish's plans. If she turned against Standish, she might easily wind up in trouble with the law herself . . . and Rebecca wasn't going to chance that.

"What do you suggest we do? Kill Bodine and Two Wolves, too?"

"A fine chance those men of yours would have of doing that," Rebecca said in a scornful tone. "They're gunfighters, and they know the West much better than any of us ever will. If you send Welch, McCracken, and Stover after Bodine and Two Wolves, all three of them will probably wind up dead." She paused. "What you really need to do is come up with some sort of distraction, so that you can move against Seymour while his friends aren't around."

Standish nodded slowly as he pondered the situation. "Perhaps what I should have done," he said, "was to kill Seymour myself, while he was just here."

"But you don't do your dirty work yourself, do you, Cornelius?"

His mouth tightened with anger. "Don't underestimate me, my dear," he snapped. "Not even you know everything that I'm truly capable of."

Rebecca believed that. She said, "Anyway, if you'd killed him, what would you have done with the body? And for all we know, Seymour told Bodine and Two Wolves that he was coming to see you. You might have fallen under suspicion if he had disappeared."

"That's certainly true. It's best that we bide our time and wait for the right moment. And as you said, that's a great deal more likely to come along if we can separate him somehow from his friends. I'll discuss it with Welch and the others."

"Good luck," Rebecca said. "As far as I'm concerned, the sooner we get out of this godforsaken place and return to actual civilization, the better." She started to turn away.

Standish stepped up behind her and placed his hands on her shoulders, bringing her to a halt. "Don't hurry off," he said as he leaned closer to her. She felt the warmth of his breath on her neck.

"I thought you were angry with me," she said.

"I can never stay angry with you for very long, my dear." He pushed her honey-blond hair aside and kissed the back of her neck.

"Are you sure this is a good idea?" she asked as his hands slipped down from her shoulders and began to roam over her body, exploring and caressing her curves.

"It's always a good idea," Standish insisted. "That is, unless you don't want to . . ." His words contained a hint of a warning.

Rebecca forced a laugh as she turned in his embrace and slipped her arms around his neck. "Of course I want to," she said. "Don't I always want to?"

One thought rang clarion clear in her mind as he kissed her.

Damn you, Seymour Standish. Damn you to hell for turning me away and giving me no choice . . .

It's your own fault you have to die.

Chapter 10

The judge in Marfa had ruled that until the legal dispute between Shad Colton and Esau Paxton could be ironed out, Colton would have to leave the creek between the two spreads unfenced. That decision had infuriated Colton, but he respected the law even when he didn't agree with it. Although the posts that had already been put up were left standing, no more were erected and the barbed wire remained unstrung.

But that didn't mean he had to let his archrival's cows drink freely from the stream.

The two Double C hands were named Rusty and Bill. One tall, one short, both were bearded old-timers who had ridden for Shad Colton for many years. Of course, for a lot of that time they had worked for Esau Paxton, too, when the two ranches were one. But they had gone with Colton when the spread split, and their loyalty was to him. Today they had been sent out to patrol the creek. Their orders were simple: If they spotted any Pax cows drinking from the stream, they were to fire their rifles into the air over the animals' heads and haze them away from the water, staying on Double C range as they did so. No damn judge could argue with that, Colton insisted.

So Rusty and Bill would do what the boss said, even though they were a mite uneasy about it. These patrols along the creek had been going on for several days, and surely Paxton and his boys had gotten wind of them by now.

"Pax ain't gonna let this stand," Bill warned as they rode toward the creek. "Say what you will about him, he's a cattleman. He won't let his cows go thirsty."

"Nothin' he can do about it," Rusty said. "As long as we stay on our side of the creek, we're within our rights to shoot guns in the air and yell at his stock."

Bill grunted. "Maybe so. But I still got a bad feelin' about this."

"Nothin's happened so far," Rusty argued.

"Could be Paxton's been tryin' to figure out what to do."

"Let him figure away. I ain't worried about it."

Rusty didn't sound completely convincing. Any time there was trouble between two ranches the size of Double C and Pax, all hell could break loose without much warning.

The two cowboys came in sight of the creek and turned their horses so they were riding parallel to the line of trees that marked the course of the stream. They hadn't gone very far when Rusty reined in, stood up in his stirrups, and pointed.

"Look yonder," he said. Several dark shapes that could be glimpsed through the trees were obviously cows. Rusty put his horse into a run toward the creek. Bill followed.

By the time they got there, at least a dozen cattle had

crowded along the far side of the creek, water splashing around their hooves as they dipped their muzzles into the stream. The Pax brands burned into their hides were clearly visible, even in the sun-dappled shade under the trees.

"Damn it," Rusty said as he drew his Winchester from its saddle sheath. The barrel was cut down to carbine length, as most of the weapons carried by working cowboys were. He worked the lever, throwing a shell into the firing chamber. "Maybe if we shot a couple o' those cows, the rest of 'em wouldn't come back."

"You heard the boss's orders," Bill cautioned as he pulled his own carbine. "We can shoot over their heads and holler all we want, but that's all."

"Yeah," Rusty replied grudgingly. He pointed the Winchester into the air.

When the shot rang out, Bill thought for a second that Rusty had fired. But then he realized almost instantly that the sound came from somewhere across the creek, not on this side. He heard Rusty grunt and saw his friend jerk in the saddle.

"Rusty!" Bill said. "What the hell happened?"

"I . . . I'm shot," Rusty said, sounding like he could hardly believe it. "Son of a—"

The tall, lanky cowboy toppled off his horse before he could finish the curse. Wide-eyed with shock, Bill stared down at Rusty and saw the blood on the front of his shirt.

Another shot crashed. Bill jerked his head up as the bullet whipped past his head. He saw a haze of powder smoke floating over a clump of mesquite about fifty yards on the other side of the creek. As he hurriedly levered his own Winchester and brought it to his shoulder, he saw another puff of smoke from the scrubby trees.

Before Bill could pull the trigger, something slammed into his right shoulder and drove him backward out of the saddle. His carbine went flying into the air as he fell.

The impact as he landed knocked the air out of Bill's lungs. His wounded shoulder didn't hurt too bad yet; it was numb right now, rather than painful. He gasped for breath, rolled onto his side, and reached across his body with his left arm since his right wouldn't work anymore. Awkwardly, he drew his pistol and then lurched to his feet, shouting curses. The racket and the smell of blood combined to make the cows that had been drinking from the creek turn and stampede away from there. Bill lifted the gun in his hand and started thumbing off shots toward the mesquites, knowing that it wasn't likely to do much good but determined to put up a fight anyway. He had seen the lifeless stare in Rusty's eyes and knew his pard was dead.

"Come on, you sons o' bitches!" he howled as the Colt roared and bucked in his hand.

He never felt the bullet that slammed into his forehead, sizzled through his brain, and then exploded out the back of his head. He was dead before he hit the ground beside Rusty.

The thirsty ground soaked up the two cowboys' blood so that it didn't run into the creek. After a while, the powder smoke drifted away and the cattle returned to drink . . . although not without casting wary glances at the two corpses sprawled on the opposite bank.

* * *

Matt and Sam were coming out of one of the stores in Sweet Apple when they heard the swift pounding of hoofbeats. They had just bought some more cartridges for their guns, years of experience having taught them it was best never to run low on such essentials.

The sound of a galloping horse usually meant trouble, so they might need that ammunition sooner than they had anticipated, Matt thought.

He and Sam swung around to see who was riding so hurriedly into the settlement. Matt stiffened in alarm as he recognized the trim shape of the rider and the long red hair that had escaped from a Stetson. The hat dangled from its chin strap at the back of Jessie Colton's head.

Jessie seemed to spot the blood brothers at the same instant as they saw her. She hauled hard on the reins and sent her horse toward them, pulling back on the lines and bringing the animal to a skidding stop as she reached the boardwalk in front of them.

"Jessie, what in blazes is wrong?" Matt asked.

She was flushed and breathless from the hard ride into the settlement, so breathless that at first she couldn't talk. When she had gulped down a couple of lungfuls of air, she was able to say, "Two of my pa's riders were killed . . . out by the creek . . . shot down from ambush . . . He thinks Paxton men did it . . . going to ride against Pax!"

Matt stepped forward and grasped the horse's reins. "Blast it, I knew no good would come of it when I heard that your pa was trying to keep Paxton's cattle away from that creek! He should've known that Paxton would fight back."

"Maybe Paxton's men didn't kill those Double C riders," Sam put in.

Matt shot him a skeptical glance. "Who else would've had any reason to do a thing like that?" Without waiting for an answer, he turned back to Jessie. "You say he's gonna attack Paxton's spread?"

Jessie nodded. "He was gathering up the men when I threw a saddle on this horse and headed for town." She was breathing easier now but still visibly upset. "I figured you and Sam were the only ones who might be able to stop him."

"Two of us against a couple of dozen fighting ranch hands?" Matt shook his head. "Not very likely, Jessie."

She grasped his shoulder. "You've got to try! Otherwise, you know what's going to happen!"

Matt and Sam exchanged a grim look. Sam said, "If your father and his men show up at Pax with their guns drawn, ready to fight, Paxton and his men will fight back. There'll be bloodshed."

"Hell, it'll be runnin' in buckets!" Matt said. "We don't have any choice. We've got to try to stop it."

Sam raced toward the livery stable to get their horses saddled, while Matt asked Jessie a few more questions. Shad Colton was gathering his whole crew for the attack on Paxton's ranch, so it was going to take a while for him to get all of them together. By now, though, the force from Double C might be on its way to Pax. It would be a long shot for Matt and Sam to reach there first.

The two murdered cowboys had been patrolling the creek to turn back any Paxton stock that tried to drink there. Their bodies had been found by Double C punchers who had come to relieve them. From the looks of it, they had been dead for several hours. One of the cowboys who found them had galloped back to the ranch headquarters to tell Colton what had happened. The other man had crossed the creek to look for sign. The closest hoofprints he'd found that belonged to horses instead of cattle had been in a clump of mesquite about fifty yards from the creek. He'd found some empty shell casings there, too. That evidence seemed to indicate that the two Double C men had been gunned down from ambush. It was a coward's way of killing and made the deaths murder, plain and simple.

The tracks led off in the direction of Paxton's headquarters. That had been all Colton needed to hear. It was time to go to war, and judges and laws be hanged!

As Jessie was finishing her story, Sam hurried up on his paint horse, leading Matt's gray stallion. Matt took the reins and practically vaulted into the saddle. "Stay here," he told Jessie.

"I want to come with you! My father—"

"We'll do our best to see that he doesn't get his fool hide ventilated," Matt promised. "But your horse is played out. You couldn't keep up with us."

He didn't add that he didn't want her getting in the way of a stray bullet, but that was part of his thinking, too. He and Sam wheeled their horses around and galloped out of Sweet Apple, heading for Esau Paxton's ranch.

They hadn't told Seymour where they were going, Matt realized as the settlement fell behind them, but it was too late to do anything about that now.

Seymour would just have to hold down the fort without them for a while.

All day, Seymour had been bothered by what happened that morning. He never would have guessed, in his wildest dreams, that Rebecca Jimmerson was interested in him—romantically, that is. Her visit to his room back in New Jersey, before he left for Texas, had puzzled him greatly, but he hadn't ever ascribed that motivation to it.

He wasn't blind. He had known how lovely she was ever since she had gone to work for his uncle. At one time, he might have been thrilled that she was attracted to him.

But not now. Not after he'd met Maggie O'Ryan and experienced the feelings he had for her. It was too late now for him and Rebecca. He wasn't interested in anyone except Maggie.

He was sorry for the pain and anger he had seen in Rebecca's eyes, however. He wished he hadn't had to hurt her.

It would have been better if Rebecca had never come to Sweet Apple. Seymour was fairly confident that Maggie understood there was nothing going on between him and Rebecca, but she might always have a little lurking suspicion . . .

These affairs of the heart were weighing heavily on Seymour's mind when the door of the marshal's office opened and Jessie Colton came in. Seymour was sitting behind the desk, his chair leaned back and a booted foot propped against the desk. He sat up hurriedly and got to his feet when he saw that Jessie was visibly upset. "Miss Colton," he said. "What's wrong?"

"Matt and Sam are on their way out to Pax," she said. "I thought I ought to let you know, Marshal, even though they didn't tell me to."

Seymour's eyes widened in surprise. "Has there been more trouble?"

Grimly, Jessie filled him in on what had happened at the creek and her father's reaction to the murder of two of his riders. "Matt and Sam headed for Pax, hell-bent-for-leather," she concluded. "If anybody can head off a gun battle, it's them, I reckon."

Seymour reached for his hat. "I should follow them—" He paused, torn by differing loyalties. "But my jurisdiction—and my responsibilities—lie here in town."

"No offense, Marshal, but I don't figure there's much you can handle that those two can't."

Seymour's mouth twisted, but he shrugged in acceptance of her statement. "I certainly can't argue about that," he said. "I suppose they'd want me to stay here and keep an eye on things in town."

"That's your job," Jessie pointed out. "Anyway, *I'm* going to Pax. They're saddling a fresh horse for me right now, down at the livery stable."

"I'm not sure that's such a good idea," Seymour said with a frown. "There may be shooting, and I don't think Matt and Sam would want you to endanger yourself."

Jessie took her hat off, settled it on her head again, and pulled the chin strap taut. "I don't care," she said. "My father's liable to wind up in danger, and I'm not going to stand by and do nothing if there's a chance I can help him. I've got a rifle, and I'm a darned good shot, if I do say so myself."

Again, Seymour was torn by uncertainty. He knew that Matt and Sam wouldn't want Jessie risking her life by riding out to Pax when a battle was imminent. For one thing, worrying about her might distract them from what they needed to do in order to head off trouble.

But he had no legal right to stop her. She wasn't

breaking any law by going out there. Seymour knew that from time to time a lawman might have to bend the law a little in order to accomplish what needed to be done, but he was too new to this business to be sure what the boundaries really were. All he could do was appeal to Jessie's good sense.

"Miss Colton, I urge you very strongly not to go out there. I know that if Matt and Sam were here, they would tell you the same thing."

A thin smile curved her lips. "I'm sorry, Marshal. I told you where those two are. Now I've got to be going myself."

Seymour lifted a hand, but Jessie ignored him and turned to stalk out of the marshal's office.

"Blast it," Seymour muttered as he stepped out of the building and watched the redheaded young woman disappear into the livery stable. The hostlers must have had her fresh horse ready for her, because a moment later she reappeared on a chestnut gelding and galloped off toward the northeast.

Seymour felt a tug on his sleeve and looked down in surprise. A small boy stood there. He'd come up without Seymour noticing him.

"Hey, Marshal," the boy piped. "You're the marshal, ain't you?"

"That's right," Seymour told him. He went down on one knee so that the lad wouldn't have to crane his neck so much to look up at him. "Is something wrong, son?"

"I dunno. Some man told me to fetch you. He gimme a nickel and told me to tell you to come down to the old barn at the west end of town."

Seymour knew the barn the boy was talking about. It was a ramshackle, patchwork affair built partially of adobe and partially of stone and wood, with a thatched roof that sagged as if it were in danger of collapsing. Seymour didn't know how long the barn had been sitting there empty and unused, but it looked as if it had been abandoned for several years at least.

"You're sure the man didn't say whether or not something was wrong?"

The boy shook his head. "Nope. Just that it was important you come down there as soon as you can."

"Very well." Seymour straightened to his feet. "Let me get my hat."

The youngster didn't care about Seymour's hat or anything else. His job was done, and he said, "I'm gonna go buy some candy with my nickel."

"You do that," Seymour said as he stepped back into the office.

He snagged his hat from the desk, and thought about taking down one of the shotguns from the rack on the wall. He decided against it, thinking that it was unlikely he would run into any real trouble right here in the settlement while the sun was still up. This wasn't like the ambush of the night before.

School had been dismissed a while earlier, but he knew Maggie would still be at the schoolhouse, wrapping up the day's work. She usually stayed at least an hour after the children went home for the day. Seymour would have liked to stop at the school and say hello to her, but just in case anything really was wrong at that old barn, he decided he'd better check it out first. He could always stop by the school when he was finished.

The barn sat by itself, a short distance from any of the other buildings on the outskirts of the settlement. It was next to what remained of the foundation of another, larger building. Seymour had no idea what it had been, but he suspected that the barn and the adjacent structure had been some of the first buildings in Sweet Apple. The settlement had gotten its start at this end of town. They probably even predated the railroad. The barn door hung crookedly on leather hinges. It was open part of the way, revealing the dark, shadowy interior.

Seymour strode up to the doorway and called, "Hello? It's Marshal Standish."

He listened, but didn't hear any response from inside. Had the man who sent the boy to summon him already left, thinking that he wasn't coming?

Or perhaps the man had been sick, or injured in some way. He could have passed out and be lying in there right now, waiting for someone to come and help him. As Seymour thought about it, he knew he couldn't ignore that possibility. He pulled the door open even farther. The top hinge broke, allowing the door to lean crazily to one side.

Seymour stepped into the barn.

There was no doubt that was what it had once been used for. Even though quite a bit of time had passed, the smell of straw lingered, mixed with other, less pleasant animal odors. Seymour paused as he heard a sudden skittering sound. Rats, he thought, trying not to shudder. He didn't like vermin.

"Hello?" he called again. "Is anyone here? This is Marshal Standish. Please speak up if you can."

The hair on the back of his neck prickled. Even though it was still daylight outside, the shadows in the barn were thick. Not much light penetrated the thick walls. The slab of sunlight that came in through the open door just seemed to make the far corners of the old building that much darker. Just as a precaution, he reached for the gun on his hip.

His fingers had just touched the Colt's ivory grips when something dropped over his head with a faint rustle and jerked tight, cutting off his air.

Matt and Sam expected to hear the sharp reports of gunfire as they approached the headquarters of Esau Paxton's ranch, but so far, the afternoon air was still, heavy with heat but quiet. They hadn't been to Pax before, but had a fairly good idea where the ranch house was located. With the unerring instincts of true frontiersmen, they rode straight toward it.

"Maybe we're gonna beat Colton and his men there," Matt said.

"It's going to be close," Sam said. He pointed. "Look there."

Matt grimaced as he saw the cloud of dust rising in the air. It took a lot of horses to kick up that much dust. And unfortunately, it was between the blood brothers and the ranch.

That wasn't the worst of it, Matt thought. If he and Sam could see that dust, then so could Paxton. The cattleman would have to be a damned fool not to realize that trouble was on the way. He would probably call together all the men who happened to be at the ranch headquarters and send somebody out on the range to round up the rest of the cowboys who rode for Pax. He would tell them to come a-runnin' . . .

And to bring their guns.

The blood brothers leaned forward in their saddles and urged more speed from their horses. The mounts responded as they always did, and stretched out in a hard gallop. The dust cloud drew closer. Colton and his men weren't wasting any time closing in on Pax, but they didn't know that possible trouble was coming up behind them.

Matt and Sam caught sight of the large group of riders sweeping down a long, shallow valley toward the Pax ranch house, which was a sprawling adobe structure in the Spanish style, with red-tile roofs on its wings that surrounded a central courtyard. A bunkhouse and other outbuildings were scattered around beyond it.

The Double C men spread out into a line and reined to a halt about a hundred yards from the Pax ranch house. A burly figure on horseback detached himself from the rest of the group and rode forward alone, stopping when he was about halfway between the rest of his bunch and the house. Matt recognized Shad Colton. He had to give the man credit for having plenty of sand. Colton had put himself out in front where he would serve as a tempting target if any shooting broke out.

Several of Colton's men heard Matt and Sam coming and wheeled around, drawing their guns as they did so. "Hold your fire!" Matt called. "We're not Paxton men!"

Colton ignored the disturbance behind him. Raising himself in his stirrups, he bellowed toward the house.

"Paxton! Come on out here and face me, you back-stabbin' murderer! You hear me, Paxton?"

The front door of the ranch house opened. Matt and Sam were close enough now to see that every window in the place had a rifle barrel protruding from it. The house was bristling with Winchesters.

The tall, lean figure of Esau Paxton stepped out, cradling a rifle in his arms. "What are you doing over here, Colton?" he shouted back at his cousin. "You know you're not welcome on this ranch!"

"I've come for justice!" Colton called in return. "Two of my men were murdered earlier today, shot down from ambush while they were doin' their jobs! But I'm not tellin' you anything you don't already know, am I, Paxton?"

Paxton stood ramrod stiff, anger radiating from him like waves of heat on a scorching day. "Are you saying that I had your men bushwhacked?" he demanded.

"Damn right that's what I'm sayin'! Give me the men who pulled the triggers, Paxton—or by God, I'll wipe you and yours right off the face of the earth!"

Chapter 11

Matt and Sam held their breath, expecting shots to roar out at any second.

Instead of whipping the rifle to his shoulder and firing, though, after a moment Paxton called, "I don't know what you're talking about, Shad! I give you my word of honor I didn't have anything to do with bushwhacking any of your men!"

"The shots came from Pax range!" Colton blustered, shaking a fist at his enemy.

"That doesn't mean Pax riders fired them!"

Under his breath, Matt said, "How about that? Paxton's actually tryin' to be reasonable."

"You believe him?" Sam asked.

Matt glanced over at his blood brother. "He sounds to me like he's tellin' the truth. And anybody could have hidden in that clump of mesquite and gunned down those Double C cowboys."

Sam nodded. "That's my thinking exactly. Come on. Let's see if we can keep those two old pelicans talking sense."

He hitched his horse into motion, riding forward de-

spite the ominous looks of warning from the Double C
punchers. Ignoring the guns pointed at him, Matt rode
after Sam. Whether Colton and Paxton continued to
talk, or if hell broke loose and bullets started to fly, the
blood brothers would face whatever it was together.

At the sound of the horses coming up behind him,
Shad Colton hipped around in the saddle. He scowled
as he recognized Matt and Sam. "You two hellions!"
he said. "What are you doin' here?"

"Tryin' to keep you from gettin' yourself shot full of
holes," Matt snapped. "I don't care all that much myself,
but I know a certain redheaded gal who'd be mighty
broken up about it if you were to get yourself killed,
Colton."

"Jessie!" the rancher snapped. "By God, that gal has
to stick her nose into everything!"

"You should be glad of that, Mr. Colton," Sam said.
"She didn't want you to do something foolish, like come
over here and attack your cousin's ranch."

"Two of my men are dead!" Colton roared.

"Yeah, but what proof do you have that Paxton's responsible?" Matt drawled, appearing a lot cooler and
calmer than he felt inside. Being in the middle of three
or four dozen guns that were primed to go off at any
second was enough to make any man a mite nervous,
even Matt Bodine.

"The shots came from his side of the creek!"

"And like Mr. Paxton told you," Sam said, "anyone
could have hidden on Pax range and shot your men. You
need more proof than that for the law."

Colton snorted in disgust. He tapped the butt of his
gun. "I don't need any more law than what I've got right

here in my holster. That was plenty when we came out here, wasn't it—"

He stopped short as he realized that he was about to ask his cousin a question concerning their shared past. With the current hostility between them, Colton obviously didn't want to bring up a time when they had been more than relatives. They had been friends and partners as well.

He scowled and went on. "Anyway, I don't care about the law, and you two don't have any authority out here! You don't work for the county sheriff or the Texas Rangers. That dude in town who calls himself a marshal don't mean squat out here on the range."

"Maybe not," Sam argued, "but we still don't want to see you or anyone else hurt or killed in a senseless battle."

"Defendin' yourself ain't senseless! Settlin' the score for two men who were gunned down in cold blood ain't senseless!"

"It is if you're not sure you're going after the men who were really responsible," Matt pointed out.

Colton glared at him. "Can you prove that Paxton *wasn't* responsible for Rusty and Bill gettin' killed?"

That was a sticky point, all right, Matt had to admit. Colton had no proof that Paxton was guilty—but Matt and Sam had no proof that Paxton was innocent either. All they had was the rancher's word, and clearly Colton wasn't prepared to accept that.

"Has anybody been messin' around that clump of mesquite where the bushwhackers were hidden?" Matt asked.

Paxton said, "This is the first I've heard about it, so I'm fairly confident that none of my men have been over there today."

"One of my riders looked the place over, found horse tracks and some shell casings," Colton said. "I don't reckon anybody's been there since then."

Sam knew where Matt was going with that question. He said, "Then let us take a ride over there and have a look around. Maybe we can find something that will lead us to the real killers."

Matt nodded. "You and your men go back to the Double C, Colton," he said. "Maybe we're not the law, but we're the closest thing to it in these parts right now. Let us investigate before you start a shootin' war."

Colton didn't like the idea. The blood brothers could tell that by the look on his face. But he was smart enough to know that they were talking sense. If a fight broke out now, even more of his men would probably be killed . . . and Colton didn't like to risk the lives of his riders.

"If there's proof that Paxton is behind what happened to your men, we'll find it," Sam vowed. "Then you can let the law take its course."

Paxton sniffed and said, "You won't find any proof, because there isn't any. Because I didn't have anything to do with those Double C men being ambushed. For God's sake, Shad, you ought to know me better than that."

"I thought I knew you," Colton said as his eyes narrowed with dislike. "You proved me wrong a while back."

"There's no point in bringing all that up again," Paxton snapped.

Colton made a curt, slashing motion with his hand. "Damn right. You showed your true colors, and there ain't no goin' back. There ain't much of anything I'd put past you now, Paxton. Your men have fought with mine before."

"Hotheaded cowboys at a dance," Paxton said.

"That's a lot different than lying in wait and gunning down men from hiding."

He had a point there, Matt thought. If Paxton men were indeed responsible for killing Colton's riders, then the feud between the two cattlemen had been taken to a whole new level. From here on out there would be nothing but death and destruction . . .

But maybe he and Sam could still head that off. He said, "Are you gonna let us take a look, or do you start killin' each other for no good reason?"

Colton and Paxton glared at each other for a few seconds; then Colton grunted and said, "Go ahead and have a look at the place where it happened. But if you find any evidence pointin' to Paxton and don't tell me about it, then you two are goin' on my list, too."

"We're just after the truth," Sam said.

"Which is that I and my men had nothing to do with this," Paxton insisted. "We've been falsely accused, and I won't forget that."

Matt fixed his intent gaze on Colton. "Turn around and ride back to your ranch," he told the cattleman. "Take all your men with you."

"We'll go," Colton grumbled, "but we'll be back once you find out I'm right about this snake-blooded bastard."

Paxton paled. "I won't be talked about like that on my own land. Get moving, Colton, or I won't be responsible for what happens."

"And I won't be ordered around by the likes of you," Colton shot back with a sneer. But he turned his horse and lifted a hand to signal to his men. "Move out, boys! We're headin' back to the ranch!"

"But what about Rusty and Bill?" one of the men called. "Ain't we gonna settle up for them?"

"Damn right," Colton said with a curt nod. "But not right now. These two hombres"—he waved a hand at the blood brothers—"are gonna take a look around and find proof that Paxton's to blame for what happened. *Then* we'll see to it that justice is done. You got my word on that."

The Double C riders didn't like it. Quite a bit of grumbling and complaining came from them. But they turned their horses around and rode away with Colton leading them back toward the neighboring ranch. Matt and Sam didn't relax until Colton's bunch was several hundred yards away. They were still within rifle range, but a battle was unlikely to break out now.

The door of the ranch house opened again and Sandy Paxton came running out, her blond hair flying in the breeze. Even though the showdown had been averted, at least for the time being, she still wore a frightened look on her pretty face.

Sam swung down to meet her, and she threw herself into his arms, hugging him tightly as she ignored her father's look of disapproval. "Thank God you and Matt got here when you did, Sam!" she said. "I thought sure Pa and Uncle Shad were going to try to kill each other."

"That man's not your uncle!" Paxton snapped. "It's bad enough he's a second cousin."

Sandy turned her head toward him with a defiant look on her face. "He was like an uncle to me when I was growing up, and you know it, Pa. The same way that you were like an uncle to Jessie."

"I haven't tried to break up your friendship with Jessie," Paxton said stiffly, "but you don't have to throw it in my face either!" He jerked a hand toward Sam.

"And for God's sake, girl, stop hugging this man! He's practically a stranger."

"Aren't you going to call him a half-breed, too?"

"You said that, not me," Paxton replied.

Sam ignored the exchange. He had long since learned to let comments about his mixed heritage roll off his back. If he took offense at them, he'd be fighting all the time, and he didn't want that. Instead, he asked Sandy, "How did you know we were coming out here?"

"I didn't," she said. "But when we realized that Uncle Shad and his men were on their way over here with blood in their eyes, I hoped you'd hear about it some way and stop them from killing each other."

"Jessie rode into town and told us what was going on," Matt said. "You've got her to thank for preventing a battle."

"A battle that neither side would win," Sandy said with a look at her father.

Paxton said, "I thought you two were going to ride over to the creek and have a look at the site of the killings."

Matt nodded. "That's right. You still say you didn't have anything to do with what happened, Paxton?"

"I most certainly do. I didn't even know any of Colton's men had been bushwhacked until he rode up and started snorting and pawing like a mad bull."

Sam patted Sandy on the shoulder and turned to his horse. "We'll see what we can find out," he promised.

"But if the trail leads here . . . we'll be back," Matt added as Sam mounted up.

"It won't," Paxton insisted, but Matt thought he saw the tiniest bit of uncertainty in the rancher's eyes. Even if Paxton hadn't given the orders, he couldn't be sure that some of his men hadn't taken it upon themselves to bushwhack the Double C riders at the creek.

The blood brothers turned their horses and headed west, leaving father and daughter standing there side by side in front of the ranch house.

"You think Paxton's tellin' the truth?" Matt asked.

Sam shrugged. "I don't know." He echoed Matt's thought of a moment earlier as he added, "Even if he is, some of his men still could have ambushed Colton's men."

"I hope we can find out one way or the other."

Sam nodded in agreement with that. They kept their horses moving at a steady pace toward the creek.

The killings had occurred not far from the spot where the previous confrontation between Double C and Pax had taken place. Matt and Sam found it without too much trouble. The bodies of the two slain cowboys had been taken back to the ranch headquarters, but their blood was still splashed on the grass along the creek bank. On the other side of the stream, about fifty yards away, was the clump of mesquite Matt and Sam had heard so much about.

They dismounted and left their horses a short distance away from the mesquite, not wanting the mounts to disturb any tracks that might have been left by the killers. They found a set of prints leading from the creek to the clump of scrubby trees. Those were made by one of the Double C hands who had discovered the bodies, Matt commented, and Sam nodded in agreement. To their experienced eyes, even the smallest sign told a story.

Another set of tracks entered the mesquite from the far side, then departed the same way. A lone rider. There had been only one bushwhacker. Whoever he was, he handled a rifle with enough skill so that he was confident of being able to kill two men. Sam knelt by the hoofprints and studied them for a long time, taking note of every nick and scratch in the iron of the horseshoes. There was nothing particularly distinctive about the tracks, but Sam said, "I might be able to pick them out if I saw them again."

Matt nodded, not doubting his blood brother's ability even for a second. "Let's see where they go," he suggested. "We know they start off toward Paxton's headquarters, but that doesn't mean they keep goin' in that direction."

Sam started to straighten, but he stopped suddenly and then reached under one of the mesquites. He picked up a small brown object that had almost blended in with a scattering of rocks about the same size.

"What's that?" Matt asked. "Some sort of animal droppin'?"

Sam lifted the thing to his nose and sniffed it, then grimaced. "Smells almost that bad, but that's not what it is." He extended his hand with the object lying on the palm. "It's part of a cigar. The bushwhacker must've bit it off and spit it out here."

"A cigar, eh?" Matt shook his head. "The hombre's not very smart. He left a cigar butt, shell casings, and hoofprints behind him. It's almost like he wanted us to track him."

Sam's eyes narrowed in thought. He stood up. "Let's see what else we can find."

No other bits of evidence were anywhere around the mesquites. The blood brothers mounted up again and followed the tracks that led toward Paxton's headquarters. After a couple of miles, the trail hit a rocky stretch and disappeared.

"Reckon he rode through there on purpose?" Matt asked as he reined in.

Sam nodded. "Yes. Maybe he's not quite as clumsy as we thought. He laid the trail he wanted to lay, pointing right at Paxton. Now he's headed somewhere else." Sam turned his paint toward the south. "He'd circle in this direction if he was going back to town."

"Why would anybody in Sweet Apple want to stir up trouble between Double C and Pax?" Matt asked with a frown.

"I don't know." Sam drew in a sharp breath as something occurred to him. "But it got us out of town in a hurry, didn't it?"

Matt saw instantly what his blood brother was getting at. "Damn it!" he exclaimed. "Seymour's back there by himself!"

The faint noise had been a warning for Seymour, but not enough of one to allow him to escape the trap. As the noose around his neck tightened, he felt himself jerked off his feet. He kicked wildly as he rose into the air. His fingers clawed at the rope as it dug into his flesh, but he couldn't get any purchase on it. Black and red starbursts exploded behind his eyes.

A small part of his brain was still functioning well enough for him to wonder if the killings out on the range had been carried out in order to lure Matt Bodine and Sam Two Wolves out of Sweet Apple. He knew the would-be assassins who had failed to eliminate him before were making that second try Matt had talked about.

Mostly, though, Seymour was terrified and panic-stricken. He was convinced he was going to die here. With that noose digging into his throat the way it was, he would choke to death within minutes. He would never see Maggie O'Ryan again, never get a chance to realize any of the dreams that he had begun to have about making a life together with her . . .

Seymour heard a loud, splintery crack and wondered if it was his neck breaking.

A second later, as his feet hit the ground and he sprawled forward in dried, ancient straw and feces, he knew the sound hadn't been his spine. But the rope was embedded so deeply in his neck that he still couldn't breathe.

Without his weight pulling all the slack out of the rope, though, he was able to work the fingers of one hand under it and pull desperately. The rope loosened just enough for Seymour to gasp and draw some precious air into his body.

He heard a rush of footsteps and kicked a foot against the ground, rolling over as he continued trying to pull the rope away from his neck even more. With his other hand he reached for the gun at his hip. The ivory-handled revolver was still in the holster. Seymour thanked his lucky stars that it hadn't fallen out. As he saw a pair of shadowy figures charging toward him from the depths of the deserted barn, he jerked the gun from its holster, angled the barrel upward, and fired.

The shot was loud in the barn, echoing back from the walls. Seymour finally tore the noose off his neck as another shot blasted, this time from a weapon wielded by one his attackers. The bullet kicked up dust next to Seymour's ear as he threw himself to the side again.

He landed on his belly this time and fired twice more. His vision was still blurred and had black and red bands running through it, but he was able to see well enough to know that the two shapes had turned and were headed for the back of the old barn. Seymour steadied his gun hand by gripping that wrist with his other hand as he drew a bead on the fleeing men. He squeezed the trigger and saw splinters fly from one of the beams around the rear door as the men ducked through the opening and disappeared.

Again, they had failed in their quest to kill him . . . but he had failed to capture them or even get a good look at them. His eyes smarted and stung from the dust that had gotten in them. Dust and God knows what else, in an old, abandoned place like this.

Seymour struggled to his feet, coughing and choking. Nearly being strangled by the noose that now lay on the ground at his feet caused him to be desperate for breath, but with each lungful of air he drew in, he also got more dust. What he really needed to do was get out of here.

He stumbled toward the rectangle of light that marked the front door of the barn. As he emerged into the late afternoon sun, he heard shouts over the pounding of blood in his head. He pulled out his bandanna and wiped his eyes. His vision cleared enough for him to make out several of Sweet Apple's citizens hurrying toward him, drawn by the sound of shots. One of them grabbed his arm and yelled, "Marshal, what the hell happened? Are you all right?"

Seymour managed a weak nod as he coughed the last of the dust out of his throat. "I'm . . . not hurt," he said.

"What in blazes happened to your neck?" another of

the townies wanted to know. "You look like you been lynched?"

"That's just about . . . what happened . . . all right." Seymour looked around at the crowd that was gathering, and wondered if the men who had just tried to kill him were among them, pretending to interested but innocent bystanders. None of them looked guilty, but he knew that didn't mean anything.

He didn't think the assassins would try again, not with this many people around. Seymour turned and started back into the barn. The citizens followed him.

Inside, once his eyes adjusted to the dim light again, he saw two pieces of a broken beam hanging down from the ceiling, their ends jagged and splintered where they had broken. From where the rope lay, Seymour knew that it had been looped over that beam and then dropped around his neck. Then the two men had hauled him up off his feet to let him dangle there until he died.

The plan might have worked, too, if the beam hadn't broken under his weight. The men had probably pulled on the rope to test the beam's strength, but they hadn't reckoned on the fact that by pulling him up as they'd done, they had added even more pressure on the beam than just his weight. The combined force had been enough to crack the old, dried-out wood. That stroke of good luck had saved him.

What if it hadn't? Seymour looked around and spotted an old, rickety, three-legged stool lying next to the wall on its side. If he had died at the end of that rope, his killers could have tied it off, set the stool next to his dangling body, and made it look like he had hanged himself. Of course, he never would have done such a thing, but did anybody in Sweet Apple know him well enough to have been certain that suicide simply wasn't in his nature?

Maggie O'Ryan. Maybe. But Seymour couldn't even be sure about that. People might have been suspicious, especially Matt and Sam, but in the end there wouldn't have been any proof that he hadn't killed himself for some unknown reason.

A shiver went through Seymour at that thought. Whoever wanted him dead was clearly willing to go to any lengths to accomplish that end. From now on he would have to be more careful than ever, since he had no idea who'd been trying to kill him.

He would talk to Matt and Sam about it when they returned from the Double C, or Pax, or wherever they were. They might have some suggestions.

And as he thought about the blood brothers, he wondered if there could be any connection between this attempt on his life and the trouble that had taken them out of town. That seemed likely, Seymour decided. Somebody could have played on the feud between Colton and Paxton to lure Matt and Sam out of Sweet Apple.

Whoever was plotting against him was truly diabolical, Seymour realized. More devil than man . . .

Chapter 12

"I don't want to hear any more excuses," Cornelius Standish said, his voice cold with anger. "This is twice you've attempted to do the job I'm paying you for . . . and twice you've failed miserably. I'm starting to believe that you three aren't the right men for the job."

Warren Welch, Daniel McCracken, and Ed Stover glared back at Standish. They didn't like having their abilities challenged that way. They prided themselves on being efficient killers.

But there was no denying that they had failed twice now to kill Seymour Standish. The young man had to be the luckiest son of a bitch on the face of the earth, all three of the would-be murderers thought.

"Maybe we tried to get a little too fancy," Welch admitted. "That beam seemed strong enough to support Seymour's weight when Ed tested it."

Stover shook his head. "Hey, don't blame this on me," he said. "It was your idea to make it look like the kid hung himself."

"I did my part," McCracken put in. "I killed those

two cowboys and got Bodine and Two Wolves out of town so you'd have a clear shot at Seymour."

Standish snapped, "Stop bickering, all of you. That's not accomplishing anything. I don't care whether it looks like an accident or suicide or divine intervention. Just make sure that little bastard dies."

"He probably won't set foot out of his office again without his pet gunfighters with him," Welch pointed out. "That's going to make it more difficult."

"Would a three-thousand-dollar bonus make it worth the risk?" Standish asked.

The three men exchanged glances. Stover said, "You mean over and above what you already promised to pay us?"

Standish nodded. "That's right. You'll all get your fee, but the man who actually kills Seymour will collect an additional three thousand."

"That's a lot of money," McCracken said.

"That's why I expect results."

"You'll get them," Welch promised.

"And soon," Standish added. He went to the table in his hotel room, picked up a bottle of whiskey, and tipped some of the amber liquid into a glass without offering any to his visitors. He tossed the drink back and continued. "The sooner I get out of this hellhole of a town, the better."

By the time Matt and Sam got back to Sweet Apple, the settlement was still buzzing about the latest attempt on Seymour's life. Pierre Delacroix, the proprietor of the Black Bull, saw the blood brothers riding past the saloon and stepped out onto the boardwalk to hail them.

"M'sieu Bodine, M'sieu Two Wolves, have you heard the news?" Delacroix asked as they reined in.

"Not really, but the town seems to be worked up about something," Matt said. All along the street, small groups of people were talking animatedly.

"Did something happen to Seymour?" Sam guessed.

"Is he alive?" Matt added with a worried frown.

Delacroix nodded. "*Oui*, Marshal Standish is still with us. But not for lack of trying on the part of two assassins a short time ago. I am not sure whether he was injured. He went into his office and has not emerged since."

"Thanks, Delacroix," Matt said with a nod to the Cajun saloon keeper. "We'd better see how he's doin'."

As he and Sam turned their mounts toward the marshal's office, both of them spotted Maggie O'Ryan hurrying along the street toward the same destination. Word must have reached the school of Seymour's mishap, whatever it was. Unable to contain herself and clearly not worried about propriety, Maggie broke into a run.

She reached the office door just ahead of Matt and Sam and threw it open, rushing in and crying, "Seymour! Seymour, are you all right?"

Matt and Sam were right behind her. They saw Seymour standing up from behind his desk, a rifle in his hands and a startled look on his face. Maggie was lucky he hadn't fired a shot when she charged in like that, Matt thought. Luckily, Seymour had been cool-headed enough to hold off on the trigger, even though he was pale and obviously tense.

"Maggie," he said as he placed the rifle on the desk.

That was all he had time to say before she threw her arms around him and enveloped him in a tight hug. Awkwardly, Seymour patted her on the back and said, "There,

there. It's all right, Maggie. I'm not hurt." His voice was hoarse and strained. "Well, not too badly, I suppose."

Matt and Sam saw the red line around Seymour's neck. "What happened?" Sam asked.

Seymour opened his mouth to answer, but before he could do so, Maggie kissed him. It was a hard, urgent kiss, and Seymour must have decided that he had better things to do with his lips for the next couple of minutes than answer Sam's question.

The blood brothers didn't particularly blame him for coming to that conclusion either.

When Seymour finally broke the kiss and went back to patting Maggie on the back as he held her, he looked over her shoulder at Matt and Sam and told them, "Somebody tried to . . . How do you say it out here? String me up?"

"You mean hang you?" Sam said.

Seymour nodded. "That's right." Quickly, he filled them in on the details of the latest attempt on his life, then concluded by saying, "The sheer good fortune of that beam breaking is the only reason I'm not dead now."

Maggie shuddered in his embrace.

"Did you see the hombres who tried to give you a necktie party?" Matt asked.

Seymour shook his head. "No, I never got a good look at them. But there were two of them, I'm certain of that, which makes me think it was probably the same two men who tried to kill me before."

"More than likely," Matt agreed. "Unless there are more folks who want you dead than we know about."

Maggie stepped back at last and looked up at Seymour. "Why?" she asked. "Why would anyone want to hurt you?"

He shrugged. "A lawman makes enemies. It's inevitable, I suppose."

"But there's nobody around here who holds a real grudge against you. You haven't—"

Seymour smiled when Maggie stopped short. "Haven't really done anything except fight that one battle against Mallory's gang and then Alcazarrio's bandits? Is that what you're trying to say?"

"Oh, Seymour, I didn't mean to hurt your feelings."

"They're not hurt," he assured her. "You're absolutely right, Maggie. Mallory's gang was wiped out, the survivors from Alcazarrio's band retreated back across the Rio Grande, and I haven't done anything else as marshal except help break up a few fights and put a drunk or two in jail for the night. That's hardly enough to warrant these repeated attempts on my life."

"That's the way we see it, too," Sam said.

"What did you do after you ran those varmints off?" Matt asked.

"Came back right here," Seymour rasped. "I loaded a rifle and sat down to wait. I'm not sure what I was waiting for, but I wanted to be ready."

With a look of concern, Maggie said, "You sound like it hurts you to talk."

He nodded. "It does, a little. My throat is rather bruised."

"Why don't you go back to the hotel and take it easy for a while?" Matt suggested. "Miss O'Ryan can bring you some supper—"

"Yes," Maggie said. "Some nice hot soup to soothe your throat. I'd be happy to do that."

Seymour put a hand on her shoulder and said, "I'd

like that. Thank you." He looked at Matt and Sam. "But I have my duties as marshal to think about . . ."

"Don't worry about that," Sam said. "Matt and I will keep an eye on things."

"And have a look at that old barn where those fellas jumped you," Matt added. "Never can tell when we might find something that'll tell us who they were."

Seymour thought about it for a few seconds, then said, "All right, I suppose that makes sense. After starting to repair my reputation in this town, though, I don't want to do anything to make people think I'm acting cowardly. I don't want them to start calling me Seymour the Lily-Livered again."

Maggie bristled with anger. "Anyone who says that around me will be sorry," she declared.

"Anyway, recovering from an attack isn't cowardly," Sam said.

"And it's not every day a fella gets lynched and lives through it," Matt added with a smile. "I reckon folks will understand if you take it easy for a little while."

"Come on," Sam said. "We'll walk over there with you, just to make sure nothing else happens."

Maggie linked her arm with Seymour's. "I'm coming, too. As soon as I know you're safe, I'll go fix that soup."

The four of them left the marshal's office together. Matt walked just ahead of Seymour and Maggie, with Sam just behind the couple. Townspeople stopped them along the way to inquire about Seymour's health and the incident that had almost cost him his life. Their concern seemed genuine.

When they entered the hotel lobby, they found Cornelius Standish waiting there, pacing anxiously. He turned toward them and said, "There you are, Seymour!

What are these rumors I hear about someone trying to kill you again?"

"I'm afraid they're true, Uncle Cornelius," Seymour said. He turned his head and craned his neck a little so that the bruises on his throat were more visible. "They dropped a noose around my neck and tried to hang me."

"Dear God! What sort of uncivilized place is this? Perhaps you should come back to New Jersey with me—"

"No," Seymour said, not waiting for his uncle to finish the suggestion. "I'm not going back. Sweet Apple is my home now, and I'm going to stay here."

"But you're going to get killed!"

"I'll just have to run that risk," Seymour said. "Besides, there are dangers back in New Jersey, too. I . . . I could get run over by a runaway milk wagon, or something like that."

"Well, I suppose your mind is made up," Standish said, scowling.

"Indeed it is." Seymour smiled. "But I appreciate your concern, Uncle Cornelius. To tell you the truth, I didn't know you cared that much."

"Of course I care what happens to you! You're family after all, Seymour."

"I'm glad to hear you feel that way. Now, if you'll excuse me . . . I'm going to go upstairs and rest a bit."

"You go right ahead," Standish told him. "If there's anything I can do for you, just let me know."

"Certainly."

Seymour and Maggie went upstairs, trailed by Matt and Sam. The blood brothers didn't turn back until Seymour was safely in his room—with the door open, as he insisted since Maggie was there.

"I won't do anything to compromise your reputation," he told her.

Cornelius Standish was nowhere in sight when Matt and Sam went back downstairs. "Nice fella for an Eastern dude, that Standish," Matt commented.

"You think so?" Sam said.

"He was mighty worried about Seymour."

Sam nodded and said, "Uh-huh," as if he didn't quite believe it.

Matt looked over at his blood brother as they reached the boardwalk. "You're not still thinkin' that Standish and those new dry-goods salesmen o' his might've had something to do with those attempts on Seymour's life, are you?"

"There's no proof of it so far," Sam admitted. "But I still find it a little coincidental that as soon as they show up in town, somebody starts trying to kill Seymour."

"Cole Halliday shot the hell out of Seymour's hat the day he got to Sweet Apple."

"Yes, but shooting somebody's hat is a lot different than shooting *him*."

Matt couldn't argue with that statement. And since he trusted Sam's instincts, he thought maybe it would be a good idea to start keeping a closer eye on Seymour's uncle and those other three dudes from back East.

They walked down the street to the old barn where the latest attack on Seymour had taken place. Inside, they found the broken beam and the rope, just as Seymour had described. Sam picked up the rope, looked at it closely, ran its rough length through his fingers.

"Nothing unusual about it," he said. "You could buy a rope like this in any general store in town. It might have even been lying around in here, left behind by whoever was the last one to use this barn."

The front and rear doors were both open, letting in quite a bit of light, but Matt scratched a match into life anyway, just to increase the illumination as he hunkered on his heels and studied the ground. He pointed to some marks in the dust and said, "Those look more like shoe prints than boot prints to me."

Sam joined him and frowned in concentration. "I think you're right," he said. "That's something else pointing to Standish and those men who work for him."

"They're not the only ones in Sweet Apple who wear shoes instead of boots," Matt said. "Fellas who clerk in the stores and men like Delacroix who own businesses do, too. Anybody who doesn't ride a horse very often, or at all, is liable to wear shoes."

Sam nodded. "That's true. But if we're talking about a preponderance of the evidence—"

"You're the one usin' highfalutin college words, not me."

"I'm just saying that after a while, things start to pile up and point in a certain direction."

Matt scratched his jaw. "How do you think Seymour's gonna react if you go to him and tell him you think his uncle is the one tryin' to kill him?"

"He's not going to believe me," Sam answered without hesitation.

"That's right. So I reckon we'd better keep lookin' until we're sure."

"Well, I know one thing," Sam said as the blood brothers straightened and Matt ground out the match under his boot heel. "I'm going to be watching Cornelius Standish. The next time trouble strikes, I plan to see where it's coming from."

That was a good idea, Matt thought.

Problem was, where he and Sam were concerned, trouble had a history of sometimes coming from two or three different directions at once.

The men reached the river in the dusk. They reined their horses to a stop on a sandstone bluff overlooking the twisting course of the stream. The western sky was a garish red from the sun that had set a short time earlier, and the water reflected that color so that the Rio Bravo looked like a river of blood as it meandered its way on down toward the Gulf of Mexico.

To the north, on the other side of the river, stretched the Texas plains, their level sweep broken here and there by mesas and rocky hills and ranges of small mountains blunted and worn down by untold millennia of sun and wind and occasional drenching rain. It was a harsh land, West Texas, rugged and starkly beautiful at first. After a while, the beauty faded and it was just ugly.

But as Hector Gallindo sat on his horse and gazed across at Texas in the fading light, he felt excitement stirring within him. Soon, and for the first time in his life, he would be leaving his native Mexico. That was something to look forward to, even though it would be dangerous. A week ago, he had been nothing but a simple farmer.

Now he was a revolutionary!

And that was very exciting, too.

For several days, the group had ridden northward with Diego Alcazarrio and Florio Cruz at its head.

Alcazarrio had visited several other villages besides the one where Hector lived, and at each place he had recruited more men for his band of freedom fighters, promising the young men who joined him that they would help him strike a mortal blow against the wicked dictator, Diaz. Hector believed him. He knew that some people considered Alcazarrio's men to be nothing more than bandits, but Hector knew that wasn't true. They served a noble cause.

Of course, it was a bit puzzling why they were going north, when El Presidente Diaz was in Mexico City, far to the south, but Hector didn't trouble himself over that. He knew that their leader had to have a brilliant plan, and sooner or later Alcazarrio would explain it. Until then, Hector was content to follow orders.

It was better than trying to scratch out a living from the rocky soil of his farm, after all. Better than listening to his mother's complaints and seeing the weary despair on the lined face of his father.

Now, when the men had come as far north as they could without leaving Mexico, Alcazarrio turned his horse around so that he could face them as he addressed them.

"We will make camp here. No fires. Even though the closest settlement on the Texas side of the river is five miles away, we do not want any gringos discovering that we are here."

That made sense to Hector. The gringos were evil; everyone knew that. Perhaps not quite as evil as El Presidente, who oppressed his own people, but still, it was best for Alcazarrio's men not to announce their presence this close to the border, Hector thought.

Following Alcazarrio's orders, the men pulled back a little, so that their camp was located at the base of the bluff away from the river, where they would not be easily spotted. Grass was sparse, but enough for the horses. As night settled down, the men made a meager meal on tortillas and beans.

Hector made sure his horse had been attended to before he worried about caring for himself. He still found it hard to believe that he had a horse and a rifle when, only a few weeks earlier, the only things he truly owned were the clothes on his back and the blisters on his hands. Of course, he supposed that the horse and the rifle actually belonged to Diego Alcazarrio, who had provided them for Hector's use, but still . . . He felt like a rich man compared to his previous existence. Was it any wonder he had thought several times that he would die for Diego Alcazarrio if he was called upon to do so?

He hunkered on his heels and began to munch on a tortilla, but he had barely started eating when a lean shadow fell over him. Hector looked up and saw Florio Cruz standing there.

"Diego wants to see you."

The words surprised Hector even more than the fact that Florio Cruz, Alcazarrio's second in command, had sought him out. So far during the time that Hector had belonged to this band of revolutionaries, neither Alcazarrio nor Cruz had ever spoken directly to him. And now Alcazarrio wanted to meet with him personally. It was a great honor, an overwhelming honor.

Hector realized he was gaping. He snapped his mouth shut and scrambled to his feet. "Of course, Señor Cruz. It will be my great pleasure. More than a pleasure. An honor, a great honor—"

Cruz's curt gesture told Hector to be silent and follow. He did so, and Cruz led him to an outcropping of rock where Diego Alcazarrio sat cross-legged on the ground with his back against the stone. He had a bottle in his hand.

"Here he is," Cruz said. "The one you wanted to see."

Alcazarrio looked up at Hector. "You are Gallindo?" he asked, even though Cruz had already pretty much said that.

"*Sí*, General," Hector said. He didn't know if Alcazarrio preferred to be addressed in that fashion, but he didn't think it would hurt anything to do so.

Then, wonder of wonders, Alcazarrio extended the bottle toward him and said, "Sit. Have a drink with me."

Hector sat down on the ground, and his hand shook a little as he reached for the bottle. He hoped that Alcazarrio didn't notice. He took the bottle, tipped it to his mouth, and tried not to gag on the fiery tequila that burned its way down his throat. It was better than the pulque made by the old men in his village.

Alcazarrio took the bottle back and did not offer again, but that didn't matter. Hector had had a drink with the great revolutionary leader. He would never forget this moment.

"I have asked around about you, Gallindo," Alcazarrio said. "I am told that you speak the gringos' tongue."

Hector bobbed his head in a nod. "*Sí*, General. When I was a boy, I helped the priest in our village. He was a gringo, and he taught me to speak English."

Florio Cruz crossed his arms over his narrow chest and scowled. "What was a gringo priest doing in a Mexican village?" he asked.

Hector shook his head. "I do not know for sure, Señor Cruz. But he was a man with great sadness in him, and a fondness for the pulque made by the old men in the village. I believe he had some dark secret in his past and wished to get as far away from it as he could."

"A sad, drunken priest!" Alcazarrio said with a laugh. "One of many such in the world, eh? What is important is that he taught you to speak the tongue of the hated gringos. Do you still understand it, Gallindo?"

Again, Hector nodded eagerly. "*Sí,* General. Though I have not spoken the words much since I was a child, I still understand them when I hear them. With practice, I am sure I would understand even better."

"You'll get your practice," Alcazarrio said, then took another swig of the liquor. "You're going across the river."

Hector swallowed. "Into Texas, General?"

"That's right. To the settlement called Sweet Apple. There you will watch and listen, pretending to be nothing more than a simple Mexican peasant."

He *was* nothing more than a simple Mexican peasant, Hector thought. Then he quickly corrected himself. He was much more than that now.

He was one of Diego Alcazarrio's soldiers of the *revolución*.

"There are things I need to know," Alcazarrio went on, "and you will find them out for me, Gallindo. Then you will return here and tell me these things."

"Of course, General." Hector hesitated, but he had to ask the question. "But General . . . how will I know what it is I need to find out?"

"I will tell you." Alcazarrio chuckled. "Lean closer, boy. Consider yourself fortunate. Tonight you will be made privy to the plans of the great Diego Alcazarrio. Tonight you will learn of the vengeance that will soon strike at the very hearts of those damned Texans!"

Chapter 13

The night passed quietly in Sweet Apple, without even a fight in the Black Bull or one of the other saloons for Matt and Sam to break up. After spending the night in the marshal's office, they went to the hotel the next morning to check on Seymour.

He opened the door of his room with a gun in his hand, even though Sam had called through the panel after knocking on it to let him know who they were. Matt grinned at him and said, "Now you're gettin' smart. Always figure that somebody's out to kill you, and you're liable to live longer."

"I'm not sure that's a fit way for a man to live," Seymour said as he holstered the revolver.

"Maybe not, but you chose it when you buckled on that gunbelt and pinned that badge to your vest."

Seymour nodded solemnly. "I'm afraid you're right."

"Any problems last night?" Sam asked.

"None whatsoever."

"How was that soup Miss O'Ryan fixed for you?" Matt asked, still grinning.

Seymour's face got pink as he replied, "It was, ah, excellent. Very soothing for the throat."

"And I'll bet the company wasn't bad either," Matt said, nudging Seymour in the ribs with an elbow.

"It was a very pleasant evening." Seymour swallowed hard. "But don't try to make anything out of that. Absolutely nothing improper happened."

"I'm sure it didn't," Sam said. He changed the subject. "We took a look around that barn where those fellas jumped you."

"Did you find anything that told you who they were?"

Sam frowned. "Not really. The rope they used could've come from anywhere. The only unusual thing was that their footprints looked like they were wearing shoes instead of boots."

Seymour's forehead creased in thought, too. "That's a bit unusual for these parts, isn't it?"

"Well, not really. A lot of folks here in town wear shoes instead of boots. All it really tells us is that the men who tried to kill you probably aren't cowboys, or anybody else who rides a horse on a regular basis."

Seymour grunted. "I suppose that eliminates some of the suspects at least."

"Yeah," Sam agreed. "In fact, I was thinking—"

Matt knew that Sam was about to mention his theory about Seymour's Uncle Cornelius and the three dry-goods salesmen being connected somehow to the attempts on Seymour's life, but before Sam could lay those cards on the table, the sound of a commotion in the street came through the hotel room's open window.

At first, it was just loud laughter, but that laughter was followed immediately by the braying of a donkey, angry voices, and then several regularly spaced gunshots.

"What in the world?" Seymour exclaimed as he swung around toward the window. He hurried over to it, followed by Matt and Sam, and looked out to see what all the ruckus was about.

Down in the street, the gunfighter named Cole Halliday had confronted a stocky young Mexican leading a burro. It was obvious that Halliday had shot the straw sombrero right off the Mexican's head. The sombrero, now with a couple of bullet holes in its tall crown, lay in the street, and every time its owner reached for it, Halliday fired again, knocking the sombrero just out of the Mexican's reach. He laughed raucously—sounding oddly like the young man's burro, in fact—as he tormented the Mexican.

"Blast it," Seymour muttered. "That's just about what Cole did to me. I thought he'd gotten over such childish antics."

Seymour swung around and headed for the door in a hurry, obviously intending to put a stop to Halliday's fun. Matt and Sam went after him. Even though they hadn't been in Sweet Apple when it happened, they had heard all about how Cole Halliday had shot up Seymour's derby the day Seymour first arrived. The story had already become part of the town's lore and legends, despite the fact that it had happened less than two months earlier.

Clearly, Seymour was angry that Halliday was resorting to such crude sport again, this time at the expense of a helpless Mexican farmer. There were plenty of them in this border country, and all they wanted was to be left alone to eke out a living for themselves and their families.

Even though Halliday had been behaving himself

lately, there was no telling what he would do if Seymour confronted him and tried to force him to stop doing what he was doing. So the blood brothers knew their presence might be necessary to keep Seymour from getting in over his head.

On the other hand, Seymour was the law in this town now, and Matt and Sam weren't going to be around to help him forever. He had to start learning how to stomp his own snakes if he was going to be the marshal of Sweet Apple.

That thought seemed to occur to Matt and Sam at the same time, because they glanced at each other and hung back a little as Seymour stormed angrily out of the hotel. They wanted to see how he was going to handle this.

Quite a crowd had gathered to watch Halliday humiliate the farmer. Some of them were laughing along with the gunslinger, while others frowned in disapproval. Another shot rang out and sent the bullet-riddled sombrero flying into the air for a few feet. Its owner stumbled after it.

Before Halliday could fire again, Seymour pushed through the crowd and stepped out into the open area in the middle of the street. One of his feet came down right beside the sombrero. "Cole!" he shouted. "Cole Halliday! Stop that right now!"

Seymour's voice was still hoarse from the attempted lynching the day before, but it carried well regardless, silencing the laughter. Halliday stared at him in surprise as smoke curled from the barrel of the Colt in the gunslinger's hand.

"Hell, Marshal, you shouldn't ought to do a thing like that," Halliday said after a moment. "I was gettin' ready to ventilate that greaser's hat again. I might've hit you by accident."

"There'll be no more shooting at this poor man's hat or anything else," Seymour declared. He reached down, picked up the sombrero, and extended it toward the Mexican, who shuffled forward and accepted it with a grateful nod.

Looking at Halliday again, Seymour went on. "In fact, if you don't holster that gun immediately, I'm going to confiscate it and place you under arrest for disturbing the peace."

"What the hell are you talkin' about?" Halliday exploded. "You're gonna take my gun and throw me in jail?" He shook his head. "I don't think so, Marshal."

"That's what's going to happen if you don't do as I say," Seymour insisted.

Halliday shook his head. A nervous hush hung over the street now, because the townspeople knew that Halliday's pride wouldn't allow him to accept this.

Matt and Sam had stopped on the hotel porch. They leaned against the posts that held up the second-floor balcony, their casual poses belying the fact that both of them were ready to go into action in less than a heartbeat if needed.

Halliday glared at Seymour and said, "I thought you had more sense than that, Marshal. I've been tryin' to steer clear of you, but I'll be damned if that means I'm gonna let you buffalo me."

"All I'm asking you to do is to cease tormenting this man and go on about your business. Whether you make it more than that is up to you." Seymour's voice shook a little, but it had an underlying core of steadiness. Everyone could tell that he wasn't going to back down either.

Halliday looked past Seymour and sneered. "I see now why you're so brave this mornin', Seymour. You've got your two pet gunfighters with you."

Matt straightened, and his voice crackled with anger as he said, "We're nobody's pets, Halliday. And Seymour called the turn. This is his dance, not ours."

Halliday looked like he didn't believe that. "You're sayin' that you'll stay out of it if the marshal and I throw down on each other?"

"That's what we're saying," Sam responded quietly.

Folks in the street began to scatter as it started to look more and more like lead would be flying soon.

"You know that if I draw on Seymour, I'll kill him," Halliday said. "And he's not Seymour the Lily-Livered anymore, so he doesn't have that to protect him."

None of the gunfighters who hung around Sweet Apple wanted to be known for killing The Most Cowardly Man in the West. That was the only thing that had saved Seymour's life during his first couple of weeks in town. But as Halliday had pointed out, that dubious reputation was no longer in place to shield him.

Matt shrugged in response to Halliday's declaration. "Maybe you will kill him," he said. "But it could be that Seymour's better with a gun than you give him credit for, Halliday. Sam and I have been helping him practice." Matt reached in his pocket and brought out a coin. "I've got a twenty-dollar gold piece right here that says he gets some lead in you, no matter what you do." He raised his voice. "Any takers for that bet?"

No one stepped forward to take the wager.

Halliday's scowl darkened even more. "Damn it, I don't want to gun down a lawman. Then every other star-packer in these parts will be after me. I'm not scared of 'em, but it'd be a damned nuisance."

"Then holster your gun and walk away," Seymour said. "It's that simple." He paused. "Anyway, Cole, I know you're not really a cruel man. We fought side by side when those outlaws attacked the town. Just don't fall back into your old habit of making trouble."

"Damn it, you're tryin' to civilize me!" Halliday swept his free hand around in a gesture that encompassed the whole settlement. "Sweet Apple used to be the most hell-roarin' place in the border country! Look at it now! It's gettin' positively tame since you came to town, Seymour!"

Seymour smiled. "Thank you. That's quite a compliment."

"I didn't mean it as a damned compliment!" Shaking his head and muttering frustrated curses, Halliday suddenly jammed his revolver back in its holster. "There! You satisfied, Marshal?"

"Indeed I am," Seymour said with a nod. "Thank you."

Halliday jabbed a finger at him. "You ain't welcome!" Still fuming, he turned and stalked toward the Black Bull, obviously intent on guzzling down some whiskey despite the relatively early hour.

What was left of the crowd started to break up. Seymour waited until Halliday had slapped aside the batwings and vanished into the saloon before he turned and walked back to where Matt and Sam waited on the hotel porch. His face was pale but composed. He managed to smile faintly as he said, "Well, that was a near thing."

"If you mean Halliday came close to blowin' a hole through you, you're right about that," Matt told him.

"Would you have let him do it?"

Sam said, "We'll be riding on one of these days, probably before too much longer. It's going to be up to you to keep the peace, Seymour. You have to be able to handle the job."

"That doesn't really answer my question."

"What I said was true," Matt told him. "I think there's a good chance you'd have got lead in him. Halliday knew that, too. That's why he turned and walked away. You pushed him just far enough, Seymour, but not too far. He knows you're the law now, and he knows you mean business. I reckon even an hombre like Halliday can respect that."

"I hope so," Seymour said with a sigh. "And I hope Sweet Apple does become civilized."

"We'll be long gone before that ever happens," Matt said with a grin.

Seymour felt a tug on his sleeve and turned to see the stocky young Mexican standing there, his ventilated sombrero in his hands. The young man had a round face and a mustache that drooped over both ends of his mouth. He nodded and said, "*Gracias, señor.* I . . . appreciate . . . your help."

His halting speech showed that he spoke English but seemed a little rusty at it, as if he hadn't used the language in a while.

Seymour smiled at him and said, "That's quite all right. It's my job to see that no one is mistreated in Sweet Apple. I don't recall seeing you in town before."

"I have not been here in . . . a long time. I have a farm . . . down by the border . . . by the Rio Bravo. I came to . . . buy supplies."

Seymour nodded. "Well, I hope this unfortunate

incident won't keep you from coming to town more often in the future, Señor? . . ."

"Gallindo," the Mexican said. "My *nombre* is Hector Gallindo. And thanks to you, Marshal, I will be able to stay in Sweet Apple until I have everything that I need."

Cornelius Standish twitched the curtain closed and uttered a disgusted curse. "I thought that gunman was about to take care of my problem for me," he said. "Then, not only would I be rid of Seymour and any possible interference with my plans, but I wouldn't have to pay that bonus I promised to those so-called professional killers either."

Rebecca Jimmerson knew that Standish had been watching a showdown of some sort in the street between Seymour and one of the local gunslingers. She had listened to the almost gleeful sound of his voice as he described what was going on. But she hadn't gotten out of bed to watch it with him.

Now, though, she stood up and wrapped a silk dressing gown around her nudity as she went over to him. "Bonus?" she said.

Standish nodded. "That's right. I told Welch, Mc-Cracken, and Stover that in addition to the fees we already agreed on, I'd pay a three-thousand-dollar bonus to whichever one of them actually kills Seymour."

"You really want him dead, don't you?"

Standish frowned at her. "I thought you knew that already. Why else do you think I came out here to this godforsaken wilderness?"

"Oh, I knew," Rebecca said. "I just didn't know how far you were willing to go."

"As far as it takes," Standish snapped.

She nodded, realizing that the same thing was true of her. She had thought that Seymour himself might represent a way out for her. That was why she had revealed her feelings to him.

And then he had rejected her. All because he was in love with that dough-faced, little half-breed schoolteacher. The memory was still like a knife in Rebecca's guts.

Well, Seymour didn't know it, but he still might represent a way for her to get away from Cornelius Standish for good. Three thousand dollars would take her a long way. With that much money, she could start a whole new life for herself.

And if Standish was willing to pay that much to one of those incompetent bumblers he had brought with him, surely he would pay it to someone who could actually deliver what he wanted to him.

Rebecca turned her back to Standish and smiled at the thought. She didn't lose the smile even when he slid the silk off her shoulders and began caressing her. Her mind was somewhere else and she barely felt his touch.

Hector led the burro toward the general store, aware that Marshal Standish and the two gringo gunfighters, Bodine and Two Wolves, were watching him. General Alcazarrio had explained who those men were—and why he hated them so.

If the general hated them, then so did Hector. But it was more difficult to do so than he had expected, because of the way the marshal had risked his own life to intervene when that other gunfighter decided to humiliate a poor Mexican farmer. Bodine and Two Wolves had stood ready to take his part, too, if they needed to.

Hector forced any thoughts of sympathy and gratitude out of his mind. Alcazarrio had sent him to Sweet Apple to carry out an important mission, and he intended to do exactly that, no matter what it required.

He certainly hadn't hesitated early this morning when he stole the burro from an old man's farm just north of the Rio. If he was going to pretend to still be a farmer himself, it would look better if he had a burro. So he had taken one from the first place he came to. Unfortunately, the animal's owner had seen Hector leading it out of the barn and had run out of the house, screeching furiously and waving around an equally ancient shotgun that probably wouldn't even fire.

Hector hadn't waited to find out if the old scattergun worked. He had used the rifle that Alcazarrio had so kindly provided for him and blown the old man's brains out.

Then, leading the burro, he'd resumed his journey to Sweet Apple. Outside of the settlement, he had found an arroyo and changed out of the new clothes the general had given him, putting on the white shirt and trousers and the sandals he had been wearing when he left his village to join the revolutionaries. He cached the better clothing there, along with the rifle and his horse. Now he was armed only with a knife, which was not an uncommon weapon for a farmer to carry. It would arouse no suspicion.

Hector went into the general store and pretended to look around. In reality, he was listening to the conversations going on among the townspeople around him. The best places to pick up useful information were stores such as this one and saloons like the Black Bull, which Hector had noticed across the street.

Diego Alcazarrio both spoke and read English. Even in hiding in the mountains of Mexico, he was able to obtain gringo newspapers from Marfa, El Paso, and San Antonio. In them he had read accounts of the battle at Sweet Apple, when the American army and the citizens of the town had prevented him from obtaining the new rifles he desired so badly. That was how he had learned of Sweet Apple's marshal, Seymour Standish, and the two gunmen Bodine and Two Wolves. The one called Two Wolves was half-gringo, half-Indian, but that didn't matter to Alcazarrio. Half-gringo was the same as all gringo as far as he was concerned, and worthy of just as much hatred as any other gringo.

The general had explained all of this to Hector in the group's camp below the border. Alcazarrio had explained as well about the ranchers named Colton and Paxton.

"They are the two richest men this side of El Paso," the general had said. "And each man has a beautiful young daughter." Alcazarrio had leaned back against the rock and laughed. "Eh? Eh? You know what I mean, Gallindo?"

"*Sí,* General," Hector had said as he bobbed his head, but in truth, he didn't know what Alcazarrio meant at all.

"Those gringos will pay handsomely to ensure the safe return of their daughters," Florio Cruz had put in.

Alcazarrio had continued to laugh and slap his thigh. "One hundred thousand American dollars for each," he had said between wheezes.

Hector's eyes had grown so wide at that, it seemed as

if they might escape from their sockets. Now he understood what the general was getting at.

Diego Alcazarrio planned to kidnap the two young American women and force their fathers to pay a huge ransom to get them back. A king's ransom, as far as Hector was concerned. He could not even imagine a sum as large as two hundred thousand dollars, let alone dream that he might be part of obtaining such a fortune for the noble cause that drove them. Why, with that much money, Alcazarrio could raise an entire army to throw out the dictator, Diaz.

"What can I do to help, General?" he had asked breathlessly.

So Alcazarrio had explained how he, Hector, would go to Sweet Apple and pretend to be nothing more than a peasant, the sort of poor farmer who was as plentiful as fleas in the border country. Once there, he would find out everything he could about the ranchers Colton and Paxton and their families. What Alcazarrio really wanted to do was to raid Sweet Apple again, this time while both girls were there. It would be too difficult to steal them from their fathers' ranches, he had explained. But an attack on the town would create much confusion, and in that chaos it would be easier to snatch the young women and get away with them.

"So you see, my young amigo, much depends on you," Alcazarrio had concluded. "You will determine when we strike. When you see Jessica Colton and Sandra Paxton together in Sweet Apple, you will ride here and tell us the time has come for the attack. Can you do this thing?"

Hector hadn't hesitated, even for a second. He had nodded and vowed, "*Sí*, General. I will do this, just as you say."

And now, as he stood in the general store in Sweet Apple, he was no less determined to carry out his mission than he had been when he arrived in the settlement. The fact that the marshal had taken his part against the gunslinger's cruelties meant nothing.

Nor could he allow the thing that Alcazarrio had said after explaining everything to deter him. Hector had asked, in all sincerity, "And after you have the ransom, General, you will let the gringo girls return to their families?"

Alcazarrio had laughed harder than ever at that. "Of course not," he had said, leaning forward to slap Hector on the shoulder. "They are young and beautiful, amigo! And for your service, you shall have your pick of them. At least, you will be allowed to take them first, before the rest of our men."

Hector had swallowed hard at that. He knew the women would never live through such a fate. When Alcazarrio's men were through with them, they would be fit for nothing except the coyotes and the buzzards. It was a harsh destiny indeed.

But that did not matter, Hector told himself, not for the first time.

All that mattered . . . was the *revolución*.

Chapter 14

Since the deaths of the two cowboys named Rusty and Bill, Shad Colton hadn't tried to keep Esau Paxton's cows from drinking at the creek between their ranches. The judge had promised a speedy hearing and a decision on the case within a week or two. Colton had decided that he could tolerate Pax cows drinking his water for that long.

Because of that, when his lawyer, Colonel Hugh Addison, drove up to the Double C ranch house in a fine buggy pulled by a pair of magnificent horses, Colton assumed the lawyer was there to tell him that Judge Wilbur had set a date for announcing his decision in the case.

Colton stepped out onto the porch and stuck his hands in the hip pockets of his jeans. "Howdy, Hugh," he called to Addison. "What brings you out here?" he asked even though he thought he already knew the answer.

The rotund, ruddy-faced lawyer climbed down from the buggy. "Got some news," he rumbled in his usual growling tones as he pulled a bandanna from his pocket to wipe sweat from his face. "Rather come up there on the porch and sit in the shade to tell you about it, though."

Colton waved him up the steps. "Sure, come on. I'll tell my missus to bring us some lemonade."

"Sounds mighty fine," Addison said as he climbed to the porch. He tapped his coat pocket with a blunt finger. "And I got a little somethin' here that'll go just fine in that lemonade, too."

Colton grinned, knowing that Addison never went anywhere without a flask on him.

They didn't talk business until they were both settled down in cane-bottomed chairs with sweating glasses of lemonade in hand. Colton took a sip of his, appreciating the way the addition from Addison's flask made the cool liquid go down even smoother.

"Now, what's this news you mentioned?" he asked. "Judge Wilbur ready to announce his decision, is he?"

"Judge Wilbur's not gonna be announcin' any decision," the lawyer replied. "He's recused himself from the case."

Colton sat up straight in his chair, confused and surprised by Addison's answer. "What in blazes does that mean?"

"Means he's taken himself off the case. A judge usually does that when he's got some sort o' conflict of interest, like one o' the parties is his brother-in-law or something. But this was for health reasons. The judge got knocked down by a runaway horse a few days ago. Broke his right leg and a couple of ribs."

Colton frowned. "That shouldn't mean he can't decide one way or the other in the case between me and Paxton."

Colonel Addison's beefy shoulders rose and fell in a shrug. "That's up to the judge, and he didn't think he was in good enough shape to render a fair and proper verdict."

Colton stood up and began to pace. "What are we supposed to do then? Wait until he's better and start the whole damned thing over?"

Addison took another swig of spiked lemonade and said, "No, there's a federal circuit judge due through these parts in a couple of days, and Judge Wilbur has transferred jurisdiction of the case to him."

"A federal judge?" Colton was confused again. "Can he do that?"

"Since the case involves water rights, he can," Addison said with a nod. "Wilbur and this new judge have already been in touch by telegram, and Judge Clark agreed to take on the case. Only hitch is that he wants to have a new hearin' so he can get the facts straight."

"You mean we've got to go to Marfa and do it all over again?" Colton asked in disgust.

"No, no, since Judge Clark is used to travelin' around, bein' a circuit judge and all, he's agreed to hold the hearin' in Sweet Apple. Day after tomorrow, in fact."

That mollified Colton a little. He had been afraid the delays might stretch out to an intolerable length. "Can you be ready for a hearing that soon?" he asked Addison.

The lawyer nodded. "Sure. The facts haven't changed since last time. All I got to do is present 'em again. And the law's still on your side, Shad. I'm sure o' that."

"Well, then . . . I reckon there's nothin' else we can do but go along with this new judge."

Addison finished off his lemonade. "That's exactly what I'm advisin' you to do as your attorney. The hearing will be at ten o'clock in the morning day after tomorrow in the town hall."

"I'll be there," Colton said with a grim-faced nod. "And maybe this blasted mess will get settled once and for all."

* * *

Since the talkative Colonel Addison had stopped in Sweet Apple on his way to the Double C and had a drink at the Black Bull, news of the developments in the legal case was already going around town. Gossip was one of the chief pastimes in any frontier settlement, and Sweet Apple was no different.

Matt and Sam heard about it while they were at the livery stable with Seymour, who had decided that he needed a horse. "Mayor Mitchell and Mr. Heathcote say that the town will provide a mount for me, as long as the cost is reasonable," Seymour had explained. "I could use some help in picking one out. I'm afraid I, ah, don't have much experience with horses. I thought maybe the two of you could go with me to the stable . . ."

"Sure, Seymour," Matt had told him, clapping a hand on his shoulder. "We've been sticking to you like a burr anyway. Might as well go to the stable as anywhere else."

It was true that Matt and Sam hadn't been far from Seymour's side during the past couple of days, following the second attempt on his life. During that time nothing unusual had happened, but neither of the blood brothers were convinced that Seymour was out of danger. Whoever wanted him dead was just waiting for another good chance to strike.

Seymour's voice had just about lost the hoarseness left over from the bruising of his throat. The mottled red and purple marks on his skin had faded, too. As he stood at the fence of the corral behind the stable, he propped a booted foot on the bottom rail and leaned on the top one, just like a real Westerner.

"How about that one?" he said as he pointed to a bay gelding inside the corral.

The proprietor of the stable, a man named Huddleston, had followed them out to the fence. He chuckled and said, "You've got a good eye for horseflesh, Marshal. That's one of my finest animals, and I can let you have him for only a hundred and fifty dollars."

Seymour looked over at Matt and Sam, both of whom shook their heads.

"That horse is too fine-boned, Seymour," Matt said. "Might have pretty good speed startin' out, but no sand."

"That's the horse you want," Sam said, pointing to an ugly, hammer-headed, mouse-colored animal with a dark stripe down its back.

"Really?" Seymour asked with a frown. "He doesn't look like much . . . not that I'd really know."

Huddleston shook his head. "I don't know, Marshal. I reckon that dun's strong enough, but he's mean. He'll take a bite out of your hide if you don't watch him mighty close."

Seymour looked back at the blood brothers, who nodded. "Could be that's right," Matt said. "But he'll run all day for you, too, and that deep chest says he's got as much speed as you'll ever need."

"You can tell all that just by looking at him?"

Matt and Sam both shrugged. "You wanted our opinion," Sam pointed out.

"Certainly. And I have no reason to doubt that you're right." Seymour turned to Huddleston. "How much for that horse?"

The stable man pursed his lips. "Fifty dollars," he finally said. "And I feel like I'm cheatin' you, at that, Marshal."

"Take it," Matt advised.

Seymour nodded and stuck out his hand to Huddleston. "You have a deal, my good man."

They were shaking hands when J. Emerson Heathcote came walking up. "Have you heard about the hearing?" the newspaperman asked.

Seymour shook his head. "What hearing?"

"I suppose I shouldn't be spreading the news verbally," Heathcote said with a laugh. "I should make everyone wait to read it in the Sweet Apple *Gazette*. But the rumors are already going around. A new judge has been appointed to settle the dispute between Shad Colton and Esau Paxton, and he's going to hold a hearing right here in Sweet Apple day after tomorrow. It'll be the biggest legal case we've ever had adjudicated here."

Matt and Sam looked at each other, and then Matt asked, "I reckon Colton and Paxton will be comin' into town for that hearing?"

Heathcote nodded. "Of course. They'll have to be on hand to testify."

Sam said, "That means you're going to have your hands full, Seymour."

"Why?" Seymour wanted to know. "I don't have anything to do with that court case."

"Chances are that Colton and Paxton will bring their families and most of their crews with them," Matt explained. "That means Sweet Apple will be full of proddy cowboys with a grudge against each other."

"And it'll be up to you to keep the peace," Sam said.

Seymour frowned and nodded. "Yes, I suppose it will. Can I count on your help?"

"Sure, we'll be around for that long," Matt said. "We

may be gettin' a little restless, but we're not in that much of a hurry to leave."

"I'm glad to hear it," Seymour said with obvious relief. He turned back to Huddleston. "Now, I suppose I'll need a saddle, too . . ."

When they had concluded the deal, they agreed that Seymour could keep his horse and tack at the stable for a nominal monthly fee. Heathcote said, "I'll speak to the mayor and the rest of the town council about paying for that expense, too, Marshal."

Seymour nodded. "I'd be much obliged."

"You're startin' to sound like you belong out here, Seymour," Matt commented with a chuckle. "Next thing you know, you'll be sayin' that it's fixin' to rain, or something like that."

The four of them headed back toward the marshal's office, with Seymour and Heathcote walking together in front and talking. Matt and Sam trailed along a short distance behind. Their eyes roved constantly over both sides of the street, searching for any sign of danger. Even though nothing had happened for a couple of days, neither of the blood brothers believed that the threat was over.

Whoever wanted Seymour dead was bound to try again sooner or later.

They were passing one of the cantinas when Sam said quietly, "Isn't that the fella Cole Halliday was hoorawing the other day?"

Matt looked and saw a stocky Mexican leaving the cantina. The young man's face was familiar, but even if hadn't been, the bullet holes in the crown of his sombrero would have identified him.

"Yeah, that's him, all right," Matt agreed. "I thought

he said he came to Sweet Apple to buy some supplies. Shouldn't he have headed back to his farm by now?"

"You'd think so."

The Mexican—Hector, that was his name, Matt recalled—stumbled a little as he went over to untie his burro from a nearby hitch rail. Matt smiled as Hector started to lead the burro out of town. He said, "I reckon that explains it. I don't see any supplies loaded on his donkey. He must've spent the past couple of days blowin' his money on tequila."

"That's too bad. He's liable to have a hard time of it now, until he can scrape up some more *dinero*."

"That's his lookout, not ours. Come on, Seymour's gettin' too far ahead of us."

The blood brothers stepped up their pace, not looking back at the raggedly clothed Mexican who was plodding southward out of Sweet Apple, leading the little burro.

It had taken a couple of days of hanging around the settlement, but things could not have worked out much better, Hector Gallindo thought as he left Sweet Apple behind. The developments he had heard about today would play right into the hands of Diego Alcazarrio.

The Coltons and the Paxtons would all be in town for the court hearing, including Jessica Colton and Sandra Paxton. And they would be in one place, making it easier for Alcazarrio to abduct them. The only drawback was that many of the cowboys from the Double C and Pax ranches would probably be on hand for the hearing, too, which meant there could be more opposition to the general's plans than there might have been otherwise.

But Alcazarrio would never get a better chance to kidnap the two girls, Hector thought. And the way things had turned out, the general would even have time to plan his raid, since it wouldn't take place until the day after tomorrow.

Each of the past two nights, Hector had checked on the horse he'd left hidden outside of town, making sure the animal had enough water and grass. This time when he reached the arroyo, he changed back into his new clothes, saddled the horse, and rode south, a revolutionary again instead of the poor farmer he had pretended to be for the past two days. He took the burro with him, not wanting to release it so close to the settlement. He didn't want anyone to come across the animal and wonder what had happened to him. Everyone needed to think he had simply returned to his farm.

Later that day, Hector reached the Rio Grande and crossed it, leaving the burro to fend for itself. As he rode up the bluff, he felt eyes watching him and knew that the lookouts posted by Alcazarrio had spotted him. They had probably already sent word to the general that he was coming.

That proved to be true when Hector reached the camp and found it in a state of suppressed excitement. The men all knew that his return meant something important was about to happen. Knowing that made a good feeling swell up inside Hector. He was important to Alcazarrio's plans. He had been entrusted with a vital mission, and he had not failed the general.

Alcazarrio and Florio Cruz strode out to meet Hector as he dismounted. "What have you found out?" Alcazarrio demanded curtly, without any greeting.

"The two señoritas will be in Sweet Apple at ten

o'clock in the morning, two days hence," Hector reported. He went on to explain about the legal dispute between Shadrach Colton and Esau Paxton and the hearing that would be held at the town hall.

Alcazarrio grinned and rubbed his hands together in anticipation. "You have done a fine job, amigo," he told Hector, whose heart swelled even more at the praise from his general.

Cruz didn't look happy, though. Instead, he frowned and said, "Many of the men who work for those gringo ranchers will be there. They will fight."

"Of course they will," Alcazarrio agreed, "but they will be no match for us. Also, we will take them by surprise. Their wariness will be directed toward each other, not toward any threat from outside."

Cruz gave an eloquent shrug. "You are right as always, Diego."

Alcazarrio thumped his chest and nodded. "Of course I am," he declared. "Come. We will talk about it and decide exactly how we will attack the gringos. And it must be made clear to all the men that no harm shall come to the two señoritas. That is most important."

"What about the man Standish, and the two gunfighters, Bodine and Two Wolves?" Cruz asked as he and Alcazarrio turned and walked away.

"Oh, they shall die," the general answered without hesitation. Hector heard him clearly. Alcazarrio went on. "I wish I could kill them myself. Perhaps I will. But all that really matters is that they not be left alive."

Hector hadn't been invited to accompany the leaders of the band of revolutionaries, so he stayed where he was. He heard Alcazarrio's words, however, and he felt a twinge of regret at them. He remembered how Marshal

Seymour Standish had defended him against that cruel gringo called Halliday. He recalled as well how Bodine and Two Wolves had stood ready to step in if necessary. All on behalf of a poor Mexican peasant that none of them knew or had even seen before. A stirring of unease inside Hector told him that they were good men—for gringos—and perhaps didn't really deserve to die.

But the general knew best, he told himself sternly, and anyway, Fate had no respect for what a person did or did not deserve. Life was capricious and cruel and dealt whatever destiny it wanted to, with no regard for the pain it caused. Every poor Mexican learned that at an early age, the first time he went to sleep at night with hunger gnawing at his empty belly, or the first time he worked for long, backbreaking hours in the hot sun so that someone else could grow rich.

Thus it was, thus it would ever be, and if Seymour Standish, Matt Bodine, and Sam Two Wolves had to die to further the cause . . . then so be it.

Chapter 15

Seymour was confused. The three men his uncle had brought to Sweet Apple to develop the sales territory here in West Texas for the Standish Dry Goods Company never seemed to do any actual work. They weren't calling on merchants in Sweet Apple, they weren't visiting any other settlements in the area . . . in short, they didn't seem to be interested in selling dry goods at all.

At first Seymour told himself that was none of his business. But of course it was, because he still owned a half-interest in the company. He knew his father never would have allowed such laggard behavior from employees. Seymour was surprised that his uncle tolerated it. Cornelius had always been the more impatient and demanding of the brothers.

So, he owed it to his father's memory, Seymour decided, to talk with his uncle and see if he could find out what was going on.

He reached that decision on the morning when the hearing on the dispute between Shad Colton and Esau Paxton was scheduled to take place. Seymour knew he would have to be there for the hearing, to keep the peace in case any trouble broke out between the two factions, but he thought he would have time to talk to Cornelius before that.

He was at the marshal's office when he reached that decision. Matt and Sam had left a few minutes earlier to go down to the café and get breakfast for all three of them. They would bring the food back to the office on trays. As far as they knew, Seymour was going to stay right there in the office until they got back.

Seymour knew he ought to do exactly that, but he found impatience gnawing at him. Once he'd made up his mind to do something, he didn't like to put it off.

The hotel wasn't very far away, he told himself. He would have time to walk over there, have a talk with Cornelius, and get back to the office, maybe even before Matt and Sam returned. He didn't think there would be any danger in walking along Main Street in broad daylight either. The morning had dawned bright and hot and clear, and the town was buzzing about the hearing that would soon take place. Shad Colton and Esau Paxton both had friends in Sweet Apple, and naturally folks took sides in any dispute. Everybody was going to be very interested to see how Judge Simon Clark was going to rule—if he even reached a decision today.

Judge Clark had reached Sweet Apple the previous evening, driving a buggy with an Appaloosa saddle horse tied on behind it. The judge was a burly man of medium height, with a salt-and-pepper beard and deep-set, intelligent eyes with bags under them that gave him a deceptively sleepy look. He had introduced himself to Seymour, Matt, and Sam, and Seymour had liked the no-nonsense jurist immediately. He had a feeling that Clark would keep the hearing moving along briskly, and probably wouldn't waste any time reaching a decision either.

Seymour put his hat on and left the office, checking up and down the street first just to make sure that no one was lurking out there, waiting to take a shot at him. Matt and Sam seemed convinced there would be another attempt on his life, but Seymour wasn't sure about that. The would-be killers, whoever they were, could have decided that getting rid of him was too much trouble and moved on instead.

As he walked toward the hotel, Seymour spotted a familiar figure coming from the opposite direction and felt pleasure and surprise go through him. He met Maggie O'Ryan on the porch in front of the hotel and asked, "Why aren't you down at the school today?"

"School is out, Seymour," she replied with a smile. "Didn't you know? I would have thought that the way the children were whooping so happily yesterday afternoon when I dismissed them for the last time would have told you."

"I'm sorry," he said with a shake of his head. "I'm afraid I didn't notice. I knew that you'd been very busy the past few days—"

"Getting everything finished up for the year," she explained.

Seymour smiled. "Perhaps now we can spend more time together."

"I'd like that," Maggie said with a shy smile of her own as she touched him lightly on the arm. "Until school starts again in the fall anyway."

Another feeling of anticipation went through Seymour as he thought about an entire summer spent getting to know Maggie better. And then in the fall—the thought popped unbidden into his mind—then in the fall, perhaps they would know each other well enough so that he could ask her a very important question . . .

Right now, though, he still had that business with his uncle to take care of, he reminded himself as he caught his breath. But he wasn't ready to desert Maggie just yet.

"I was wondering," he began, "I was wondering if perhaps you'd like to take a buggy ride with me sometime."

Her face lit up with delight and that made her even prettier, as far as Seymour was concerned. "That sounds wonderful," she said. "I could pack a picnic lunch for us."

He nodded. "Yes, of course. Wonderful indeed. We'll talk about it later and decide where and when. Right now . . . I'm sorry, but I have to tend to some business."

"I understand," Maggie said. "You'll be at the hearing later?"

"Of course."

"I'll see you there." She came up on her toes and brushed her lips across his in a kiss. To do such a thing in broad daylight, on a public street, was pretty brazen— but Seymour liked it.

His heart was pounding hard as he left Maggie and went into the hotel. More than ever, he thought that perhaps he had found the woman with whom he wanted to spend the rest of his life.

He stopped short as he saw Rebecca Jimmerson standing in the lobby, her arms crossed and an icy look on her face. Seymour glanced over his shoulder and realized that if Rebecca had been standing where she was a moment earlier, she had probably been able to watch through the hotel's front window as Maggie kissed him.

His contacts with Rebecca had been few since the day she had revealed her romantic interest in him. Seymour thought that keeping his distance from her was best under the circumstances. But since they had known each other for years and she was standing there less than a dozen feet away, he couldn't very well ignore her now.

Seymour forced a smile onto his face and nodded politely to her. "Miss Jimmerson . . . Rebecca," he said. "How are you today?"

"I'm fine," she said, but her chilly tone of voice didn't make her sound fine at all. "I don't suppose I need to ask how you are, Seymour. I could see that perfectly well for myself just now."

She *had* seen Maggie kiss him, he thought as he felt his face growing warm. But there was nothing wrong with two people who cared about each other sharing a kiss, he reminded himself. To think otherwise would be disrespectful to Maggie.

To change the subject, Seymour said, "I'm looking for my uncle. Have you seen Cornelius this morning?"

"I certainly have. He's upstairs in his room . . . with those so-called salesmen of his."

"So-called? . . ." Seymour felt his pulse quicken. Did she think there was something wrong about Welch, McCracken, and Stover, too? Excitedly, he asked, "What do you mean by that, Rebecca?"

She shrugged. "I don't know. It's just that they don't seem to be very interested in selling dry goods, do they? They hang around here at the hotel, and at that saloon called the Black Bull, and as far as I can see, they haven't done a lick of work since they came to Sweet Apple."

She was saying the very same things he had thought earlier, Seymour realized. He knew now that his suspicions weren't just the products of his own imagination, as he had worried that they might be. Rebecca shared his concerns, too.

"This is incredible," he said. "I was about to go talk to Uncle Cornelius about the very same thing. I didn't know that you were worried about it, too."

Rebecca lost some of her chilly demeanor as she came closer to him. "You can't talk to him right now," she said. "Those men are in with him discussing God knows what." She put a hand on Seymour's arm. "Come up to my room with me. It's right across the hall from Mr. Standish's room. We'll be able to hear them when they leave, and then you can go talk to him."

Seymour considered her suggestion, the wheels of his brain turning over rapidly. What Rebecca said made sense, but if he went along with her, he would be gone longer from the marshal's office than he had intended. Matt and Sam might get back there before he could return, and then they would worry that something had happened to him.

But he was a grown man, after all, and the marshal of Sweet Apple, for goodness' sake. He didn't have to ask permission to go and talk to his uncle. As long as he concluded his discussion with Cornelius in time to reach the town hall before the hearing got under way, everything should be fine.

Seymour took his watch out, flipped it open, and checked the time. Five minutes after nine. Almost an hour was left before the hearing started. There should be plenty of time, he decided, and if Welch, McCracken, and Stover stayed closeted with his uncle for too long, well, he could always leave and come back to talk to Cornelius later, Seymour decided.

"All right," he said to Rebecca with a nod. "That's a good idea."

She smiled. All the coolness was gone from her now. She took his arm and said, "Come along then. It'll be nice to visit while we're waiting for those men to leave."

As they started up the stairs, Seymour felt a momentary surge of uneasiness. He was going to be alone with Rebecca in her hotel room for an undetermined amount of time. Given what had happened on the last occasion when they were together like that, this might not be such a good idea after all. Of course, he knew that nothing improper would happen, because he wouldn't allow it to. But if Maggie heard about it . . .

There was no reason for her to hear anything of the sort, he told himself. Anyway, there was nothing going on between him and Rebecca. This was strictly business.

Still, he was glad the lobby and the second-floor corridor were deserted at the moment, so that there was no one to see him going into Rebecca Jimmerson's room. No one to see the door closing behind them . . .

"What the hell?" Matt said as he came into the marshal's office carrying one of the breakfast trays.

Sam was right behind him with the other two trays, one in each hand. "What's wrong?" he asked when he heard Matt's puzzled exclamation.

"Seymour's not here!"

The marshal's office was empty. They set the trays on the desk and took a quick look around, but there weren't that many places to hide in the small office—and no reason for Seymour to be hiding in the first place.

"He might've gone out back to the privy," Sam suggested.

"You take a look there, while I check up and down the street and see if I can spot him."

Sam nodded and went out the office's rear door. Matt left by the front and stopped on the boardwalk to peer both directions along the street, searching for Seymour.

He hadn't found the marshal by the time Sam came back through the office and reported a similar lack of results. "He's not in the privy. Where could he have gotten off to?"

"I reckon he could've gone over to the hotel to see his uncle." Matt shook his head. "Don't know why he would have, when he knew we were expectin' him to stay here . . . but he's Seymour. Can't always tell what he's gonna do."

"That's right," Sam agreed. "Let's go over there and see if we can find him."

Breakfast was forgotten as the blood brothers started down the street toward the hotel. In all likelihood, there was an innocent explanation for Seymour's absence and he wasn't in any real danger, but Matt and Sam couldn't forget the two previous attempts on his life.

The sound of hoofbeats—a *lot* of hoofbeats—distracted them before they reached the hotel. They stopped and swung around to see a buckboard and more than twenty riders entering the settlement. A big, red-headed man on horseback led the procession. Matt and Sam recognized Shad Colton. The rancher had arrived early for the hearing, bringing his family and what looked like most of his crew with him.

"I figured practically the whole Double C bunch

would show up," Matt said. "Didn't think they'd get here quite this soon, though."

"That's not the problem." Sam nodded past the Coltons and their men. "They're not the only ones riding in early."

Matt saw the dust rising into the clear morning sky, just outside the settlement. A group of roughly the same size was coming into town, and it could only be Esau Paxton and his family and riders.

"Damn it," Matt grated. "We need to keep those two bunches apart, or there may be trouble before the hearing ever gets started."

"Yeah," Sam agreed. "Let's hope Seymour's all right, because we don't have time to go looking for him now."

"He'll show up," Matt said, wishing that he felt as confident as he sounded.

They strode quickly down the street. The Colton party had come to a halt in front of the town's meeting hall. Carolyn Colton and Jessie were on the buckboard, with Carolyn handling the reins. Both women wore dresses and sunbonnets. Matt thought that Jessie looked like she would have preferred wearing boots and jeans and a Stetson and making the trip on horseback like her father, but he supposed she was trying to look like a lady since the family was going to court.

Sam walked quickly along the street to intercept the Paxton party. Matt lifted a hand in greeting as Shad Colton swung down from the saddle. "Mornin', Mr. Colton," he said. "You're here a mite early."

Colton's eyes narrowed. "Didn't want Paxton tryin' to steal a march on me. I don't know this new judge. Paxton might try to make friends with him, or even bribe him."

Matt shook his head. "I don't think that's gonna happen. We met Judge Clark yesterday evenin', and he strikes me as the sort of hombre who's gonna be fair, come hell or high water."

"We'll see about that." Colton turned to the buggy to help his wife down from the vehicle.

Jessie didn't wait for anybody to help her, although Matt would have if she'd given him the chance. She stepped down from the buggy on her own, and as Matt went over to her, she said, "I hope you and Sam plan on going to the hearing. The boys are a mite proddy this morning."

Matt could see that for himself. The Double C hands were all wearing six-guns and had tense looks on their faces, as if they were spoiling for a fight. It wouldn't take much of a spark to set off an explosive ruckus.

"Don't worry," he told Jessie. "We'll be there, and we'll see to it that things don't get out of hand."

Jessie looked around. "Where's the marshal?"

Matt shrugged. He wished he could answer that question.

The Double C punchers started for the double doors that opened into the town hall. Before they got there, the doors swung open and a formidable figure barred the way. Judge Simon Clark stood there in a dusty black suit, with a shotgun tucked under his right arm.

"Gentlemen," Clark's powerful voice boomed out, "for the duration of the hearing this morning, this town hall is now a federal courtroom! And as such, no guns are allowed amongst the spectators."

Loud, angry voices were raised in protest.

That didn't seem to faze Clark. He stood there calmly, letting the reaction run its course. When the uproar died down, he continued. "You'll all be required to turn in your firearms if you want to attend the hearing."

Shad Colton pointed at Matt. "What about Bodine and Two Wolves?" he demanded.

"I'm hereby appointing them deputy United States marshals," Clark said.

Matt's eyes widened in surprise. He didn't recall asking to become a deputy U.S. marshal, and he was pretty sure Sam hadn't either.

"Hold on a minute, Judge—" he began.

"These appointments are temporary," Clark said, "for the duration of this case or until I otherwise rescind them, but they *are* legal and binding. Therefore, Mr. Bodine and Mr. Two Wolves have full authority to enforce my orders, and my first such order is that they collect the guns from anybody who wants to come into my courtroom."

Colton's jaw was thrust out belligerently. "Does the same thing go for Paxton and his bunch?"

"You're damn right it does," the judge snapped.

A muscle jumped in Colton's tightly clenched jaw. "Sort of a high-handed hombre, aren't you?"

A grin appeared on Clark's bearded face. "I'm a federal circuit court judge." He tapped the shotgun that he held. "And before I took up the law, I carried this very same Greener as a shotgun guard for a stagecoach line. So, yeah, I reckon you could say that I'm used to gettin' my way."

That seemed to mollify Colton a little. He knew now that Judge Clark wasn't some dude who didn't understand how things were done in the West. Clark was a product of the frontier just like the rest of them.

Colton jerked his head in a nod and turned to his

men. "All right, boys, you heard what the judge said. Shuck those shootin' irons as you go in."

Matt heaved a mental sigh of relief as Colton handed over his revolver and then took his wife's arm to lead her into the town hall. Jessie followed them. Matt supposed that the younger Colton children had remained on the ranch with the cook and the skeleton crew that had been left behind.

The Double C hands filed in. Matt took their guns as they went by. He wasn't prepared for such a chore and didn't have any place to put them, so he wound up with his arms full of revolvers. He was grateful when Abner Mitchell came up with a bushel basket from the general store.

"I saw your dilemma, Matt," the mayor said. "Put the guns in here. I'll bring another basket for Sam to use when he disarms Paxton's group." Mitchell looked as relieved as Matt felt. "Disarming those cowboys will go a long way toward keeping the peace, won't it?"

"Can't hurt," Matt said.

Sam had held the Paxton bunch down the street until everyone from the Double C had gone inside. Esau Paxton didn't look happy about it when Sam finally allowed them to ride on to the town hall. His wife Julia and daughter Sandy were in a buggy, as Carolyn and Jessie Colton had been, but the twins, sixteen-year-old Royce and Dave, were on horseback like their father and the rest of the men. They were packing guns like the rest of the men, too.

Matt quickly filled Sam in on Judge Clark's edict about no guns in the courtroom other than theirs—and that old Greener, Matt supposed. Sam nodded and turned to Paxton. "You heard the rules, sir," he said.

"You and your men will have to turn in your guns before you can go inside."

"And put ourselves at the mercy of that renegade Colton and his pack of thieves?" Paxton shook his head. "I don't think so."

"Mr. Colton and his men gave up their guns," Matt said. "This hearing's gonna be nice and peaceful."

"I suppose you don't *have* to attend," Sam put in. "Your lawyer can represent you."

Paxton reached for the buckle of his gunbelt. "If Colton's in there, I'm going to be in there!" he said. "Here. Here's my damned gun."

"Esau," his wife said in a warning tone. "You know the doctor said you don't need to get all worked up. It's bad for your heart."

Paxton snorted, but he didn't say anything else as he took Julia's arm to escort her into the town hall. The Pax riders followed the same course as the Double C men had, filing into the building and surrendering their guns as they did so.

When everybody was inside, Matt and Sam left the baskets containing the weapons on the boardwalk in front of the town hall. Nobody would bother them. The blood brothers stepped through the open doors and saw that the hall was crowded. Colton's bunch had congregated on the right side of the room, while Paxton and his family and riders had gone to the left. They had scooted their chairs away from each other so that an aisle that hadn't been there earlier had been formed.

At the front of the room, Judge Simon Clark sat behind a table on which lay the shotgun and a gavel, as well as a Bible, some blank sheets of paper, and an inkwell and pen. At one end of the table was an empty chair—for witnesses, Matt supposed.

It was pretty noisy in the room as cowboys from both ranches talked among themselves. Clark let the hubbub continue for a while, then pulled a pocket watch from his vest and opened it.

"The lawyers for both parties aren't here yet, or I'd go ahead and get started," he announced. "Keep the racket down. Court's not in session yet, but I'll still have some decorum in my courtroom."

Matt and Sam took up positions to either side of the doors and waited. A few minutes later, Colonel Hugh Addison, Colton's lawyer, arrived. He was followed a few minutes after that by Everett Sloane, Paxton's attorney. The room was already so crowded that there was no room for more spectators, but J. Emerson Heathcote slipped in, nodded to Matt and Sam, and stood along the back wall, pencil and pad in hand, ready to take notes for his newspaper story.

The two lawyers conferred briefly with the judge, then went to chairs in the front of the room. They didn't sit down, though, because Clark reached for his gavel and said, "All rise." Everyone else got to their feet.

In the rustle of people getting up, Matt looked over at Sam and said, "I sure as hell wish I knew where Seymour was."

Sam didn't have time to reply before the gavel banged down and Judge Clark announced, "This court is now in session!"

Chapter 16

Rebecca told herself to ignore the pounding in her chest. This was one time she had to listen to her head and not her heart. Three thousand dollars was a fortune to her, and it could change her entire life.

She put a smile on her face as she watched her visitor fidgeting. "Don't be so nervous, Seymour," she told him. "Believe it or not, you're not doing anything wrong."

He pulled at the collar of his shirt. "I know," he said. "I just hope that it won't be long before those men leave Uncle Cornelius's room. I'm anxious to talk to him, that's all."

"Oh. I thought you were worried about being alone with me in my hotel room."

"Not at all," he said unconvincingly. "We're friends. Nothing wrong with friends being together. Right?"

"That's right," Rebecca said. She wished that Seymour hadn't mentioned that about them being friends. What she had to do was going to be difficult enough without thinking about such things.

There was no point in delaying the inevitable. It was just going to get harder if she waited. She moved closer to him, still smiling, and asked, "What shall we do to pass the time?"

He began to look even more flustered. "I, uh, I don't really know . . . I suppose we could talk."

"It might be better if we didn't," Rebecca whispered. "Someone passing by in the hall might hear us."

Seymour shook his head in confusion. "So?"

"Well . . . just because we know there's nothing improper going on, that doesn't mean everyone else would know, too." She was very close to him now. She laid a hand on his chest and said, "Maybe we should do something else."

Seymour's eyes widened. "Rebecca, I . . . I thought we had settled this," he stammered. "There can't be anything . . . anything romantic between us."

She shook her head as she looped her left arm around his neck. "I'm not talking about romance," she said. "I'm just talking about a pleasurable way to pass the time."

He was starting to sound a little desperate as he said, "But I can't—"

"Of course you can," Rebecca said. She forestalled any further conversation by pressing her lips to his.

She thought for a second he was going to pull away or push her back a step. But for all his high-flown morals, he was human, after all, and male to boot, which meant that after stiffening for a second, he began to relax and enjoy what was going on.

With her right hand, she slipped the knife from the pocket of her dress. The blade was long enough to reach his heart. All she had to do now was plunge it into his back with all her strength, between his ribs, and into the organ she could feel slugging against her as she molded her body to his. He would die without a sound, because she intended to keep her mouth pressed to his until he was finished.

Then she could go across the hall and interrupt Standish's meeting with his hired killers. She could just imagine the shocked look on his face when she informed him that she had done the work that three men had failed to do. Welch, McCracken, and Stover could earn their fee by disposing of Seymour's body, since that was really out of Rebecca's line.

With the three-thousand-dollar bounty she would claim, she could leave Sweet Apple and never have to see Cornelius Standish again, never have to endure the touch of his hands on her body. All it would take to achieve that goal was one thrust of the knife. It probably wouldn't even hurt Seymour very much, she told herself. He would be dead before he knew what was happening.

So why couldn't she do it?

Three thousand . . . three thousand . . . three thousand . . . The refrain echoed in her brain. She lifted the knife until it was poised to strike.

Someone rattled the doorknob.

Rebecca jerked back and gasped as she broke the kiss with Seymour. She had turned the key in the lock without him noticing, and then slipped it into the same pocket where the knife was concealed. Now someone was trying to get into the room. Standish? Probably, but she couldn't be sure about that. As a surprised and guilty-looking Seymour started to turn toward the door, Rebecca stepped back and hid the knife behind her.

She gasped again as someone struck the door a heavy

blow from the other side. "Good Lord!" Seymour exclaimed. "What in heaven's name—"

He didn't have time to finish the question. Whoever was in the corridor rammed into the door again, and this time the wood in the jamb around the knob splintered. The door flew open.

Maggie O'Ryan stumbled into the room, clutching the shoulder she had obviously just used to break the door open. She forgot any pain she was feeling, though, in the surge of anger that reddened her face as she glared at Rebecca and said, "You! I knew you were up to no good, you . . . you trollop!"

Rebecca pulled herself up and gave Maggie a haughty stare as she said, "You have no right to break into my room like that, Miss O'Ryan. Seymour, you're the marshal. Arrest her!"

Seymour's mouth opened and closed without any sound coming out. That, and the stunned, pop-eyed look on his face, gave him a vaguely fishlike appearance.

Maggie pointed a finger at Seymour and said, "You can arrest me when I'm through with her, and with you! That's right, Seymour Standish, I have some things to say to you, too! But first . . ." She advanced on Rebecca, stalking forward like a cat after its prey. "When I saw you taking Seymour up here, I knew you were still after him. I should have known better than to ever trust him. I certainly didn't trust you!"

Seymour finally found his voice. "Maggie, I . . . I promise you, nothing happened—"

"For God's sake, Seymour, what sort of fool do you think I am? Your face is red, you were breathing hard—"

"You startled me," he said.

That was actually a reasonable explanation, Rebecca

thought, but Maggie was clearly too angry to accept it. Rebecca's fingers flexed around the handle of the knife. The crash of the door being broken open like that was bound to attract attention. She had only seconds to act, if she was going to. Killing once had been difficult for her; could she kill twice?

Of course, with Maggie O'Ryan, it might be easier, Rebecca thought as she started to bring the knife from behind her back.

Maggie never gave her a chance. She leaped forward, throwing a punch like a man, and her fist crashed into Rebecca's jaw.

Seymour had never been more shocked in his life than at the moment when the door of the hotel room burst open and Maggie stood there. Not only was he not expecting to see her, but also he never would have dreamed that a delicate slip of a girl like her could wreak such destruction.

Of course, she wasn't really that delicate, he realized. And her life growing up here in the border country had toughened her considerably. Still . . .

His stunned brain was working just enough for him to understand that Maggie must have looked through the hotel's front window just as Rebecca was leading him upstairs. He'd thought that she had gone on, but obviously she had turned back for some reason. And she had seen what he would have given almost anything for her not to have seen. The only thing that could have been worse was if she had actually witnessed Rebecca kissing him.

It wasn't really fair either to characterize what had

happened that way, because after the first few seconds, he had been kissing Rebecca just as much as she had been kissing him. He hadn't wanted to . . . he knew better, Dear Lord, but he knew better! It was just that her lips were so warm and soft and insistent . . .

What happened next drove even those thoughts from Seymour's brain. He made a grab for Maggie as she launched herself forward, but he was taken by surprise and too late. The crack of Maggie's hard little fist against Rebecca's jaw stunned Seymour beyond belief.

Rebecca was stunned, too, physically at least. The punch's impact drove her backward against a dressing table. A knife that must have been lying on the table clattered to the floor at her feet. Seymour didn't have time to wonder what the knife had been doing on the table. He lunged at Maggie as she swung another blow at Rebecca's head.

This one didn't land, not because of Seymour's efforts, but because Rebecca recovered enough of her wits to duck underneath it. With an angry screech, she threw herself at Maggie, fingers hooked into claws that lashed out. The two young women crashed together and then slammed into Seymour. It was like he'd been run over by a mauling, clawing, hair-pulling buzz saw. With his arms flailing, he went over backward and landed on the floor with such force that all the breath was knocked out of his lungs.

He rolled over, gasping for air, and saw that Maggie and Rebecca had fallen, too. The impact had knocked them apart. Rebecca scrambled to her feet first and fled, dashing out the open door.

Maggie went after her, ignoring Seymour's choked

cries for her to stop. He struggled to his feet and stumbled after the two women.

Several people were in the hallway, their attention drawn by the commotion. Among them were Cornelius Standish and the three men who claimed to be dry-goods salesmen. Standish grabbed his nephew's arm and demanded, "Seymour, what in blazes is going on here?"

"No time to talk, Uncle Cornelius!" Seymour cried as he jerked free and ran along the corridor toward the second-floor landing, where Maggie had caught up to Rebecca. They were fighting again, Rebecca's arms windmilling as she slapped at Maggie in an attempt to hold off the other young woman's attack. Maggie brushed aside Rebecca's blows and grabbed her by the throat, evidently intent on choking the life out of her.

She might have done it, too, if they hadn't been perched at the edge of the stairs. Suddenly, Rebecca fell, and since Maggie didn't let go, she went with her. Seymour's eyes widened in horror as he shouted, "No!"

He dashed toward the stairs as Rebecca and Maggie tumbled over and over down the flight. Seymour thought surely they would stop before they reached the bottom, but they didn't. Instead, they fell all the way to the lobby, and when they reached the bottom of the stairs, they lay there in two huddled, moaning heaps.

At the top of the stairs, Seymour stared at them, a little surprised that both of them were still alive, praying that neither of the young women was badly hurt. As he started down toward the lobby, Rebecca pushed herself up onto hands and knees and then weaved upright. She seemed stunned and not really sure where she was or what was going on, but something, probably instinct, started her toward the front door of the hotel. She was still trying to get away.

"Maggie!" Seymour cried as the young schoolteacher got up and went after Rebecca. Maggie was unsteady on her feet, too, but her anger drove her on.

Rebecca ran out of the hotel with Maggie right behind her. Seymour reached the bottom of the stairs and went after them. He made it to the hotel porch in time to see Maggie bring Rebecca down with an unladylike tackle that sent both of them sprawling in the dust of the street.

Rebecca lashed out with a foot, and Seymour winced as the kick caught Maggie in the jaw with a resounding crack. Maggie rolled over and over and came to a stop on her belly. This time, instead of fleeing, Rebecca went after her. She landed on Maggie's back with a knee, grasped the other woman's long dark hair, and jerked Maggie's head up only to drive her face back down against the ground. She was about to do it again when Maggie bucked upward like a maddened bronco and sent Rebecca flying through the air.

"Maggie! Rebecca!" Seymour shouted. "Stop! Stop that!"

He didn't know what to do. If it had been two men whaling away at each other in a drunken saloon brawl, he would have been tempted to draw his gun and wallop them over their heads, knocking them senseless so that they could be hauled off to jail.

But he couldn't do that to females. He might hurt them too badly. After all, they were the delicate flower of womanhood—

"Man-stealing whore!" Maggie screamed at Rebecca. "Little slut!" The insults were followed by a torrent of border Spanish that Seymour could only assume was profane in nature.

"Crazy bitch!" Rebecca howled right back at Maggie. "I'll kill you!"

Then they were at it again, scratching, biting, clawing, punching, and kicking in a wild melee that sent them careening back and forth in the street.

Out of instinct, Seymour reached for his gun. He still didn't plan to pistol-whip them, but he thought that maybe firing a shot into the air would startle them into settling down.

His hand found only an empty holster. He realized that the gun must have fallen out when they knocked him down in the hotel room, when the fight started.

With no weapon, he ran toward them, empty hands outstretched, and called, "Ladies! Ladies, please! You have to stop this madness!"

He didn't know if his pleading ever would have gotten through to them or not. He didn't have a chance to find out.

Because that was when people began to yell and scream, hoofbeats thundered in the street, and the sudden roar of gunshots filled the air.

"I'll hear opening statements from counsel," Judge Simon Clark said. He pointed the gavel at Hugh Addison. "You first, Colonel."

Matt and Sam didn't pay much attention to the eloquent oratory of Addison or Everett Sloane, Esau Paxton's attorney. Instead, they watched the crowd, alert for any signs of trouble. The cowboys from the Double

C and Pax kept their seats, content for the moment just to glower darkly at each other.

When the opening statements were over, Judge Clark said to Addison, "Very well, Colonel, you may present your case."

"Thank you, Your Honor," Addison said as he hooked his left thumb in his vest and reached down to the desk in front of him to pick up several sheets of paper. "Our case is quite simple. When the CP ranch, owned jointly by my client and Esau Paxton, was split up into the Double C and Pax ranches, Mr. Paxton signed away any and all rights in perpetuity to any use whatsoever of the stream that forms part of the boundary line between the aforesaid ranches."

Esau Paxton shot to his feet and said loudly, "That's a dad-blasted lie! That creek is the boundary between the ranches. That means we can both use it."

Judge Clark pointed his gavel at Paxton and snapped, "Sit down, sir! Mr. Sloane, I advise you to keep your client under control."

Sloane was already tugging at Paxton's sleeve, trying to get him to take his seat again.

"I'll hear from you in due time, Mr. Paxton," the judge went on, "and if you try to jump the gun again, I promise you you'll be sorry you did." Clark turned back to Addison. "Go on, Colonel."

Addison raised the document he held in his hand. "This contract is all the proof of our claim that we need, Your Honor," he said. "I enter it into evidence as our first and only exhibit, and when you examine its provisions, you'll see for yourself that Mr. Paxton's land ends at the eastern bank of the stream in question, meaning that the stream itself and all the water therein belong to my client, Mr. Shadrach Colton."

Paxton shook his head stubbornly, but stayed in his chair and didn't say anything.

"Furthermore, Your Honor," Addison went on, "you will see Esau Paxton's signature on this contract, signifying his agreement to those very terms."

Paxton couldn't hold it in. He didn't stand up, but he said, "That's not what I meant. And if that's what it says, that's not what I thought it said. That's not what we agreed it would say beforehand."

The slender, dignified Everett Sloane rose to his feet and said, "Your Honor, I apologize for my client. But I ask you to understand how upset he is over what has now been revealed as the fraud perpetrated by his former partner."

"Fraud!" Shad Colton bellowed as he shot to his feet. "What the hell do you mean by fraud?"

"Mr. Colton!" Judge Clark thundered in a voice that threatened to shake the town hall's rafters. "There will be no profanity in this courtroom unless I'm the one usin' it, damn it!"

He began to pound the gavel on the table as the cowboys from the rival ranches shouted and shook fingers at each other. Matt and Sam watched tensely, ready to step in if any of the punchers left their chairs and tried to start a brawl, but the crashing of Clark's gavel finally began to quiet down the uproar.

When the judge could be heard again, he said, "Fraud's a mighty serious charge, Mr. Sloane. What do you mean by making it?"

"It's quite simple, Your Honor," Sloane replied, echoing what Colonel Addison had said earlier. "My client and Mr. Colton *agreed* before that contract was drawn up that the water from the creek would be split equally, but then Mr. Colton or his attorney *changed* the terms of the agreement and fooled Mr. Paxton into signing it."

"That's a lie!" Colton shouted. "I never did anything o' the sort! Hell, I never even read the contract after it was drawed up! I don't reckon Esau did either. We knew what it was supposed to say."

"I warned you about the profanity." The judge leaned forward in his chair. "But I'm going to let it pass for now because I want to hear more about this agreement you made with Mr. Paxton. *Was* it your intention to share the water from the creek?"

"Don't answer that, Shad," Addison said quickly. He turned back to the judge and waved the papers in his hand. "Your Honor, I submit that any further discussion of anything that was said before this contract was executed is irrelevant and immaterial. Any verbal agreements—and I am *not* stipulating that such agreements did in fact exist—were superceded by this written, signed contract, which does in fact contain language specifying that it is the sole and binding agreement between Mr. Shadrach Colton and Mr. Esau Paxton concerning the division of property theretofore held by them jointly!"

The words came out of Addison like a rushing river and left him even redder in the face than usual when he was finished. He plucked a handkerchief from his breast pocket with his free hand and used it to mop sweat off his forehead.

The big room was filled with considerable hubbub again. Judge Clark gaveled the spectators into silence once more, then gazed with narrow, steely eyes at Addison and said, "I have a question for you, Colonel. Did *you* draw up that contract?"

Addison shook his head. "I did not, Your Honor."

"Then who did?"

Colton said, "Am I allowed to answer, or do I still have to keep my trap shut?"

Clark jerked the gavel at him to indicate that he should go ahead.

"Old Marcellus Reilly drew up the contract," Colton said. "He was my lawyer before the colonel here took over the job."

"And where is Mr. Reilly now?" Clark asked.

"In the graveyard over at Marfa."

"Mr. Reilly passed away last year, Your Honor," Addison explained. "That was when I began to represent Mr. Colton."

"So you don't know if this fella Reilly changed the terms of the agreement to favor his client and then slipped it past Paxton, is that right?"

Addison said, "With all due respect, Your Honor, you're engaging in pure speculation and as such, it's irrelevant and immaterial to the case at hand." He brandished the contract again. "All that matters is what is written here, including the signatures of Mr. Colton and Mr. Paxton. It was Mr. Paxton's responsibility to make certain that the terms of the contract were what he had agreed to before he signed it."

Paxton's face was gray and drawn now. Matt thought he looked like a man who knew he was beaten.

It was pretty clear what had happened, Matt figured, even to somebody like him who wasn't educated in the law. Colton's original lawyer had pulled a fast one. He'd changed the agreement when he wrote it up so that

Colton owned the creek. If Paxton had noticed that and refused to sign, Reilly could have claimed it was an honest mistake in the wording and had the contracts redrawn. Nothing ventured, nothing gained, as the old saying went.

But Paxton *hadn't* noticed and had signed the contract the way Reilly drew it up, and that was that. The creek belonged to Colton, and Paxton's cows had no right to drink out of it.

Whether or not Colton had known all along what his lawyer was up to, Matt couldn't have said. He knew there was plenty of bad blood between the ranchers. But somehow, trying a sneaky legal trick like that didn't sound like something Colton would do. It was possible that Colton hadn't even known about it until after old Marcellus Reilly was dead. Then he might have looked over the contract and discovered what it really contained. That seemed like the most likely explanation to Matt.

The question now was, what would the judge do about it? Clark couldn't very well set aside the contract and give Paxton part of the ranch. Like Addison had said, checking the contract before he signed it was Paxton's lookout.

Clark leaned back in his chair and didn't even try to quiet down the racket in the town hall this time. His high forehead corrugated in a frown of consternation. Whatever he decided here, one side or the other was going to explode in outrage.

Then, suddenly, everyone in the room turned to look at the open windows as somebody started screaming in the street outside. "What the hell?" Matt muttered as he turned toward the doors. The caterwauling sounded like a couple of panthers going after each other.

Or a couple of really angry women, he realized as he stepped out onto the porch with Sam and saw the battle taking place down the street. One of the combatants, he saw to his surprise, was that Eastern girl who had come to Sweet Apple with Seymour's Uncle Cornelius. The other was Maggie O'Ryan, who was going after Rebecca Jimmerson with all the hot-blooded ferocity she'd come by honestly with her Irish and Latin heritage.

Seymour was trying to break them up, but not having any luck at it. The way he was dancing around, he really didn't have any idea what to do to stop the two young women from fighting.

Matt couldn't help but grin as he watched. After a second, he said, "You reckon we ought to go give Seymour a hand?"

Sam was smiling, too. "I reckon we should," he said. "Otherwise, those ladies are liable to really hurt each other."

The blood brothers had just stepped down from the porch to the street when they heard the hoofbeats. Their heads jerked around, instinct warning them that all hell was about to break loose. They saw the riders, two dozen, maybe more, sweep around a corner and charge down the street, guns blazing. They seemed to be headed straight for the town hall, and Matt recognized the burly, bearded figure in the lead.

"Alcazarrio!" he yelled as he slapped leather.

Chapter 17

Seymour recognized Diego Alcazarrio from the *bandido* chieftain's previous attack on Sweet Apple, but Alcazarrio's identity barely had time to sink in before an even more urgent realization hit Seymour.

Maggie and Rebecca were right in the path of the galloping horses. In a matter of seconds, they would be ridden down, crushed under the slashing hooves.

He had no gun, so he couldn't even hope to stop the raiders. The way they were charging down the street, he couldn't have turned aside their attack even if he had been armed.

So Seymour did the only thing he could. He lunged at Maggie and Rebecca, who had stopped fighting and were staring at Alcazarrio's men in shock. Grabbing an arm of each girl, Seymour began trying to hustle them out of the way, half-urging them to run, half-dragging them.

He saw the boardwalk right in front of them, twenty feet away, then ten, then five . . . the hoofbeats were deafeningly loud now, as were the shots that rang out . . . as Seymour shoved Maggie and Rebecca toward safety.

The next instant something crashed into his shoulder

and sent him flying through the air. One of the horses had struck him as it galloped past. He slammed into the edge of the boardwalk and felt pain shoot through him. Dust clogged his mouth and nose, making it impossible to breathe as he landed in the street.

As Seymour rolled over a huge shape loomed above him. One of the bandits had reined in, and now the man's horse reared up on its hind legs, its steel-shod front hooves pawing at the air and threatening to come down and crush the life out of Seymour. He scrambled frantically out of the way as the hooves thudded against the street where he had been a second earlier. Seymour ignored the pain that filled his body. There was no time for it.

He caught hold of the edge of the boardwalk and pulled himself up. As he came upright, panting with exertion and agony, he heard a harsh voice say, *"Hasta la vista, gringo!"* and looked up to see the Mexican raider pointing a gun at his head. Seymour's eyes barely had time to widen in shock and fear before flame spouted from the barrel of the revolver.

Both of Matt Bodine's Colts fairly leaped into his hands as he opened fire on the onrushing bandit horde. Beside him, Sam's revolver roared defiance, too. Behind them, the cowboys from the Double C and Pax began to hurry out of the town hall to see what all the shooting was about. Howls of surprise and outrage came from their mouths as they reached for their guns, only to remember that they had surrendered their weapons as they went into the hearing.

The baskets containing the guns that had been collected were still sitting right there on the boardwalk.

The delay required to retrieve the guns was crucial, though. The bandits overran the building while many of the would-be defenders were still unarmed. Horses leaped onto the boardwalk. Men screamed as they went down before the trampling hooves. Glass shattered as a fusillade of shots drove several men back through the front windows, their bodies filled with lead. Diego Alcazarrio himself led the charge into the town hall, leaping his horse to the porch and then ducking his head so that the mount could crash on through the doors and into the building.

Matt and Sam had gone down in the first few moments of the battle, creased in several places by flying bullets. Neither was seriously hurt, but the press of people kept them from getting up. They were in imminent danger of being crushed by the crowd as the melee spread along the front of the town hall. Both of them were big, strong young men, though, and at last they were able to fight their way back to their feet. Matt had emptied his Colts, but he used them as clubs, swinging them in powerful strokes against the heads of the mounted bandits. Several of the *bandidos* came crashing down from their saddles.

Sam had drawn his bowie knife and was using it to carve out an open space around him in the middle of the battle. Blood flew through the air and spattered his face as the razor-sharp blade sliced through the flesh of his foes. It must have been like this in the middle of the chaos atop the ridge overlooking the Greasy Grass, during the epic battle in which Medicine Horse had lost his life after counting coup on Yellow Hair.

There was no counting coup here, only killing. And trying to stay alive . . .

* * *

Maggie O'Ryan found herself on the porch of Mayor Abner Mitchell's general store. She hurt all over from the tumble down the stairs and the damage that Rebecca Jimmerson had inflicted on her during their fight. But she couldn't even think about that, because when she picked herself up and turned around after Seymour had practically thrown her and Rebecca onto the porch, she saw one of the bandits about to shoot the man she loved.

She didn't waste time screaming Seymour's name. Instead, she snatched up a shovel from a barrel that sat on the porch and held an assortment of farming implements for sale. The price tag hung from a string tied to the handle of the shovel. Maggie flung the tool like a spear, putting all her strength behind the throw.

The shovel's blade hit the raider in the throat just as he pulled the trigger. Although it didn't hurt him badly, that was enough to make him jerk the gun a little to one side as it exploded. Seymour fell anyway, blood streaming from his scalp.

Now Maggie screamed, *"Seymour!"*

The bandit leaped from his horse. He was bleeding from a scratch on his neck where the shovel had hit him. "You damned little hellcat!" he growled at Maggie. He reached for her, but she sprang back and grabbed another tool from the barrel, this time a pitchfork. The bandit lunged at her again, trying to knock the pitchfork aside with his gun. He failed, and his eyes bugged out in horror as Maggie rammed the sharp tines into his belly. She put all her weight behind the blow and drove the pitchfork deep.

The mortally wounded bandit cursed and fell to his

knees. He tried to lift his gun again so that he could kill this spitfire who had just struck him down, but blackness engulfed him before he could pull the trigger. He started to pitch forward, but stopped before he could fall all the way to the boardwalk, propped up by the handle of the pitchfork buried in his belly.

Still terrified and shocked by the knowledge that she had just killed a man, Maggie started to turn away, only to have strong arms wrap around her. A grinning face leered into hers from only inches away. "You are coming with me, little one," the *bandido* said, and then his fist crashed into Maggie's jaw, knocking her out cold before she could even begin to struggle against his cruel grip.

Rebecca Jimmerson stumbled along the street, looking for a place to hide. She had lost track of where Maggie was, and didn't care about that jealous, crazy bitch anyway. Maggie had ruined everything by bursting into the hotel room just as she was about to kill Seymour and earn that three thousand dollars.

At the moment, Rebecca wasn't thinking about the blood money Cornelius Standish had promised to pay for his nephew's death. All she cared about was finding someplace where she would be safe from all those marauding Mexicans. She reached the corner of a building and turned to run down an alley.

She hadn't even gotten started, though, before an arm like a steel band went around her waist and scooped her right off the ground. She shrieked as she felt herself lifted into the air.

Then with an impact that seemed to jolt every bone in her body, she was dropped down onto the back of a galloping horse. The man who had snatched her up still had hold of her. His arm was so tight around her that she couldn't struggle, couldn't even breathe. Her head swam dizzily from lack of air.

Dust filled her nostrils, along with the smell of horse and unwashed human flesh. She would have gagged if she'd had any breath to do it with. A voice chattered something in her ear, but she didn't understand the words. She didn't know if her captor was speaking Spanish or if her brain was just so stunned that it refused to work.

She passed out, fully expecting that she would never wake up.

Guided by some instinct, Matt Bodine and Sam Two Wolves moved as they fought their way through the chaos in front of the town hall until they found themselves back-to-back. Matt threw a glance over his shoulder, saw Sam's bloody, grinning face, and grinned right back at him. They were ringed by bandits who had dismounted and were now closing in on them, guns ready. This looked like the end. In a matter of seconds, the blood brothers would be filled with lead.

But at that moment, a man on horseback leaped his mount through the window behind them. All the glass had already been broken out or shot out, but the window frame exploded in a shower of splinters. Matt was directly in the path of the horse, but Sam shoved him out of the way with a swift hand to the shoulder. The horse clipped both of them with glancing blows that knocked them off their feet.

A deep voice bellowed orders in Spanish, saying to

follow him. The words were punctuated by a woman's frantic screams. Matt rolled to the side, and as he did so, bullets chewed up the ground next to him. He was about to spring to his feet when a heavy, suffocating weight landed on top of him, driving him back down to the ground. Matt felt whatever it was jerk several times, probably from bullets thudding into it.

Unable to breathe, Matt squirmed over onto his back and found himself staring into the dead face of Colonel Hugh Addison, Shad Colton's lawyer. Addison's body was riddled with bullets and a good-sized chunk of his head had been shot away. He'd probably been dead when he fell on Matt. Realizing that and remembering the way Addison's corpse had soaked up more lead, Matt knew that even dead, the lawyer had saved his life.

Matt got his hands on Addison's shoulders and rolled the lawyer's body aside. A lot fewer guns were going off now, but hoofbeats still filled the air. As Matt struggled up to his knees, he saw that the raiders were streaming out of Sweet Apple, departing as swiftly and unexpectedly as they had shown up. A few of the bandits turned in their saddles to fling a few final shots at the town.

Matt swayed to his feet and grabbed a nearby hitch rail to steady himself. The wooden rail cracked and broke. It had been shot up until it was barely standing. Matt stumbled over to the boardwalk, looking for Sam. Finding out whether his blood brother was dead or alive was the only thing in Matt Bodine's mind right now.

"Matt! Matt!"

Then Sam was there beside him, covered with blood but still on his feet. They grabbed each other, slapped each other on the back. Sam pulled away and asked, "Are you all right?"

Matt took stock. He hurt all over, but his arms and legs worked and as he flexed his fingers, he knew he could still hold a gun. "I got nicked in a few places and beat all to hell," he told Sam, "but I reckon I'm not hurt too bad. How about you?"

"Same here," Sam said with a nod.

"You look like you lost a lot of blood."

"Most of it's not mine."

Matt managed a tight grin. "Yeah, I saw you usin' that bowie knife like you were the Grim Reaper and it was your scythe. I hope you sent a lot of those bastards straight to hell." He looked around. The street was littered with bodies, and more corpses were piled up on the porch in front of the town hall. Matt heard wounded men groaning. "Or maybe that's where *we* are."

"No, this is still Sweet Apple," Sam said. "We'd better try to find Seymour."

Both of the blood brothers had been too young to take part in the Civil War, but they had heard Matt's father speak in hushed tones about the aftermath of the great battles. The scene in Sweet Apple's main street was like something out of one of the elder Bodine's war stories, although on a much smaller scale than the carnage at places like Chancellorsville or Gettysburg. Despite that, both Matt and Sam felt horror welling up inside them as they hurried among the wounded and the slain, looking for Seymour Standish.

This was the second time in recent months they had seen what was left after a town had been raided by a gang of killers. It had happened up in the Panhandle, too, and that attack on the settlement of Buckskin by Deuce Mallory's gang was what had started Matt and Sam on the trail that eventually led them to Sweet Apple. Mallory and his men had done more widespread damage; the attack by Alcazarrio seemed to have been concentrated on one specific spot—the town hall. That thought made Matt frown. Why would a Mexican revolutionary target a hearing to resolve a legal matter over water rights, if that was indeed what had happened? And how had he known it would be going on at this particular place and time?

Matt had no answers for those questions, and he put them aside anyway as Sam exclaimed, "There's Seymour!"

The marshal was struggling to sit up as he leaned against the boardwalk in front of Abner Mitchell's general store. A sheet of blood covered one whole side of Seymour's face. Matt and Sam ran over to him. Each of them got hold of Seymour under an arm and lifted him to his feet.

"How bad are you hurt, Seymour?" Sam asked as the marshal sagged in their grip.

"I . . . I don't know." Seymour lifted a trembling hand to his head. "I remember there was a shot . . ."

Matt looked at the shallow, bloody furrow in Seymour's scalp, an inch and a half above his left ear. "Looks like you got creased," he said. "Head wounds bleed a lot, and you've probably got a hell of a headache, but maybe you're not hurt too bad."

"Got any other bullet holes?" Sam added.

"I . . . I don't think so." Seymour steadied a little as the blood brothers held him up. "No, I'm all right. Just a little dizzy, and like Matt said, my head hurts." He looked around at the devastation along Main Street, and his voice cracked as he asked, "My God, what happened here?"

"Alcazarrio," Matt said.

Seymour blinked. "That Mexican bandit? Yes, I . . . I remember now. I saw him leading the charge into town. But why would he attack us again? The first time he wanted to steal those army rifles, but now . . . there's no good reason . . ."

Suddenly, as if something had just occurred to him, Seymour jerked around, pulling out of their grip. His eyes desperately searched the boardwalk in front of the store.

"Maggie!" he cried in a choked voice. "She was right here!"

Well, she wasn't now, Matt saw. In fact, he didn't see any sign of Maggie O'Ryan anywhere up and down the street. He remembered how she had been fighting with Rebecca Jimmerson when the *bandidos* attacked. It appeared that the Jimmerson girl had vanished, too. Matt supposed that he ought to be grateful the bodies of the young women weren't lying there, killed in the battle. But at the same time, he had a bad feeling about their disappearance.

"I have to find her," Seymour said. He started stumbling along the street, looking for Maggie.

Matt and Sam glanced at each other. The same thoughts that had gone through Matt's head had occurred to Sam, too. "If those girls are gone, it's probably because some of Alcazarrio's men grabbed them," he said.

Matt nodded in agreement. "I don't reckon they raided the town just for that, but they weren't gonna pass up the chance to kidnap a couple of good-looking young women either."

They started to join Seymour in looking for Maggie and Rebecca, but they were sidetracked by Mayor Mitchell and J. Emerson Heathcote, who came up to them looking stunned. The newspaperman was limping and had a bloodstain on the left leg of his trousers. He had been nicked in the fighting, too.

"Dear God, what are we going to do?" Mitchell asked. "What happened? Why . . . why did those Mexicans attack the town?"

Matt shook his head and said, "I don't know why they hit us, but the first thing you need to do, Mr. Mayor, is see about helpin' the wounded. Anybody who's not hurt too bad should be carried into the town hall."

"The doctor's already here," Heathcote said. "He heard the shooting and came to see what had happened. Come along, Mayor, we'll give him a hand." He put a hand on Mitchell's arm and led him away. The mayor still seemed to be stunned and distracted by this second outbreak of unexpected death and violence in his town.

Matt and Sam started after Seymour again, but then they heard horrified screaming coming from inside the town hall. They exchanged a look and then started trotting in that direction, wondering what fresh outrage they would find in there.

Esau Paxton and Shad Colton both appeared on the porch of the building before Matt and Sam got there. Paxton had his right hand clamped over his upper left arm. The blood that oozed between his fingers told Matt and Sam that he had been wounded there. Colton seemed to be unharmed, just extremely upset. He saw Matt and Sam hurrying toward him and yelled, "They took the girls!"

The blood brothers bounded onto the porch, ignoring the steps. "What?" Sam asked. "You mean—"

"Sandy," Paxton choked out between teeth gritted against the pain of the wound in his arm. "Those bastards took Sandy."

"And Jessie," Colton added, his voice every bit as

bleak as that of his cousin and former partner. "The big one, and a hawk-faced son of a bitch who was with him, they rode up and grabbed Jessie and Sandy, like that was all they wanted."

Matt and Sam looked at each other again, and suddenly things were a little clearer to both of them. Matt remembered how single-mindedly Alcazarrio had ridden right into the town hall. During the bloody chaos, the bandit leader and one of his men had been able to snatch Jessie and Sandy and get away with them. Was it possible that the two young women had been the real targets of the raid all along?

"What about the rest of your families?" Sam asked.

"My boy Dave was wounded," Paxton replied, "but I reckon everybody else is all right."

"A lot of my men were shot down," Colton snapped. He glared at Matt. "They couldn't even defend themselves because they didn't have their guns."

"That was Judge Clark's decision, not mine . . . but if it had been up to me, I'd have taken your guns, too, Colton." Matt frowned at both of the cattlemen. "If you two old pelicans had been able to get along, there wouldn't have been any need for this hearing in the first place!"

For a moment, it appeared that both Colton and Paxton were going to react angrily to Matt's words, but then Colton shrugged and said, "What're you gonna do about this, Bodine? A posse's got to go after those bastards and try to get our girls back."

Matt nodded. "That's exactly what's gonna happen, as soon as we can get it organized."

"Not hardly," came a growl from the doorway. Judge Simon Clark limped out of the town hall, using his shotgun as a crutch. His right leg was covered with blood from the knee down. "Somebody show me where the telegraph office is, so I can send some wires and get the army after those bandits."

"The nearest army post is in El Paso," Paxton objected. "Troops can't get here in time. Those raiders will be back across the border long before the army shows up."

"What about the Texas Rangers?" Clark asked.

Colton shook his head. "Same problem. They're too far away to help us."

Matt spoke up, saying, "Chances are that Alcazarrio and his men are already across the Rio Grande, or they will be soon, no farther away than it is." He shook his head. "We'll have to go into Mexico to rescue those prisoners."

"You're talking about an illegal incursion into another sovereign nation," Clark warned.

"You got a better idea, Judge?"

"Yeah. Let me go along, too." Clark's lips drew back from his teeth in a grimace. "I been fightin' outlaws since before you was born, youngster. Just let me throw a saddle on my horse . . ."

As the judge started to turn, his wounded leg gave underneath him. He would have fallen if Sam hadn't caught hold of his arm.

"Looks to me like you're hurt too bad to go chasing after *bandidos,* Your Honor," Sam said as he steadied the judge. "Why don't you go back inside and get off that wounded leg?"

"Damn it—" Clark started to protest. Then he sighed and shook his head. "You're right, young man. The shape I'm in, I'd just hold you back, and I don't want to do that. You mind givin' me a hand?"

"Not at all." Sam helped the judge back into the town hall.

While Sam was doing that, Matt heard his name being called. He turned and saw Seymour stumbling toward him. "They're gone," Seymour said in a hollow voice as he came up to the porch.

"You mean Miss O'Ryan?" Matt asked.

Seymour nodded. "And Miss Jimmerson. They're both gone. I found some people who saw them grabbed up by the bandits and carried away." He covered his face with his hands and asked in a strained, muffled tone, "Dear Lord, what are we going to do?"

"First thing you're gonna do is buck up, Seymour," Matt said, deliberately hardening his own voice. "You're the law here. Folks are gonna be lookin' to you to lead the posse."

Seymour lowered his hands and blinked. "Posse?"

"That's right. You didn't think we were gonna let those bastards get away with what they've done, did you?" Matt pulled his right-hand Colt from its holster and started reloading it with fresh cartridges from the loops on his gunbelt. "We're going after Alcazarrio. We're gonna get those prisoners back safe and sound, and we're gonna settle the score for what that son of a bitch did to Sweet Apple." Matt snapped the gun's cylinder closed. "You with me, Seymour?"

Seymour had straightened as Matt was talking. His face was still ashen under the blood that was drying on it, but he was able to swallow, nod his head, and say, "I'm with you, Matt. All the way, as far as it takes."

Chapter 18

It was past noon before things started to settle down in Sweet Apple. By that time, Matt and Sam had been able to get a pretty good idea of the toll taken on the town by Diego Alcazarrio's raid.

Four young women had been kidnapped: Jessie Colton, Sandy Paxton, Maggie O'Ryan, and Rebecca Jimmerson. Eleven people were dead: eight men, two women, and a ten-year-old boy who had been trampled by some of the raiders' horses. Twenty-seven more men, women, and children had been wounded, many of them seriously. Without a doubt, the death toll would rise as the hours and days went by.

There was only one doctor in the settlement, but a couple of barbers and an old Mexican who was known to be a *curandero* were pressed into service to help the sawbones. The town hall had been turned into a makeshift hospital for the most badly injured. The walking wounded had been treated and sent home.

Since Matt and Sam had as much experience at patching up bullet wounds as many medical men, they tended to each other's injuries, cleaning the creases with whiskey and bandaging them. They changed into clothes that weren't bullet-torn and bloodstained, then went to the marshal's office and found Seymour loading the rifles from the rack on the wall. The dried blood had been swabbed off his face, and a white strip of bandage was tied around his head.

"How are you doing, Seymour?" Sam asked as he and Matt came in.

Seymour nodded. "The doctor says that I should go to my hotel room and lie down. He thinks I should take it easy for the next few days, maybe for as long as a week. He says it's not wise to take chances with head injuries."

"And what do you say?" Matt asked.

Seymour worked the lever of the Winchester he was holding. "I say we've got bandits to track down and prisoners to rescue."

Matt grinned and said, "That's the spirit," but Sam frowned in concern.

"Are you sure about that, Seymour?" he asked. "You don't want to get off somewhere in the middle of nowhere and then not be able to go on."

"I'll be able to go on, don't you worry about that." Seymour laid the rifle down and picked up another one to load. "I won't come back without Miss O'Ryan."

"You know that'll mean crossing the border? You won't have any legal jurisdiction down there in Mexico."

"I'm aware of that. Do you think the Mexican authorities would help us if we contacted them?"

"The *rurales*?" Matt shook his head. "I reckon there must be some good, honest men among 'em, but by and large they're almost as bad as outlaws like Alcazarrio's bunch. Alcazarrio calls himself a revolutionary, but mostly revolutions in Mexico mean one bunch o' bandits is tryin' to replace another bunch."

"Then it's very much up to us, isn't it?"

The blood brothers both shrugged, and Matt said, "That's about the size of it."

"I'd say we have no choice but to pursue them," Seymour declared. "And I'm prepared to do whatever is necessary to rescue those women. Why would Alcazarrio go to so much trouble just to kidnap four young women?"

Matt and Sam had been thinking and talking about that very question. Sam said, "We don't think Alcazarrio planned on kidnapping Miss O'Ryan and Miss Jimmerson. That's just something that his men did in the heat of the moment."

"What about Miss Paxton and Miss Colton?"

"Reckon they're the ones he was really after," Matt said. "It takes money to start a revolution, even when you're really just a bandit, and the fathers of those two gals are a couple of the richest men between San Antonio and El Paso."

Understanding dawned in Seymour's eyes. "He's going to hold them for ransom!"

"I'd be mighty surprised if he didn't," Matt said.

"Will Mr. Colton and Mr. Paxton meet Alcazarrio's demands?"

"We don't know," Sam said.

Matt added, "But I've got a hunch that givin' in to a polecat like Alcazarrio will rub those two the wrong way. Men who can carve out homes for themselves and their families in a place like West Texas, fightin' weather and outlaws and Indians the whole way, aren't the sort to just go along with it when they're hit. They hit back."

"You think they'll want to join the posse?"

"I'd say it's pretty likely. We haven't talked to them yet, but—"

The door of the marshal's office opened then, breaking into what Matt was saying. Cornelius Standish stalked into the room, followed by Warren Welch, Daniel McCracken, and Ed Stover.

"Seymour!" Standish said. "Is it true what I've heard? Miss Jimmerson has been abducted?"

"That's right, Uncle Cornelius," Seymour replied. "I'm not seriously wounded, by the way."

"I knew you were all right," Standish snapped. "I asked about you after that terrible uproar. All that shooting!" He shuddered. "Things like that never happened back in New Jersey, or anywhere else that's civilized!"

"Well, this part of Texas isn't exactly civilized yet, at least not completely," Seymour said. "That's why it would be a good idea for you to go back home, Uncle Cornelius. You don't belong out here."

"And you do?"

Seymour finished loading the rifle in his hands and worked the weapon's lever. "I'm starting to, I hope. Don't worry about Miss Jimmerson. We're going after those brigands, and we'll bring her back safely, along with the other prisoners."

"I'm going with you."

Seymour stared at his uncle. "What?"

"I said, I'm going with you." Standish gestured toward his companions. "So are they."

Matt grunted. "Appreciate you fellas volunteerin', Mr. Standish, but I reckon we can get along without a handful of dry-goods salesmen."

"I was in the war, sonny," Stover snapped. "Killed

plenty of Johnny Rebs at Petersburg. I don't suppose killing greasers is that much different."

"And I can handle meself in a fight, never you doubt it," McCracken added. Welch didn't say anything, but his calm smile showed that he was confident in his abilities, too.

"You have extra firearms, don't you?" Standish asked.

Seymour shrugged. "There are several extra rifles here, and Mayor Mitchell has said that the posse can take whatever weapons and supplies it needs from his store. Arming you won't be any problem."

"What about horses?"

"Plenty of mounts on the Double C and Pax," Matt said. There was no real argument against Standish and the other men coming along, except for their inexperience. "We'll be ridin' pretty hard and fast, though. You'd have to keep up."

Standish took a cigar from his vest pocket and clamped it between his teeth. "Don't worry about us keeping up," he said. "Just find the men who kidnapped my secretary. How soon will we be leaving?"

Seymour looked to Matt and Sam for the answer to that question. Matt said, "I hope we'll be ready to ride in another hour or so."

Standish nodded. "Get us horses and guns. We'll be ready to go."

The four of them turned and left the office. Matt, Sam, and Seymour stood there in silence for a moment, before Sam finally said, "Seymour, I'm not sure if them coming along is a good idea."

"Neither am I," Seymour said. "But once my uncle makes his mind up, you can't sway him from his course."

"That's sort of what we're worried about," Matt said. "Will he take orders, or will he try to run the show once we get across the border?"

"He'll take orders, or he'll turn around and come back." Seymour looked at the blood brothers. "You have my word on that."

Before they could discuss it any more, the door opened again, and an excited J. Emerson Heathcote looked in at them. "There's a message coming in down at the telegraph office!" the newspaperman said. "It's from Alcazarrio!"

Once the holes where a bullet had passed through Judge Simon Clark's calf had been patched up, the judge had spent most of the time at the telegraph office, burning up the wires between Sweet Apple and Marfa, San Antonio, and El Paso. The army was going to send a cavalry patrol from Fort Bliss, and Major John B. Jones, commander of the Frontier Battalion of the Texas Rangers, agreed to dispatch a troop of Rangers from San Antonio.

"Too damned late to do any good," Judge Clark grumbled as his stubby fingers used a pencil to scrawl another message on a telegraph flimsy. The office was crowded with men, most of them members of the town council. "But they have to make a show of trying to help, I suppose."

The telegrapher looked up from his key with a startled expression on his face. "Line's gone dead, Judge!" he announced.

Clark frowned. "Are the wires down?"

"Either that or somebody cut 'em."

"It's Alcazarrio's doing!" Mayor Mitchell exclaimed. "He's trying to isolate us from the rest of the world so that we can't summon any help."

Clark shook his head. "Too late for that. We've already notified the army and the Rangers, and Alcazarrio has to know that we'd do that right away."

"Then what's the point in cutting the wires?" somebody asked.

That question was answered a moment later when the key began clicking and the telegrapher said, "What the— It's workin' again." He snatched up his pencil and began taking down the message.

Using a cane now instead of his shotgun, Clark stumped over and peered past the man's shoulder as the pencil printed out the words. "It's from Alcazarrio!" the judge said. He turned and looked at Heathcote. "Find the marshal, and Bodine and Two Wolves!"

It was obvious now what had happened. Alcazarrio, or some of his men, had cut the telegraph wires, all right, but only so they could tap into them and send a message of their own. One of the *bandidos* must have had some experience as a telegraph operator and still possessed a key for sending messages.

"He ain't much of a hand," the telegrapher in the Sweet Apple office commented as he continued to take down the message, "but I can make out what he's sendin'. Most of it anyway."

Matt, Sam, and Seymour hurried into the office a moment later, just as the key fell silent.

"Have they stopped sending?" Clark asked.

The telegrapher nodded. "Seems like it."

"Try to raise them again."

A couple of minutes of key-pounding proved to be

futile. The man looked up at Clark and shook his head. "They're not answerin', and neither is anybody else. The line's dead again."

Clark extended a hand. "Give me the message."

With a worried frown on his face, the telegrapher hesitated. "No offense, Judge, but I ain't sure I should. It's addressed to Shad Colton and Esau Paxton. If they're still in town, I ought to give it to them."

"We're right here, damn it," Colton said from the doorway as he and Paxton forced their way into the crowded room. "Give that paper to the judge and let him read it." Beside him, Paxton nodded agreement with that decision.

The telegrapher handed over the message. Clark took it, hesitated, then slipped a pair of reading glasses from his vest pocket and put them on. A hush fell over the room as he read the message in his deep, powerful voice.

"'To Paxton and Colton. If you wish to see your daughters alive again, bring two hundred and fifty thousand dollars in gold to Villa Rojo before three days have passed. They will not be harmed unless you fail to pay this ransom. If you fail to pay or if you try to trick me, your daughters will die.'" Clark looked up from the paper. "Then it says General Diego Alcazarrio."

Shad Colton snorted. "General, my ass! He's nothin' but a two-bit bandit!"

"A two-bit bandit who has our daughters," Paxton reminded him.

Seymour stepped forward and cleared his throat. "Does it say anything about Miss O'Ryan or Miss Jimmerson?" he asked.

Judge Clark shook his head and said, "I'm sorry, Marshal, but it doesn't." He glanced at the telegrapher. "You said you had a little trouble with some of it?"

"Yeah, but just a word here and there," the man said. "I didn't miss anything as big as the names o' them two other gals."

Seymour's face fell. "Oh."

Matt put a hand on his shoulder. "Don't worry, Seymour. They've got a good reason to keep Jessie and Sandy alive and in good shape, so I reckon they'll take care of the other two ladies, too."

Seymour swallowed and looked at him. "But you said it yourself, Matt . . . They *don't* have any reason to do that."

Matt couldn't argue with him.

Wherever they were right now, Maggie O'Ryan and Rebecca Jimmerson were probably having to fend for themselves.

Maggie had never hurt worse, or been more scared, than she was right now. She had been on the back of this horse for what seemed like hours, forced to straddle it like a man as she rode in front of the saddle, and the insides of her thighs were rubbed raw. Every muscle in her body ached, and to top it all off, she had been forced to endure the humiliation of being pawed by the bandit whose arm was looped around her waist like a steel band. From time to time his rough, dirty hand had strayed up to her breasts and mauled them through her dress. Every time that happened, a part of her wanted to sob in fear and shame. Another part wanted to turn around and punch the son of a bitch in the face.

She did neither of those things. Instead, she rode stoically, not saying anything as she kept her face expressionless.

That wasn't true of the other prisoners. Rebecca Jimmerson sobbed and wailed so much that Maggie was afraid their captors would get tired of listening to her and kill her just to shut her up. Jessie Colton spent her time cursing and railing against the bandits, telling them how sorry they'd be that they ever laid their filthy fingers on her, while Sandy Paxton tried without much success to keep her friend calm.

Alcazarrio and his men didn't seem to care what the prisoners said or did. They were focused on one thing only, and Maggie knew what it was because she had been able to overhear the conversation between Alcazarrio and his chief lieutenant, a man named Cruz. She spoke border Spanish as fluently as any of them, so she had no trouble understanding what the bandits were saying.

Their plan was to take the prisoners to their stronghold in Mexico and hold Jessie and Sandy for ransom. Alcazarrio was going to demand a combined quarter of a million dollars from the girls' fathers, or else Colton and Paxton would never see their daughters again.

Maggie wasn't sure if the ranchers could raise that sort of money on short notice, but she had a feeling they probably could. Both the Double C and Pax were large, successful spreads. Alcazarrio might get the fortune he wanted to finance his revolution against El Presidente Diaz.

The question that loomed in Maggie's mind was . . . how much were she and Rebecca worth?

And the answer was—not much.

Cornelius Standish might be willing to pay something to get his secretary back. Maggie knew from talking to Seymour that Standish was fairly well-to-do. But Maggie seriously doubted that Standish would fork over a hundred thousand dollars or more to save Rebecca. It wasn't like she was his daughter or anything.

As for *her* . . . she was just a schoolteacher. She didn't come from a wealthy family. They had been poor, in fact, and she had no wealthy relatives. There was Seymour—she knew he cared for her—but really, how much cash could he raise on short notice?

No, she decided with a grim sigh, she and Rebecca weren't worth much to the bandits as far as collecting any ransom was concerned. She was sure that the men would find other ways to justify carrying them off.

She shuddered as she thought about what those ways were likely to be.

Before Alcazarrio's band reached the Rio Grande, he sent a couple of his men racing off to the east. Maggie knew from what Alcazarrio said to Cruz that those men were supposed to tap into the telegraph line between Sweet Apple and Marfa and send a message to the settlement containing the ransom demands. The other bandits, including the ones who carried the prisoners on their horses, continued southward, splashing across the border river into Mexico. Flat, mostly empty wasteland stretched in front of them, although some rugged hills were visible in the distance.

Finally, after what seemed like a painful eternity, Alcazarrio called a halt so that everyone could rest. The prisoners were allowed to slide down from the horses. Maggie stumbled and almost fell when her feet hit the ground. She caught herself and looked around, wishing there were some shade. The midday sun beat down mercilessly.

Rebecca was having just as much trouble getting around. Jessie and Sandy, who were accustomed to riding, were in better shape. The two younger women hadn't been engaged in a knock-down, drag-out fight just before the raiders attacked either, so they weren't beaten up to start with. Sandy came over to Maggie and said, "Let's go sit on those rocks over there, Miss O'Ryan. I'll give you a hand."

"Thank you," Maggie said. "I think you should call me Maggie, though."

Sandy managed to smile as she took Maggie's arm to help her. "All right."

Jessie assisted Rebecca over to the rocks, which were small boulders just big enough to sit on. As the prisoners sank gratefully onto them, Jessie said quietly, "Don't worry, those bastards are gonna get what's comin' to them."

"How can you think that?" Rebecca asked, her voice cracking with strain. "We're their prisoners. We're in Mexico now. There's no one to stop them from doing whatever they want with us."

"You're wrong about that," Maggie said. "Seymour will stop them."

She wasn't sure where that statement came from. But even as the words left her mouth, she knew they were true. Seymour would come after the bandits and rescue her and the other prisoners.

Rebecca just stared at her for a second before saying, "Seymour? Seymour Standish? Are you insane? What can he do against . . . against monsters like those bandits?" She nodded toward Alcazarrio's men, who were pouring water from canteens into their sombreros and letting the horses drink.

"He won't be alone," Jessie said. "Matt Bodine will come with him."

"And Sam Two Wolves," Sandy added.

"And they won't be alone either," Jessie went on. "You think Sandy's pa, or mine, will let them get away with this?" She gave an unladylike snort. "I'll bet there's a posse already on the way after us."

"How do you know any of them are still alive?" Rebecca asked. "They might have been killed in the attack."

Stubbornly, Jessie shook her head. "I know it in my bones."

Maggie understood that feeling. She was convinced that Seymour was still alive, too, even though she had seen him shot. She knew he had survived. She knew he would come after her. And she was convinced that Jessie and Sandy were right about Matt Bodine and Sam Two Wolves, too. They were too tough to let themselves get killed by a motley group of *bandidos* like Alcazarrio's men.

All she and the other three prisoners had to do was stay alive until help arrived. Maggie was going to cling to that belief with every fiber of her being.

Because to do otherwise would be to admit that they were doomed to a terrible fate, in the hands of as ruthless and bloodthirsty a crew of *bandidos* as the border country had ever seen.

Chapter 19

Back in Sweet Apple, it wasn't taking Shad Colton and Esau Paxton long to come to an agreement, despite the long history of contention between them.

"I'll be damned if I'm gonna *pay* some son of a bitch for stealin' my daughter!" Colton declared, and Paxton nodded.

"I'll have to leave a few of my hands on the ranch to take care of things," Paxton said, "but the rest of the men are coming with me to Mexico! It shouldn't be too hard to track those beasts."

Along with Matt, Sam, Seymour, Judge Clark, Mayor Mitchell, and J. Emerson Heathcote, the two ranchers had come back to the marshal's office to discuss the situation. The rest of the Colton and Paxton families were over at the hotel, trying to get some rest. The doctor had given Carolyn Colton and Julia Paxton something to help them get through the ordeal of having their daughters kidnapped.

"Wait just a minute," Clark said to the cattlemen. His wounded leg was extending stiffly in front of him as he sat on one of the chairs. "This fella Alcazarrio was smart enough to find out when both of you would be in town with your families, so that he could grab those girls. He's probably smart enough to have left somebody behind to keep an eye on the town and report back to him. If you go charging out of here with a posse and no ransom, and Alcazarrio finds out about it, he's liable to decide to cut his losses and get rid of his prisoners."

Colton glared at him. "I haven't forgotten it was your fault my men were unarmed when those bandits hit, Judge . . . but I reckon you might be right about that part of it. What do you figure we ought to do?"

"Take the ransom to Alcazarrio," Matt said.

The other men all looked at him in surprise, except for Sam, who knew what his blood brother was getting at with that idea.

"We just said we weren't going to pay him," Paxton pointed out.

"But you can make him *think* that you're going to," Sam said, taking up Matt's suggestion. "Alcazarrio demanded the ransom in gold, right?"

The rest of the men nodded.

"That's a sizable hunk of coin," Matt said. "Put a pair of chests big enough to hold that much money on a couple pack mules and head south with it for that Villa Rojo place. Take enough men with you to make it look like you're guardin' the ransom, but not your whole crews."

Colton scowled. "We've got to take enough men so we'll have a chance against that bunch."

Sam shook his head and said, "Let the main body of the posse trail behind, out of sight. That way, when you rendezvous with Alcazarrio, they can swoop in at the right time and keep the bandits from getting away."

Colton and Paxton looked at each other for a long moment before Paxton finally shrugged and said, "It might work."

"I guess we can give it a try," Colton agreed with a nod. "The posse'll have to have a good scout with it. Someone who can keep an eye on the bunch that's supposed to be carryin' the ransom."

"That's a job for Sam," Matt suggested. "I'll ride with you two and the money."

Sam looked over at him and said, "That means you'll be riding right into the jaws of what's more than likely a trap."

Matt smiled. "Yeah, I know. I get the job that's more fun. But I called it first, so that's your tough luck, pard."

Judge Clark spoke up again. "Being an officer of the federal court, I have to advise you men that the plan of action you're discussing constitutes a highly illegal incursion into another sovereign nation. My official position is that you should wait here for the army and the Texas Rangers to arrive, then attempt to arrive at a peaceful solution by diplomatic means."

"And what's your *un*official position, Your Honor?" Matt asked.

Clark shook his head and sighed. "I wish I was in good enough shape to go with you. Shoot a few of the sons o' bitches for me, boys."

Matt chuckled and looked at the marshal. "What about you, Seymour?"

"I've already told you what I plan to do," Seymour said. "I'm coming with you."

"You should be in charge of the posse then," Sam suggested, "since you're the only real lawman here, even though you'll be out of your jurisdiction."

Seymour considered that for a moment and then nodded. "All right. How many men are going in the advance group?"

"No more than a dozen or so," Matt said. "Me, Colton, Paxton, and five or six men from each of their ranches. That's a big enough bunch to make it look like we're really deliverin' the ransom, without spookin' Alcazarrio."

"Sounds good to me," Colton agreed.

"And me," Paxton put in. "We'll start putting the group together."

Matt nodded and turned to Mitchell. "Mr. Mayor, have you got chests in your store that's big enough to hold a quarter of a million dollars in gold coins?"

"I certainly do," Mitchell said.

"We'll load them with rocks to make them look heavy enough."

"Let's get a move on," Colton snapped. "We've already wasted enough time jawin'."

"You sure you know what you're doin', Standish?" McCracken asked as he snapped a match into life with his thumbnail and held the flame to the tip of the stogie clenched between his teeth.

"You don't have to come along if you don't want to," Standish said. He looked down into the amber liquid in the glass he held, then abruptly threw the whiskey down his throat.

Damn Rebecca anyway, he thought. Why did she have to go and get herself carried off by Mexican bandits? It wasn't that he cared for her particularly. She had her uses, of course, but there was nothing she could do that dozens, no, hundreds of other women couldn't do just as well or better. But to preserve appearances, he had to act like he was worried about her, when really her captivity was just an unwanted complication.

But as soon as he'd heard what happened, Standish had seen immediately that he might be able to turn this situation to his advantage. Seizing the moment was what had allowed him to become a successful business-man. That was why he had gone to the marshal's office and volunteered himself and his companions to go along on any rescue mission.

Surely *something* fatal could happen to Seymour while they were all below the border. Something that couldn't be traced back to Standish or the three men who had come to Texas with him.

"I'm not sure how well suited we are for an adventure like this," Welch said now as the four of them gathered in Standish's hotel room.

"There won't be anything to it," Standish said with a shake of his head. "We'll just ride along with the others, and when the inevitable battle breaks out with those Mex-icans, just make sure that my nephew doesn't emerge from it alive. He probably shouldn't be shot in the back, though. I don't want anything suspicious about his death."

"What about those greasers?" Stover asked. "You expect us to actually join in the fight with them?"

Standish poured himself another drink. "I don't give a damn about that," he said. "We'll make it look good, then get the hell out of there once Seymour is dead."

"What about Miss Jimmerson?" Welch said. "Should we try to rescue her?"

"Only if it's not too much trouble. We'll be there to get rid of Seymour, that's all."

Welch looked at him for a moment, then said, "You're a cold-hearted bastard, aren't you, Mr. Standish? No offense meant."

"None taken," Standish said, then downed the drink he had just poured.

The group delivering the "ransom" gathered at the livery stable a short time later. The rest of the posse wouldn't assemble for a while, just in case Alcazarrio had spies watching the town, as seemed likely. Those spies would follow the smaller group, unaware they were being trailed by a much larger bunch. That was the hope anyway. This plan stood a better chance of working than if everyone rode together.

Colton brought six of his men, Paxton five. With the two ranchers and Matt, that made fourteen in the party. It was a good number, Matt thought. Better than thirteen anyway—not that he was superstitious or anything.

He and Sam hoisted wooden chests onto the back of three pack mules and lashed them into place. The rocks inside made them obviously heavy, although Matt and Sam had had to guess about the weight. They didn't know exactly how much a quarter of a million dollars in gold coins would weigh, but they'd determined it would take three mules to carry the load. But the actual weight didn't really matter since the chests were just for show.

The blood brothers shook hands. "Be careful," Sam said.

"Aren't I always?" Matt asked with a smile.

"Hardly ever. As far back as I've known you, you've been prone to recklessness."

"Yeah, but I've lived this long."

"But this time it's not just you and me we have to worry about. The lives of those four girls depend on us, too."

Matt sobered. "You don't have to tell me that," he said. "I know it."

Sam nodded and clapped a hand on his longtime friend's shoulder. Then he stepped back as Matt swung up onto the back of the rangy gray stallion. The rest of the men were already mounted.

"I'll be keeping an eye on you," Sam said.

Matt nodded and lifted a hand in farewell. He wheeled his horse and led the way, riding out of Sweet Apple and heading south. Behind him, Shad Colton held the lead mule's reins and led the pack animals. Paxton and the rest of the group rode around him in a protective circle. Townsmen who had gathered to watch the group's departure called encouragement after them.

The riders from the Double C and Pax had put aside all the hard feelings between the two crews. Like members of a squabbling family, they had closed ranks due to the threat from outsiders. Now all their anger and hatred were directed toward Diego Alcazarrio and his men, rather than each other. It might not stay that way once they got back to Texas—assuming they got back—but for now the feud between the two ranches was over.

All the members of both crews had volunteered to go along, and the ones who hadn't been picked to ride with Colton and Paxton had grumbled about it. But they would be coming along behind with the posse, and before the mission into Mexico was over, they ought to all have their chance to get in on plenty of action.

In addition to the men from Double C and Pax, the posse would include Sam Two Wolves, Seymour Standish, Cornelius Standish and the three men who had come with him from New Jersey, and several men from Sweet Apple, including the gunmen Cole Halliday, Ned Akin, and Jack Keller. They had made life miserable for Seymour when he first arrived in Texas, but now, once again, they would be siding with him in a fight. The group numbered about thirty men. Combined with the smaller advance party, they might outnumber Alcazarrio's force.

But Alcazarrio would be fighting on his home ground, from a position of strength. Numbers weren't everything, as Sam knew quite well. He and Matt had come out on top in previous battles when they had been outnumbered.

Figuring out the plan and getting everyone together, mounted and armed, had taken some time. It was mid-afternoon when Matt and the men with him reached the Rio Grande. Matt had been keeping his eyes open and hadn't seen any signs of anyone watching them. That didn't mean they weren't there, though, and as he led the way across the border river, the horse's hooves splashing in the shallow, slow-moving stream, he caught a glimpse of sunlight reflecting off something in the distance. Maybe a spyglass, he thought, being used by one of Alcazarrio's men who had been left behind. It was a good sign, although Matt knew it didn't *have* to mean anything.

He dropped back a little so that he was riding beside Esau Paxton. "Know anything about this Villa Rojo place where we're supposed to take the ransom?" he asked.

Paxton nodded. "I've been there once. Went down to buy a bull from a Mexican who had a ranch near there. There wasn't much to it then, just a little village in some hills. Probably less now, because the village depended on the ranch for its existence, and Don Alviso, the *hacendado,* died about a year later. From what I heard, he had no heirs, so bandits moved in and stripped the place of all its stock. The village was abandoned."

"So what you're sayin' is that it's a Mexican ghost town."

"That's about the size of it," Paxton agreed.

"How far is it from here?"

"It's a good fifty miles below the border. We can make it in the three days that Alcazarrio gave us, but the trip will take most of that time."

Matt nodded as he frowned in thought. It sure sounded like they might be riding into a trap. Alcazarrio probably figured that once he had his hands on the gold, none of the gringos would ride out of Villa Rojo alive.

The so-called general was in for a surprise—or at least, Matt hoped so.

The main body of the posse rode out of Sweet Apple about an hour after the group led by Matt Bodine. Sam Two Wolves and Seymour Standish headed up this bunch, followed by the contingent from the settlement and the cowboys from the Double C and Pax.

The two ranchers had made it clear to their men that Sam and Seymour were in charge, and that the lives of Jessie and Sandy might depend on obeying their orders. Sam didn't expect any real trouble from the punchers except maybe for a little hotheadedness—and he knew how to deal with that, having ridden with Matt Bodine for so long.

Bringing up the rear were Cornelius Standish, Warren Welch, Daniel McCracken, and Ed Stover. Sam wasn't going to be surprised if the Easterners fell behind and eventually turned back once they saw how much of a long, hard ride they had in front of them, but for now at least, the four men were keeping up fairly well.

Before leaving Sweet Apple, Sam had conferred with the ranch crews and found several men who knew where Villa Rojo was located, at least approximately. Sam didn't think they would get lost. He figured Matt would be able to track the *bandidos,* and he didn't anticipate having any trouble following the trail left by Matt's group. But it was nice to have an idea where they were going, just in case.

Sam glanced over at the man who rode beside him and asked, "Are you all right, Seymour? You're still looking a mite peaked. You didn't have to come along, you know."

"Yes, I did," Seymour said as he jerked his head in a nod. "I couldn't stand not knowing if Maggie is all right, or not doing everything I can to help her. Besides, if there are any . . . legal repercussions for this expedition, the blame will fall on me. As a duly appointed lawman, the responsibility for our actions is mine."

"Suit yourself," Sam said. "But if you pass out and can't go on, somebody's going to have to take you back to Sweet Apple."

"I won't pass out," Seymour vowed. "I'm fine."

He didn't look all that fine, but Sam didn't argue with him. Seymour was a grown man and could make his own decisions.

Besides, Sam knew how he felt. Sam was mighty worried about Sandy Paxton, and from what he had seen, Seymour and Maggie O'Ryan were a lot more serious about each other than he and Sandy were.

After they had ridden a while longer, Sam broached another subject. "Seymour . . . what do you think about your uncle and those other hombres from New Jersey coming along with us?"

Seymour hesitated, then said, "I'll admit I'm a little surprised by them volunteering. But I suppose Uncle Cornelius is worried about Miss Jimmerson. She's worked for him for quite a while, you know. And I suppose the others came along because Uncle Cornelius did."

"Does something about them strike you as a mite funny?"

Seymour glanced sharply over at Sam. "What do you mean by that?"

"I just mean they don't seem much like dry-goods salesmen to me. But I reckon you'd know more about that than I would, since you were in the business for such a long time."

Again, Seymour didn't answer for a moment. He looked at the trail ahead as he finally said, "The same thought has occurred to me, Sam. And earlier today, when I was talking to Rebecca—I mean, Miss Jimmerson—some of her comments led me to believe that she had her doubts about them as well."

Sam turned around in the saddle enough so that he could look over the group of riders strung out behind them. Standish and the other three Easterners were still at the rear. Sam said to Seymour, "Well, then, if they're not drummers, what *are* they?"

"I don't know. Bodyguards for my uncle perhaps?"

"Maybe. But nobody was trying to kill you, Seymour . . . until your uncle and his friends came to Sweet Apple."

Seymour's eyes widened in shock. "You can't mean . . . That's insane! Uncle Cornelius couldn't be behind those attempts on my life. He's my uncle, for heaven's sake!"

"If I recall my Shakespeare correctly, Hamlet's uncle tried to have him killed."

"That was just a play," Seymour argued.

"Maybe so, but folks have tried to get rid of their relatives plenty of times in real life."

"I suppose that's true, but still . . ." Seymour shook his head. "I just can't believe it."

Sam shrugged. "Something to think about, that's all."

Seymour might not want to believe it. Sam wasn't sure about his suspicions himself.

But he knew he was going to keep a close eye on Standish and the other three Easterners, just in case. Getting those kidnapped women away from Alcazarrio was going to be difficult enough without having to worry about danger from within their own ranks.

Except for a couple of brief stops, Alcazarrio had kept his men moving fast all day, ever since they'd galloped out of Sweet Apple and headed for the border. When night began to fall, the bandit leader signaled another halt.

The man on whose horse Maggie was riding laughed in her ear. "Now, little bird," he said, "you and Esteban will have a chance to get to know each other better."

Maggie remembered the way this man had been pawing her for hours, and thought she didn't want to get to know him any better than she already did. What she really wanted was the opportunity to plant a knife in his guts. She would twist the blade and take great pleasure in the twisting . . .

But she had no knife, and the bandits were probably too watchful to ever let her get her hands on one. For now, she had to concentrate on staying alive, not on the desire for revenge that burned inside her.

Esteban dismounted first, then reached up to haul her off the horse. She was shaky from pain and exhaustion and fear, and she swayed a little as he set her on the ground. His grip tightened on her waist and he pulled her against him. She smelled tequila and peppers on his breath as he leaned over her. With a leer, he said, "It will be a good night," and nuzzled his lips against her neck as she tried to shrink away from him.

"Let go of her, damn you!"

Maggie heard Jessie Colton's voice, followed by the smack of a hand against flesh. Esteban jerked in surprise and turned away from Maggie to glare at Jessie, who stood there with an angry, defiant look on her face after slapping him. A torrent of curses poured out of his mouth as he reached for the redheaded girl.

"Esteban!"

That sharp voice belonged to Diego Alcazarrio, who strode toward the confrontation, trailed by Florio Cruz. "What is going on here?"

Esteban pointed at Jessie. "This gringo bitch struck me!"

"He was trying to assault Miss O'Ryan," Jessie shot back. "I just told him to stop."

"Señorita Colton . . ." Alcazarrio spread his hands as if he were trying to reason with her. "I have told you that you and Señorita Paxton will be kept safe, but I cannot promise as much for these other two." He waved at Maggie and Rebecca, who had also been lifted down from horseback by one of the bandits. "The hills are lonely, and my men have been without women for a long time."

"I don't care," Jessie said. "I demand that Miss O'Ryan and Miss Jimmerson be treated with the same respect that Sandy and I are."

"Señorita . . . you in no position to make demands." The words came from Florio Cruz, and his voice held a snakelike hiss.

Alcazarrio shrugged and said, "My amigo is right. Besides, if you insist on being treated equally, perhaps I will give you and your friend to my men as well as these other two."

Jessie shook her head. "You won't do that. You know that if you do, our fathers will never pay any ransom for us. Not only that, but they'll hunt you down and kill you like a dog, no matter how long it takes."

Alcazarrio's jaw tightened. "You gringo women should learn to keep a civil tongue in your heads when you talk to men. But that is the fault of your fathers, for not beating you enough." He made a curt slashing motion with his hand. "For tonight, you will be spared. The other two as well."

"But General—" Esteban began to protest, as mutters of complaint came from some of the other bandits who had envisioned molesting the attractive young prisoners.

"I have made my decision!" Alcazarrio roared. "Let none dispute it!"

That quieted the rest of the men.

He turned back to Jessie. "Does this satisfy you, Señorita Colton?"

"For now," Jessie said with her best haughty look. "We'll see about tomorrow."

"Yes," Alcazarrio said with a slow nod. "Tomorrow may be very different."

Maggie swallowed. She didn't like the sound of that.

But there was nothing she could do about it, and for now, at least, she was safe, along with Rebecca, Jessie, and Sandy.

She prayed that wherever Seymour and Matt and Sam were, it wouldn't take them long to catch up with the bandits.

Chapter 20

Matt, Colton, Paxton, and the men with them made it about ten miles into Mexico that afternoon before the shadows of night closed in and forced them to call a halt.

"We should keep goin'," Colton argued. "We know where we're headed. We don't have to follow the tracks those bastards left."

"Unless Alcazarrio tries to pull some sort of double cross," Matt said with a shake of his head. "Maybe he won't go to Villa Rojo. Maybe he's got a stronghold somewhere else and plans to hold the girls there while some of his men collect the ransom in the village."

"We still have to deliver the chests there," Paxton pointed out. "I'm sure he'll have men watching us, and watching the village as well."

Matt nodded. "Yeah, that's true. But if he's up to anything fancy, I want to know about it as far ahead of time as possible, so we can make plans of our own."

"I thought Two Wolves said you were reckless and hotheaded," Colton complained.

"Yeah, but I'm not a damn fool," Matt replied with a grin. "We'll make a cold camp, and post guards for the night. Alcazarrio could try to grab the ransom before we ever get to Villa Rojo. There are still some bands of renegade Apaches down here below the border, too."

As a matter of fact, it hadn't been very many years since the cavalry had chased the Apaches out of West Texas. Both Colton and Paxton had fought off their share of Indian raids in the not-so-distant past. Matt recalled Jessie talking about how she and Sandy had even taken part in some of those battles, despite being young girls at the time.

With fourteen men in the group, it was easy to set up short shifts with two men always on watch. Matt took the final turn himself, along with Gil Cochran, Paxton's foreman. Matt knew that Cochran didn't like him much, but that didn't matter as long as the man could stay awake and alert. Matt hadn't come down here below the border to make friends.

The eastern sky was turning gray with the approach of dawn when Matt thought he heard something in the distance. He wasn't sure, but it could have been a faint clinking, as if a steel-shod hoof had just stepped on a rock, or a horse had tossed its head and caused a harness chain to bump something else.

Early in the morning like this was a good time for an ambush, when most men were still groggy from a night's sleep. On the lookout for some sort of treachery on Alcazarrio's part, Matt moved swiftly to Shad Colton's side and knelt to put a hand on the cattleman's shoulder. Colton started up out of sleep, opening his mouth to yell in alarm, but Matt's hand clamped over his mouth before any sound could come out.

"Quiet!" Matt whispered as he leaned over to bring

his mouth close to Colton's ear. "I think some riders are out there."

"Alcazarrio?" Colton asked tensely as Matt took his hand away.

"Could be, but there's really no tellin'. Let's wake everybody up, but be quiet about it." He paused, then added, "It's nearly time to get up anyway."

Colton rolled out of his blankets, and he and Matt moved quickly through the camp, rousing the other men from sleep as noiselessly as possible. Gil Cochran, hearing the others moving around, came in from his guard post and asked, "What's goin' on?"

"Bodine thought he heard something," Paxton told his foreman.

Cochran gave a little snort and said, "He did, did he? Well, I didn't hear anything, and there's nothin' wrong with my ears."

"Nobody said there was," Matt told him. "I might've been mistaken." He didn't want the distraction of an argument with Cochran right now. "It won't hurt anything to get ready for trouble anyway."

He detailed a couple of the men to keep an eye on the horses and mules. It would be well nigh catastrophic if their mounts, pack mules, and the horses they had brought along for the prisoners were stampeded.

In the fading shadows, Matt suddenly heard the sound of hoofbeats approaching. This noise was distinct and grew steadily louder.

"Just two men, I make it," Colton said in a whisper.

Matt nodded. "That's what it sounds like to me, too. But don't let your guard down. Where there are two men, there could be more."

Everyone clutched their rifles, and an air of tension

gripped the camp. A moment later, the hoofbeats stopped, and a man's voice called softly in Spanish, "Hello the camp! All right to come in?"

"Come ahead," Matt replied in the same language, "but don't try anything."

The man who had spoken chuckled and said in English, "I can tell by your accent that you are a gringo, Señor, no?"

"That's right. What do you want?"

"My amigo and I are only a pair of lonesome travelers, Señor. We would share your coffee and your company, *con permiso*."

The soft hoofbeats sounded again, and two tall shapes loomed up out of the darkness. The pair of riders both wore low-crowned sombreros. Matt could tell that much about them, but not much else. He recalled that most of Alcazarrio's men had worn the taller, steeple-crowned sombreros, but that didn't have to mean anything.

"We don't have any coffee brewing," Matt said as the strangers reined in. "You should've been able to tell that by the smell."

"Ah, perhaps it was wishful thinking on our part, as you gringos say. Well, if you have no coffee, perhaps you would be willing to share what is in those chests over there on the ground, next to the horses."

That was what they'd been after all along, Matt thought, getting close enough to make sure this was the party from Sweet Apple delivering the ransom to Diego Alcazarrio.

Several of the men reacted to the challenging words by lifting their rifles, and Shad Colton said, "You just keep your cotton-pickin' paws off those chests, mister."

If the spokesman was worried about being threatened, he didn't show it. The sky was light enough now for Matt to start making out some details about him and his companion. The men were roughly dressed, looking more like farmers than bandits. They were armed with rifles and six-guns and had bandoliers full of ammunition slung across their chests.

"You do not want to cause trouble, amigo," the man said with his eyes fixed on Matt, obviously sensing that he was the leader of the group. "My men are hidden in the brush with their rifles pointed at you, and if anyone fires, all of you will be cut down immediately."

"Sounds like a bluff to me," Paxton said in a cool voice. "How do we know you're telling the truth?"

"How do you know I am not?" the man replied. "The price for guessing wrong will be your life, amigo."

"I'm not your friend, damn it!"

The man shrugged. "True. Shall we conduct our business?"

"We don't have any business with you," Matt said. "Our business is with Diego Alcazarrio."

The stranger leaned over in the saddle and spit contemptuously. "Alcazarrio!" he said. "People speak of him as if he were the only important man in this part of Mexico."

"Then you're not part of his bunch?" Matt asked.

"We are our own men!" There was a note of fierce pride in the stranger's voice. "And we want what is in those chests!"

Matt saw how it laid out now. He'd been afraid that something like this might happen. Sweet Apple had a large Mexican population, being so close to the Rio Grande, and a lot of those Mexicans had family south of the border. The story of Alcazarrio's attack on the settlement and the kidnapping of the four young women had already spread, and by now there were probably plenty of folks down here who knew that Matt and his companions were escorting chests full of gold coins to Villa Rojo.

If these strangers weren't members of Alcazarrio's band—and Matt believed that they weren't—then they had to be local, freelance *bandidos,* probably half-starved and desperate. Desperate enough to try to bluff a much larger group in order to get their hands on that gold?

"All right," Matt said to his companions. "Lower your guns."

Paxton and Colton and several of the other men stared at him in disbelief. "Have you gone loco?" Colton demanded. "We can't give those chests to them!"

"It doesn't matter how many men they have," Paxton said. "We'll fight if we have to."

"They've got the drop on us," Matt said. "It won't help anybody for you fellas to get wiped out." He moved over to the chests and stood beside them. "We'll make this between these two hombres and me instead."

"Señor!" the spokesman said sharply. "What foolishness is this?"

"No foolishness. You want what's in the chests, you'll have to come through me to get it. But these other fellas will stay out of it, so there's no need to hurt them. You got that, Colton? Paxton? Whatever happens, you don't interfere."

"You *are* insane, Bodine," Paxton muttered.

Matt kept his attention focused on the two men on horseback. "Well, what's it gonna be?" he challenged them.

The second man, who hadn't spoken during the encounter, suddenly spit out a curse in Spanish and clawed at the gun on his hip. The spokesman yelled, "Pablo, no!" but it was too late. His partner's gun was already flashing up.

That revolver never got the chance to speak. Matt didn't even seem to move, but in the shaved instant of time between two heartbeats, both Colts had appeared somehow in his hands. The right one blasted first, sending a bullet smashing like a pile driver into the chest of the man who had drawn first. The slug's impact knocked the man backward off his suddenly skittish horse.

The other bandit must have hoped that he could get his own gun out and firing while Matt was distracted with killing his companion. If that was the plan, it was a complete failure. Matt's left-hand gun roared hard on the heels of the first shot. This bullet didn't quite go where Matt wanted it to. He'd figured on putting it through the second man's heart, but the hombre had time to move a little and the slug ripped through his right lung instead. The bandit slewed around in the saddle but didn't fall. Even as he began drowning in his own blood, the hatred he felt for this gringo made him try again to lift his gun and squeeze off a shot.

Head shots were tricky in this uncertain light, but Matt had time since to his battle-heightened senses his opponent seemed to be moving in slow motion. Matt fired a second shot from his right-hand Colt. The bullet smashed through the bridge of the bandit's hawklike nose, bored through his brain, and exploded out the back of his skull. The man was dead before he hit the ground like an empty bundle of clothes.

Matt was the only one left standing, because the rest of his party had hit the dirt in case the bandit had been telling the truth and riflemen were hidden in the brush to open fire on them. They would make a hard fight of it if that proved to be the case.

Instead, the only sounds in the early morning stillness were the echoes of the shots Matt had fired, rolling away across the wasteland. After a moment, Shad Colton climbed to his feet and said, "You guessed right, Bodine. There were only two of 'em."

"But you couldn't have known that for certain," Paxton snapped as he got up, too. "You could have gotten us all killed, and then where would our daughters and those other two young women be?"

"Sam would've stepped in and gotten them away from Alcazarrio," Matt said with complete confidence in his blood brother. "But I hadn't heard a damned thing from out there in the brush, and I didn't think they could sneak up on us like that without making some sort of sound."

"That's a hell of a lot to wager on your hearin'," Cochran said. "I don't like folks bettin' with my life."

"Well, you'd better get used to it," Matt said as he holstered his left-hand Colt and began reloading the spent chambers in the right. "We're all wagerin' our lives in this game, and we have been ever since we crossed the border."

Sam lifted his head and stiffened as he was about to lift his saddle onto his horse. Seymour was beside him, getting ready to saddle the dun, and he noticed Sam's reaction.

"What's wrong?"

"I heard something. Sounded like pistol shots. Three of them."

"From up ahead?" Seymour asked.

"Yeah. The direction Matt and the others are."

Sam and Seymour had talked at length the night before about the dangers they might be facing down here in Mexico. It wasn't just Alcazarrio's band of so-called revolutionaries they had to worry about. There was also the threat of renegade Apaches and other bandits. If word had spread about the ransom being delivered to Villa Rojo—and it seemed likely that it had—other greedy men might try to get their hands on it.

"Just three shots? That's all you heard?" Seymour's face wore a worried frown as he asked the question.

"Yeah. That's a good sign. If somebody jumped Matt and the others, they must have taken care of them without much trouble."

Seymour shook his head. "I didn't hear anything. My senses will never be as keen as yours, Sam."

"Well, I wouldn't worry about that," Sam said. "I wouldn't have any idea how to get along in New Jersey."

That wasn't strictly true. Sam had been educated back East, in one of the finest colleges, and he possessed the uncanny knack of being able to fit in wherever he was, in whatever sort of society he found himself. He could have donned evening clothes and gone to the opera and been just as comfortable as if he'd been wearing buckskins and attending a Cheyenne ceremony. Well, almost. But Seymour didn't have to know that.

"Rise and shine," Sam called as he moved through the camp. "It'll be light soon, and we'll hit the trail."

Quite a few complaints came from Cornelius Standish and his three companions. They weren't used to riding that much, and they certainly weren't accustomed to sleeping on the ground with only a blanket roll to lie on and a saddle for a pillow. All four of them hobbled around cursing for a while before their stiff, sore muscles began to loosen up a little.

Sam didn't pay much attention to their bitching, since it would have been all right with him if they had gotten discouraged and turned around to go back to Sweet Apple. He still didn't trust any of them as far as he could throw them. But Standish and the others managed to saddle their own mounts, and when Sam called for everybody to mount up and move out, the four of them were ready to ride.

A short while after sunup, Sam caught a whiff of something and hipped around in the saddle to see that Daniel McCracken had lit a cigar. Sam motioned for Seymour to keep going and then turned his paint, falling back so that he was riding alongside McCracken.

"Better put that out," he said, nodding to the stogie.

"Why the hell should I do that?" McCracken snapped.

Sam explained, "We're in hostile country now. There could be fifty Apaches out there watching us right now, and you'd never catch sight of them unless they wanted you to."

"And what the devil does that have to do with me enjoyin' a smoke?"

"Well, maybe there *aren't* any Apaches out there. If that's the case, we'd like to keep it that way. That cigar's got a pretty potent aroma to it, and an Indian could smell it from a long way off."

McCracken sneered. "Yeah, and you'd know about that, wouldn't you, Two Wolves?"

Sam didn't let the man's words bother him. He'd heard much worse in his life. He just said, "I've never smelled one quite that strong before, that's all."

"It's a special blend," McCracken said. "Expensive."

The smoke from the stogie smelled like burning garbage to Sam, but he didn't say that. He just said, "Put it out. It's dangerous to all of us for you to smoke it."

Cornelius Standish had been listening to the exchange as he rode nearby. Now he snapped, "For God's sake, put it out, McCracken. If I can do without smoking while we're down here, so can you."

McCracken glowered, but he pinched out the cigar, stuck it back in his vest pocket, and said, "It's my last one anyway. I'll save it until we're done with this fool's errand."

"Fine," Sam said. He gave the man a curt nod and heeled the paint into a trot that carried him up beside Seymour again.

"What was that about?" Seymour asked.

"I didn't want McCracken smoking that stogie," Sam explained. "The smell might've drawn attention that we don't want."

"I'm glad you're along, Sam," Seymour said. "I never would have thought of that."

"If you ever find yourself in a situation like this again, you'll remember," Sam predicted. "You learn pretty fast, Seymour."

He didn't explain what *he* had just learned. The smell of McCracken's stogie had taken him back several days, to that clump of brush where the man who'd bushwhacked the two Double C cowboys had hidden. Sam had found a cigar butt there that must have come from the man who'd killed Rusty and Bill, and while he hadn't really noticed anything about it at the time other than the fact that it stank, now that he'd smelled that gasper McCracken set fire to, he knew they were the same. And the tobacco was a special blend, McCracken had boasted, meaning that he was probably the only one in these parts who smoked it . . .

That was proof enough as far as Sam was concerned. McCracken had ambushed and killed the two cowboys in order to stir up more trouble between the Double C and Pax. That ruckus had gotten Matt and Sam out of town, and while they were gone, a second attempt had been made on Seymour's life. There was no doubt about it now. Those three "dry-goods salesmen" were really hired killers.

And there was only one man they could be working for. Cornelius Standish.

As if Sam and the posse didn't have enough to worry about, trying to rescue those prisoners from Alcazarrio, they had also taken four vipers into their bosom, so to speak, Sam thought.

That was all right, he told himself. He and Matt had stomped plenty of snakes in their lives. When the time came, they would stomp these scaly varmints, too. He didn't think Standish and the others would make their move until they got to Villa Rojo. But when the fighting started, that would be a prime opportunity for them to get rid of Seymour.

Still, he would have to take some extra care between now and then, just in case Standish tried his double cross early.

Seymour would be safe enough here in broad daylight, with all the members of the posse around him, Sam decided. He said, "I'm going to scout on ahead and see if I can tell how Matt and the others are doing."

"Be careful," Seymour admonished him. "Don't let any of Alcazarrio's spies spot you."

Sam smiled. "Don't worry about that. I may not be an Apache, but I'm pretty good at not being seen unless I want to be, too."

He found two hastily dug graves where the group with the "ransom" had camped the night before. Sam sat his saddle and frowned at the two mounds of dirt and rocks for several moments before he sighed and dismounted. It didn't take him long to uncover the faces of the two dead strangers. With a sense of relief, Sam scraped the dirt back into the graves.

He hadn't figured that Matt was one of the dead men. The bond between the two blood brothers was so strong that Sam knew each of them would be aware of it when the end came for the other, even if they weren't together at the time. But he'd wanted to make sure that Paxton or Colton or one of the other men hadn't been killed.

The distant shots he'd heard had been spaced very close together. Sam thought that these two must have tried to steal the ransom, and Matt had taken care of them before they ever got a shot off. Such a display of gun-handling wasn't unusual at all for Matt Bodine.

Sam pushed on, riding through arroyos and along the base of ridges, never skylining himself and taking advantage of every bit of cover he could find. When he came to a spire of rock, he dismounted and climbed it, leaving his field glasses in his saddlebags because he didn't want to take a chance on a reflection from the lenses.

His naked eyes were enough to spot the plume of dust maybe a half mile ahead. It was just the right size to be made by the horses of the party delivering the "ransom." Sam lifted his eyes to the horizon. He wasn't sure, but he thought he saw something far ahead, maybe ten miles or more away.

Alcazarrio, he thought. The *bandidos* were out there, still moving south, heading for Villa Rojo and the fateful rendezvous that would take place there.

And as Sam gazed out into the hazy miles that lay before him, he couldn't help but wonder about Sandy Paxton and the other prisoners. Were they still alive? Were they still unharmed?

Only time would tell.

Chapter 21

Despite the orders Alcazarrio had given, Maggie didn't really believe that the *bandidos* would leave her and Rebecca alone during the night. But that was what happened, and when they crawled out of their blanket rolls early the next morning, they were stiff and sore from the long ride but otherwise unharmed.

The sun was not up yet, but there was enough gray, predawn light in the air for Maggie to be able to make out the features of the stocky young man who came over to the prisoners and brought them tortillas for their meager breakfast. He had a round face and a drooping mustache, and there was something familiar about him. Maggie frowned as she looked at him and tried to figure out what it was.

After a moment, she got it. "I know you," she said as he handed her one of the tortillas. "You're the man Seymour—Marshal Standish—helped when Cole Halliday was harassing you."

It was true. The man was wearing better clothes now, instead of the farmer's garb he had sported in Sweet Apple, but he was undeniably the same man.

He looked away, refusing to meet Maggie's eyes. "Take the food, Señorita," he muttered.

She cast her mind back over the things Seymour had said about the incident, and dredged up the man's name from her memory. "You're called Hector."

He thrust tortillas into the hands of the other prisoners and then stalked off. Maggie could tell that he wasn't angry, though.

It was more like he was embarrassed.

She filed that away in her mind. She didn't delude herself into thinking that the young man might help them; he was obviously a loyal member of Alcazarrio's band. But it couldn't hurt to have one of the *bandidos* feeling a little bad about what was going on.

Also, this explained how Alcazarrio had known when to attack. The whole settlement had been buzzing about the hearing that Judge Clark was going to hold to decide the dispute between Shad Colton and Esau Paxton. The time and place of that hearing had been common knowledge, and so was the fact that Colton's and Paxton's families would be in town with them. Alcazarrio must have sent Hector into Sweet Apple to spy for him, and the young man had gone back and told the bandit chieftain about the hearing. It all made sense now.

But figuring that out didn't help her situation one bit, Maggie told herself as she gnawed on the tortilla. It didn't really matter how she had come to be taken prisoner. What was important was that she was in the hands of a gang of ruthless, hardened outlaws.

Shortly after that, the group mounted up and resumed their southward journey. Rebecca Jimmerson had calmed down and was no longer crying and fighting. Either she had found some inner strength somewhere, or else she was just resigned to her fate, whatever it might be. Jessie Paxton was as defiant as ever, and Sandy was calm, staying close to her best friend and utilizing an occasional quiet word of advice to keep Jessie from pushing their captors too far.

Maggie rode with Esteban again. Evidently, since he was the one who had snatched her up during the raid, he was claiming her as his own, at least until he tired of her. He was sullen today, and the smell of tequila that wafted from him told Maggie that he was probably hungover. That was fine with her, because he simply held her in front of him on the horse and didn't paw her as he had the day before.

Alcazarrio kept the band moving at a fast pace all day. That night they camped again, and once again the prisoners were guarded closely but otherwise left alone. The next day, Rebecca was more withdrawn than ever, and Maggie began to worry about her mental state. She wasn't sure why she cared; she didn't like Rebecca at all, as their brawl back in Sweet Apple had demonstrated. But things were a little different now. This ordeal they were sharing couldn't help but make Maggie sympathize a little with the young woman from New Jersey.

That afternoon, they reached a village in the foothills of the mountains. When Maggie spotted the red tile roofs of the buildings in the distance, for a moment hope flared inside her. Maybe someone there would help them.

But then she realized how unlikely that was. The inhabitants of the village would be afraid of Alcazarrio. The self-styled revolutionary general had this whole region under his thumb. None of the common people would dare to cross him.

And then as the riders drew closer, she realized it was all moot anyway. The village was deserted, doors hanging open and swinging back and forth on rotting hinges in the wind.

"Villa Rojo," Alcazarrio announced. "Our new home. Once we have the ransom, we will buy enough guns and supplies so that men will flock here to join our army from all over Mexico. Our fame will spread, and this humble village will be the birthplace of a new day for our land! The beginning of the end for El Presidente! Freedom and liberty!"

Noble words, Maggie thought, but they meant nothing. They were a mere smoke screen for Alcazarrio's naked lust for wealth and power. He was a bandit at heart and would never be more than a mere *bandido,* no matter how much high-flown rhetoric he spewed out to his men.

They knew it, too, because most of them were just like him. Maggie had seen it all before. Those who spoke the loudest about helping the common man were the greediest when it came to increasing their own power. Even if Alcazarrio succeeded in overthrowing Diaz, nothing would change. Not for the farmer and the shopkeeper and the wagon driver. There would just be a different group of hogs gorging themselves at the trough of power.

She put those thoughts out of her head. They meant nothing now. She had to concentrate on staying alive until someone came for her . . . Seymour, and Matt Bodine and Sam Two Wolves. They would not turn their backs on the captives. Somehow they would thwart Alcazarrio's plans.

Now, as the group entered the deserted village of Villa Rojo, Jessie Colton said to Alcazarrio, "You're crazy if you think our fathers are going to pay you one red cent for letting us go. You made the worst mistake of your life when you grabbed us, mister."

Alcazarrio laughed. "You had better hope you are wrong about that, Señorita. Because if your fathers refuse to pay, then *they* will be making the worst mistake of *your* lives . . . what little remains of them."

Hector Gallindo watched as the four young women were taken into one of the old buildings. Guards were posted at both doors and all of the windows to make sure that none of them tried to get away. He wished that there was something he could do for them, some way to reassure them that they would be all right.

But of course, there wasn't, because in truth he didn't know if they would be all right. Señorita O'Ryan and the other one—Hector wasn't sure of her name—were lucky that they had not been assaulted so far. They had the strong-willed Señorita Paxton to thank for that. But their good fortune would only last so long. Already, many of the men were complaining that they had not been allowed to pleasure themselves with the women. Eventually, the general would have to give in or face a rebellion among his own forces.

Hector wished that the extra two prisoners had not been taken during the raid, and he knew from conversations he had overheard between Alcazarrio and Florio Cruz that the general felt the same way. The women were an added complication, an unwanted distraction. But before the attack on Sweet Apple, Alcazarrio had neglected to order his men not to take any prisoners except the two ranchers' daughters. Esteban had given in to impulse when he snatched Miss O'Ryan, and Raoul had done likewise when he grabbed up the young woman with hair the color of honey. Now the situation had to be dealt with as best it could.

Hector told himself that he would stay near the building where the prisoners were being held. If things began to get out of hand, perhaps he could put a stop to them. He wasn't sure if he would dare step in, but he liked to believe that he would.

Late that afternoon, a couple of revolutionaries galloped into Villa Rojo and reined their mounts to a halt in front of the cantina that Alcazarrio had taken over as his headquarters. Hector saw them and recognized them as two of the men Alcazarrio had left behind to watch their back trail and make sure the gringos were coming with the ransom. The men dismounted and hurried into the building. After a moment, Hector walked over there to see if he could find out what was going on.

He stopped just outside the door where he could hear the men making their report to Alcazarrio. Hector felt his pulse quicken as one of them said, "The three chests are heavy. That much we could tell when they lifted them down from the mules carrying them each time they camped."

Alcazarrio grunted and said, "*Bueno!* Gold is heavy. How many of the gringos are there?"

"Fourteen, General. We came close enough to count them."

"They did not see you?" Alcazarrio snapped.

"No, General. We were very careful."

"Your other two amigos are still out there?"

"*Sí.* They will warn us when the gringos draw close to Villa Rojo, but you said you wanted to know how many of them there are, and whether or not they had brought the ransom with them."

"You have done well, my friends." Hector heard the sound of Alcazarrio slapping the men on the back. "You deserve a drink for your hard work."

"And a woman?" one of the men asked hopefully.

For a moment Alcazarrio didn't answer, and Hector found himself holding his breath as the general hesitated. But then Alcazarrio said, "Not yet. But soon, I promise you. After the ransom is ours. After we have taken the money and killed the gringos, then all four of the prisoners will be turned over to the men."

Hector had expected no less, but still the blood seemed to grow cold in his veins. Treachery came naturally to Alcazarrio, he supposed. The man was a general and fought in a noble cause, but yet he had human failings like everyone else. He could not bring himself to deal honorably with the hated gringos.

Normally, that would not have bothered Hector, because he hated the gringos, too. Or at least he had before the marshal in Sweet Apple had stepped in to help a Mexican farmer who was unknown to him, at the risk of his own life. Those two gunmen, the ones called Bodine and Two Wolves, would have defended him, too, if they needed to. Hector had sensed that about them, that they were good men who would not see anyone who was innocent or helpless be harmed if there was anything they could do to stop it.

Why had these things happened to confuse him so? It should have been so simple. He followed his general against all enemies. That was how it was supposed to be. Hector had no need for doubts.

But need them or not, they had begun to gnaw at his

brain like rats. He walked slowly back toward the building where the prisoners were held, and on the way he pondered many things.

Following the encounter with the two bandits who had tried to bluff their way into the possession of the chests they believed to be full of gold, the group headed by Matt Bodine didn't run into any more trouble the rest of that day.

Colton and Paxton hadn't particularly wanted to take the time and trouble to bury the two dead men, but Matt had insisted. Sure, they'd been thieves and their hands were probably stained with the blood of many innocents, but Matt couldn't be sure of that and preferred to err on the side of laying them to rest properly.

The posse expected to arrive at Villa Rojo late the next day, so there was an air of anticipation about the camp as the men rose that morning. They were deep in Mexico now, and as Gil Cochran ran a hand over his beard-stubbled jaw, he said, "I sure hope that pard of yours and the rest of the posse are still back there, Bodine. If they ain't, we'll be bad outnumbered when we go to waltzin' into Alcazarrio's stronghold."

"Don't worry about Sam and Seymour and the others," Matt said. "They'll be there when we need them."

He didn't know what was going on a few miles to the north, however. If he had known, he might not have been quite so confident.

Sam and the larger group had made camp at the base of a rocky butte that jutted up from the plain. As they were getting ready to break camp, one of the men hurried over to where Sam and Seymour were saddling their horses and said, "Somebody's comin', Marshal. Somebody afoot. Looks like it might be a woman."

Sam and Seymour looked at each other and frowned. Sam knew that a woman shouldn't be wandering around by herself on foot in this wasteland, and even a relative newcomer like Seymour could figure out the same thing without much trouble. "We'd better see what this is all about," Sam said.

As they walked across the camp, Cornelius Standish called, "What's going on, Seymour? Trouble?"

"I don't know, Uncle Cornelius," Seymour answered over his shoulder. "But I intend to find out."

Now that Sam was convinced Standish and the other three Easterners were behind the attempts on Seymour's life, for whatever reason, he had been keeping a close eye on the men. They hadn't done anything suspicious, and even though they were cranky and sore from riding, they hadn't slowed the posse down any. They were biding their time, Sam thought, waiting for just the right moment to try to kill Seymour again—and Sam was equally determined not to let that happen.

Right now, though, he wasn't as concerned about Standish and the others as he was about whatever *new* trouble might be headed their way. Because his instincts told him this wasn't going to be anything good.

Sam tipped his hat back, stared out across the flat, semiarid, brush-dotted land, and saw the figure stumbling toward the butte. Beside him, Seymour exclaimed, "Good Lord! It *is* a woman!"

"Or somebody in woman's clothes anyway," Sam said. "It could be a trick, Seymour. Stay here."

He walked forward, motioning for Seymour to stay

where he was. Seymour started to follow, then stopped and did as Sam told him. He drew his gun.

So did Sam, as he approached the figure. As he drew closer, he saw that the stranger really was a woman. The shape under the ragged, low-cut blouse and long skirt was definitely female. She had long black hair that hung most of the way down her back. Her eyes were downcast, and she didn't seem to see Sam until only a few yards separated them. Then she suddenly cried out in fear and fell to her knees, begging him in Spanish not to kill her.

"Don't be afraid, Señorita," Sam said. "I'm a friend. I'm not going to hurt you. Are you alone?"

He had to ask the question twice before it penetrated her fear. Then she jerked her head in a nod and fluttered a hand in the direction she had come from—west—as she said, "*Sí*, my family is back there, at my father's rancho . . . where the Apaches are!"

Sam's jaw tightened as a chill went through him. The Apaches were widely feared down here. They had been run out of West Texas, but they had found new prey on the far-flung ranches of the Mexican settlers.

He could see now that the girl was young, no more than fifteen or sixteen. Her feet were bare and covered with scratches from running through the brush, as were her arms. Sam holstered his gun, confident now that this was no trick, and stepped forward to help her to her feet.

She flinched away from his touch at first. Staring up into his face, she said, "You are *indio*."

"Half," Sam said. "But my people are the Cheyenne, who live far from here and are not the enemies of your people, Señorita. I am not an Apache."

His kindly voice and his white man's clothes must

have convinced her. She let him help her up, and then he led her toward the posse's camp.

"Somebody bring a canteen!" he called. "I'll bet this girl is mighty thirsty."

One of the men hurried over with a canteen. Sam set the girl down on a rock, gave her the canteen, and let her drink for a moment before he eased it away from her mouth. He didn't want her to guzzle down so much water that it made her sick.

"Now," he said as the men gathered around, "what's this about the Apaches being at your family's ranch?"

She nodded shakily. "They attacked . . . early this morning, before dawn. We have a tunnel . . . that leads from the house to an arroyo . . . there is much brush in the arroyo, and someone crawling through it cannot easily be seen. I didn't want to go, but my father told me I must. He said perhaps I could find help." She looked around at the members of the posse, who were listening with great interest to her story, those who understood Spanish anyway. "And now I have."

"What's she saying?" Seymour asked Sam, who had a grim expression on his face.

"Her family's ranch was attacked by Apaches early this morning, before sunup," he explained. "She got away and has been looking for help."

"And fate led her to us." Seymour nodded. "If she can show us where the ranch is, we can send those Apaches packing in short order."

"It may not be that easy, Seymour," Sam warned. "Anyway, several hours have gone by since the attack. It's possible the Apaches have overrun the place and killed everybody on it by now."

Seymour's eyes widened. "Good heavens! What a horrible prospect!"

Sam nodded and turned back to the girl. "How many fighting men on your ranch?" he asked in her native tongue.

She thought about it for a moment, then said, "Eleven. And several women who will fight, including my mother."

"Were they forted up good?"

She nodded. "*Sí*. Our house is sturdy, with thick adobe walls and rifle slits."

"Food? Water? Ammunition?"

Again she nodded. "My father has fought the Indians before. He says that a wise man is always prepared for calamity."

Sam summoned up a smile. "He sounds like a wise man, all right." From what the girl had just told him, the situation might not be as dire as he had believed at first. There was at least a chance that the ranch's defenders had been able to hold out. "How far away is it, and can you take us there?"

Her head bobbed eagerly as she waved to the west. "Five miles, perhaps six or seven. I can show you the way."

Sam patted her arm. "All right. We will go and see if we can help your family. You have to be prepared, though, for the possibility that we may be too late."

She swallowed and said, "I know. I have thought of nothing else since I left there."

Sam turned to the men and said, "Saddle up. We're riding west to see if this girl's family is still holding out against the Apaches."

"Wait just a damned minute," one of the men from the Double C protested. "We came down here to get the boss's daughter back, along with the Paxton girl and those other two ladies. Nobody said anything about fightin' any Apaches."

"You knew we might run into some renegades."

"But we didn't run into 'em," the cowboy said. "We're goin' out of our way to get into a ruckus with 'em."

"That's right," another man said, this one from Pax. "We can't risk those gals' lives on account o' some greasers who're probably dead and scalped already."

The girl must have understood the word "scalped." Her eyes widened in horror.

"We won't be risking the lives of the prisoners," Sam insisted. "The ranch isn't far off. We can be there in less than an hour."

"Maybe so, but that'll put us that much farther behind the bunch with the chest. What if we get to Villa Rojo too late because o' this wild-goose chase?"

The same question had already occurred to Sam, but he had pushed that worry aside. He had confidence in Matt to handle whatever needed handling until the rest of them could get there. And the simple fact of the matter was that he couldn't just ride off and abandon this scared, scratched-up little girl to her plight.

"That's not going to happen," he said, putting some steel into his voice. "You know that Colton and Paxton told you men to follow my orders. I say get ready to ride. We're going to see if we can help this girl's family."

For a tense moment, he thought he might have a mutiny on his hands. Then Cole Halliday spoke up, saying to the ranch hands, "What the hell is wrong with you boys? I never knew a Texan who'd turn his back on a Indian fight!"

Several of the cowboys muttered grudging agreement

with that, and the tide turned. The men scattered to finish saddling their horses. Within minutes, they were ready to ride.

"I hope you're right about this, Sam," Seymour said as he grasped his horse's reins. "I can't help but think about Maggie . . . Miss O'Ryan."

Sam swung up into the saddle. "I know, Seymour. But some things you just can't ride around. We'll get back on the trail to Villa Rojo just as fast as we can, I promise you." He extended a hand to the girl and helped her climb up onto the paint in front of him. He asked her, "What's your name?"

"Maria," she told him, no surprise since half the girls in Mexico seemed to have that name.

"Well, Maria," Sam said, "let's go see if we can help your family."

Chapter 22

They had ridden several miles when Sam thought he heard a faint popping sound in the distance. He signaled a halt so that he could hear better. Sure enough, his ears hadn't been playing tricks on him.

"Listen," he told Seymour as his pulse quickened. "Gunshots."

"That means Maria's family is still holding out against the Apaches?"

"Got to be," Sam said with a nod. He waved the posse forward and called, "Let's ride!" The men sent their horses racing over the level landscape.

A short time later, they came in sight of a patch of green at the base of a hill. That vegetation marked the course of a stream, Sam knew, and the probable location of the ranch. Maria confirmed that with a pointing hand and a cry of "My father's rancho!"

Sam saw an adobe hacienda nestled in the cotton-woods and aspens that lined the creek. Several outbuildings were scattered beyond it, and flames and smoke rose from their thatched roofs. The house itself was roofed with tile, so the Apaches hadn't been able to fire it.

A haze of powder smoke drifted through the air around the hacienda, though. Puffs of gray smoke spurted from the walls, and Sam knew the defenders were making good use of those rifle slits Maria had mentioned. If everyone had managed to get inside the house when the Apaches attacked, they stood a good chance of survival, at least for a while.

Unfortunately, they were outnumbered and wouldn't be able to hold out forever. As Sam and the rest of the posse drew closer, he estimated the number of Apaches as between twenty and thirty, a good-sized war party. Using wagons, trees, rocks, and some of the outbuildings for cover, they fired steadily at the house. The *crack-crack-crack* of Winchesters filled the air. Some of those shots had to be finding the rifle slits. Eventually, enough slugs would ricochet around inside the house to take down some of the defenders. That sort of attrition would wear them out. Sooner or later, the Apaches would breach a window or a door, and then the savages would pour into the house and kill everyone inside.

Unless Sam and his companions could stop them.

He raised a hand to signal a halt while they were still about five hundred yards away. The Apaches didn't seem to have noticed them yet. Sam took hold of Maria's arm and helped her slide down from the horse.

"Stay here," he told her. "We'll come back for you when the Apaches are gone."

She clutched his leg for a second. "Be careful, Señor."

Sam gave her a confident smile and told her, "Don't worry. You'll be reunited with your family soon."

Then he turned to the other men and began to issue orders.

"Spread out in a line as we charge. Those Apaches

are pretty well scattered around the ranch house, so we'll have to split up, too. If we can drive them out of their cover, the riflemen in the house can pick them off. We'll have to mop up the ones that the folks in the house don't get."

Nods of understanding came from most of the men. Standish and his three companions looked noticeably nervous. They had come along hoping for a chance to kill Seymour, Sam knew. They hadn't signed on to do any actual fighting, and certainly not against the Apaches.

Sam arranged his forces so that Standish, Welch, McCracken, and Stover were at the other end of the line from Seymour. They didn't want to go, but they didn't have much choice if they didn't want to reveal their true motives in being there. As the group trotted forward, spreading out into a long line of riders, Sam kept Seymour close to him.

"You all right?" he called over the growing sound of hoofbeats.

Seymour managed a nod. "It's always something new out here in the West, isn't it?" he said. "Some fresh danger you haven't faced before."

"I've fought Apaches in the past, and after today, you will have, too, Seymour. You'll do just fine."

"Yes," Seymour said. "I think I will."

After that, there was no more time for talking, because the horses broke into a gallop and the posse swept toward the ranch.

Sam had told the men to hold their fire as long as they could. They didn't want to warn the Apaches that they were coming. He would fire the first shot and trigger the assault when he felt that the moment was right. He knew the Apaches would see them coming sooner or later, but he wanted to get as close as possible before that happened.

Sam spotted a couple of the Indians in their dark blue shirts and bright red headbands as they darted from behind a building and dashed over to several more Apaches who were clustered behind an overturned wagon. When he saw the way they gestured frantically and turned toward the onrushing possemen, he knew the time had come. Guiding the savvy, experienced paint beneath him with his knees, he brought his rifle to his shoulder and fired.

The hurricane deck of a galloping horse was no platform for accurate shooting, but luck and instinct guided Sam's bullet as the Winchester cracked and bucked against his shoulder. One of the Apaches slammed back against the wagon as if he had just been slapped by a giant hand. He bounced off and pitched forward onto his face and didn't move again.

In the heartbeat following Sam's shot, a ragged volley rang out from the line of charging possemen. From the corner of his eye, Sam saw Seymour crank off a round, then awkwardly work the rifle's lever while he held on to his mount's reins. Seymour might not be smooth about it yet, but he got the job done, raising the rifle for another shot. If he had stayed back in New Jersey, chances were he never would have discovered that within him beat the heart of a fighting man.

A grin plucked at Sam's mouth for a second as that thought crossed his mind. Most folks were capable of a lot more than they ever dreamed. A hero lived inside nearly every man, emerging only in the right circumstances. The moments of heroism allotted to each individual might be limited . . . but they were there.

No time for philosophy now, though, Sam told himself as he triggered another round toward the Apaches, who were now scurrying for new cover as they became the attacked instead of the attackers. He was rewarded by the sight of one of the warriors tumbling to the ground, leg shattered by Sam's bullet.

The hot air was filled with the roar of gunfire. The shots coming from the house increased as the posse's assault forced the Apaches to show themselves. Caught between two fires, more and more of them stumbled and fell. Sam was close enough now to use his Colt, so he slid the rifle back into its sheath and drew the revolver. He turned in the saddle as a bullet whistled past his ear, spotted the warrior who had fired it, and put a .45 slug in the Apache's chest. The Indian went over backward, his stolen rifle flying into the air as he collapsed.

Seymour started using his six-gun, too, spraying lead toward some trees where several Apaches lurked. His hat flew off his head, plucked into the air by a bullet. Seymour grimaced and emptied his Colt into the Apaches. Two of them went down, while the third man, wounded by one of Seymour's shots, tried to limp away. He made it a few steps before a shot fired from the house exploded his head and dropped him like a rock.

Most of the Apaches were gunned down in a matter of moments, taken by surprise as they were. A few managed to escape into the desert. Sam didn't expect them to come back any time soon. They would retreat to their hiding places in the mountains and spend quite a while licking their wounds before venturing out on another raid. And they would think twice about coming back here at all, Sam figured. As fierce as the Apaches were, they were also pragmatic and chose their battles carefully.

As the shooting died away, the posse regrouped. A few of the men had been nicked, but none of them were seriously wounded. Hitting hard and fast as they had, they hadn't given the Apaches a chance to put up much of a fight.

Sam heard someone calling, "Señor! Señor!" and turned his head to see Maria running toward the rancho from the spot where he had left her. She was smiling broadly with relief. Sam dismounted as she came up to him, and she threw her arms around him, pressing herself tightly to him.

He felt a warm flush spreading over his face. He knew Maria was grateful to him for his help in saving her family, but she was a mite too young to be hugging him this way . . . especially considering the fact that people were starting to emerge from the house now, among them surely Maria's father and mother. Gently, he disengaged himself from her embrace, held her off with a hand on her shoulder, and said to her, "You'd better go see if your folks are all right."

She nodded and ran over to the defenders who had come out of the house. A stocky, middle-aged man hugged her, and then a woman who was crying tears of joy did the same. These parents had probably been convinced that they would never see their daughter again.

Seymour swung down from the saddle and smiled as he stood next to Sam and watched the joyful reunion. "I think this moment is worth the extra time and risk," he said.

Sam nodded. "That's the way I had it figured, too. I hope this won't have any effect on our real job, but I couldn't turn my back on these folks once I'd heard Maria's story."

"Nor could I have. But now that they're safe, we shouldn't delay any longer than necessary."

"That's just what I was thinking," Sam said.

Maria's father came over, expressing his gratitude effusively. He would have welcomed all of the posse members to stay at the rancho as long as they liked, but Sam explained politely that they had to be moving on, that they had a job to do.

He didn't explain what that job was, though. Even though it was unlikely there was any connection between the people on this ranch and the *bandidos* led by Diego Alcazarrio, he didn't want to take a chance on revealing their true purpose. It was risky enough that these folks knew a large group of gringos was riding through the area, heading south.

But there was nothing he could do about that now, Sam told himself as he got the men mounted up again and waved for them to head out. Some risks had to be run. Nothing in life was guaranteed.

And if it had been, Matt Bodine would have said if he'd been there, then that wouldn't be any fun at all.

Matt wasn't the sort of man to get nervous, at least for himself. He had long since learned that if he didn't like what life threw at him, he would just fight like hell to change it. And if he failed . . . well, at least he would go down battling to the end—although he never really considered failure to be an option.

But in this case, more was riding on him than just his own life, or even that of his blood brother Sam. Four young women were counting on him to rescue them from the clutches of as foul a bunch of hombres as Matt had ever run across.

They were down there somewhere, Matt thought as he reined in at the crest of a small ridge and looked at the huddled, slate-roofed buildings of Villa Rojo, about a mile away. Those roofs shone red in the late afternoon sunlight, which must have been what gave the village its name.

Matt glanced over at Shad Colton and Esau Paxton, who had brought their horses to a stop alongside him. Strain pulled taut the ranchers' faces. No doubt each of them was thinking about his daughter.

"Take it easy," Matt told them in a quiet voice. "I know you want to go chargin' in there with all guns blazin', but that won't get your girls free. We've got to pretend to play along with Alcazarrio a little while longer."

"How do you suggest we go about that?" Paxton asked.

"The rest of you are going to stay here while I ride into the village and parley with Alcazarrio. We'll set up a swap—the girls for those chests full of gold."

"Which aren't actually full of gold," Paxton pointed out.

Matt shook his head. "Alcazarrio won't know that until it's too late. He won't get his hands on the chests until we have Jessie and Sandy and Miss O'Ryan and Miss Jimmerson."

"How you gonna make sure of that, Bodine?" Colton said.

"That's the only deal I'll agree to."

Colton grunted. "What if Alcazarrio just shoots you and then *we* have to deal with him?"

"He won't shoot me," Matt said, "because he'll know that if he does, he'll die, too. Even if he has sharpshooters with rifles lined up on me, they can't pull trigger fast enough to keep me from getting lead in him."

"You're mighty confident about that."

Matt shrugged and said, "Man who's got no confidence in himself's got no business doin' what I do."

Colton and Paxton couldn't argue with that. Paxton said, "You'll be riding into a lion's den, you know that, don't you?"

"Yeah." Matt grinned. "Maybe it ought to be Colton here who goes, since he's named Shadrach. Don't have any punchers named Meshach and Abednego, do you?"

"Get on down there before we lose the light," Colton growled.

Still grinning, Matt hitched the gray into motion. He rode toward Villa Rojo without looking back.

On the way, he mulled over the plan, which was pretty simple. Make the swap for the prisoners. Then protect them when Alcazarrio discovered he'd been tricked, which he was bound to do. Then fight their way out of the village, while Sam and the rest of the posse swooped down, took the *bandidos* by surprise, and wiped them out, or at least hurt them bad enough so that there wouldn't be any pursuit as everybody from Sweet Apple lit a shuck for the border. Matt was confident it would work, but first he had to get those young women away from Alcazarrio.

He felt a crawling sensation on the back of his neck as he approached the village, and knew that hostile eyes were watching him. He didn't let it bother him. When he reached the buildings, he rode openly down the broad, dusty street between them. The foothills of the mountains loomed above him, cloaked in green pines that filled the air with their sweet scent, even down here below.

No one was in sight, which came as no surprise to Matt. Alcazarrio must have ordered all his men to stay inside. But a glimpse of a corral full of horses as the other end of town confirmed for Matt that the *bandidos* were here. He brought his own horse to a halt in the middle of the street and called, "Alcazarrio! Come on out and let's talk!"

A man appeared in the doorway of a building. The word CANTINA was painted over the arched opening in faded letters that were barely discernible now, after years of neglect. A gust of wind whipped up a little plume of dust that danced in front of the man for a second as he strode forward a few feet and then stopped.

Matt recognized the burly, bearded form of Diego Alcazarrio. And he knew from the hatred burning in Alcazarrio's eyes that the bandit chieftain knew him, too. Matt waited, and after a moment Alcazarrio said, "There is nothing to talk about, hombre. You have the ransom?"

Matt smiled thinly. "Not on me, but it's close by. You have those four young women?"

"Not on me," Alcazarrio replied with an ugly grin. "But they, too, are close by."

"Unharmed? All four of them?" The questions came sharply from Matt.

"What if I told you my men have had their way with them?" Alcazarrio gibed. "What would you do then, gringo? Would you refuse to pay for their lives? Would you turn and ride away with the ransom and tell those gringo *hacendados* that their daughters are no longer worth paying for?"

Slowly, Matt shook his head. "Nope. I'd kill you where you're standing first."

Alcazarrio stiffened. His breath hissed between

clenched teeth. He cursed in Spanish and snapped, "A dozen men have rifles trained on you at this very instant, gringo dog! A flick of my hand and you die!"

"In the time it takes you to flick your hand, *you* die."

The tense duel of wills continued for a couple of tense, silent seconds; then Alcazarrio threw his head back and laughed. "You are courageous, Bodine. A fool, but a courageous one. Tell me what you want."

"The ransom's loaded on pack mules. Give me the prisoners. I'll take them out of the village and send the mules back in with the chests of gold coins on them."

Alcazarrio laughed again. "You know that is unacceptable. You bring the ransom to me, and once I have examined it, I will turn over the prisoners to you."

Matt shook his head. Not for a second had he believed that Alcazarrio would go along with his first suggestion. That was why he'd made it so outrageous. "I don't have any more reason to trust you than you do to trust me," he said. "We'll bring the chest into town—all of us." He jerked a thumb over his shoulder. "We'll stop at that end of the street. You bring the prisoners out and start them toward us. We'll start the mules toward you. Everybody gets what they want. Fair enough?"

Alcazarrio thought it over. It was a classic swap between adversaries, rife with possibilities for a double cross on both sides, but still workable if everybody played fair.

Matt didn't expect Alcazarrio to play fair. He just wanted to get close enough to those girls to grab them and keep them safe when the shooting started.

Finally, Alcazarrio nodded. "It will be as you say, Bodine. But if there are any tricks, you and all the men with you will die—and then those women *will* know the attentions of my men."

"Fair enough," Matt said, "and if *you* try any tricks, you won't live to spend any of that ransom."

Alcazarrio grunted and waved a hand. "Bring the ransom."

Matt turned his horse and started out of the village. Again, the skin on the back of his neck crawled. Before, it had been an assumption, but now he *knew* that cold-blooded killers had their rifle sights lined on him.

They wouldn't fire, though, not while Alcazarrio still didn't have that loot he wanted so badly. For the moment, the bandit's greed outweighed his hate.

When that changed . . . *that* was when all hell would break loose.

"I hope you're not far off, Sam," Matt whispered to his blood brother. "Gonna be needin' you mighty soon now."

Chapter 23

It had been a long, tense day as the prisoners waited for their fate to be determined. The heat in the little building was stifling, and flies buzzed around them. There was no furniture, so the women had to sit on the hard-packed dirt floor. In fact, the only item in their makeshift prison was the bucket in which they had to relieve themselves, in humiliating fashion right out in the open.

The guards had brought them food and water several times, but not enough to do more than barely stave off hunger and thirst. That was probably deliberate, Maggie thought as she leaned against the adobe wall, which thankfully held a little coolness. Their captors wanted to keep them weak and disoriented, so they would be less likely to cause any trouble or try to escape.

Maggie's eyes were closed. To help distract herself from her current plight, she thought about her life back in Sweet Apple—the children she taught in school, the friends she had . . . and Seymour Standish. She wished she knew for certain that he was all right. Her instincts told her that he was, but she didn't know how much she could trust them. Maybe it was just wishful thinking.

She wished she could be with him right now, that was for sure. She wished she could feel his arms around her again . . .

The sound of soft sobbing broke into her reverie. She opened her eyes and looked over to see that Rebecca Jimmerson, who had been sitting with her back against the wall a few feet away, had slumped down until she was lying on the ground. Rebecca's back shook as she cried from pain and terror and exhaustion. Maggie knew those were the causes of Rebecca's sobs, because she was experiencing the same things herself. It took a strong effort of will for her not to collapse into tears as the girl from back East had done.

Even though she didn't like Rebecca, Maggie reached over to touch her shoulder. "Don't cry," she said. "It'll be all right. You'll see."

Rebecca jerked away. "N-no, it w-won't be!" she choked out between sobs. "They're going to rape us and kill us! You know they are!"

"No, I don't know that," Maggie insisted. "I still think someone will come to save us."

Without looking up, Rebecca flipped a trembling hand toward Jessie and Sandy, who sat on the other side of the single-roomed hut. "Those two maybe, but not us!"

"We won't leave here without you, ma'am," Jessie said. "You've got my word on that."

Rebecca finally lifted her head to glare across at the young redhead. "Oh? How are you going to make those bastards go along with what you want?"

Jessie couldn't answer that. She just frowned and didn't say anything.

Maggie tried again to comfort Rebecca. "I have faith that Seymour will do something—"

"Seymour!" Rebecca interrupted with a scornful laugh. "Seymour can't do anything! He's helpless. He always has been. For God's sake, he doesn't even have any idea that his uncle's been trying to kill him!"

Maggie's eyes widened in shock. *"What?"*

Rebecca pushed herself back to a sitting position and wiped the back of her hand across her nose and eyes. "It's true," she said. "Cornelius wants Seymour dead because he's afraid that Seymour will interfere with his plans for the company. It's more than just a matter of wanting to grab Seymour's share of the profits for himself. I think Cornelius has something criminal in mind, and he's worried that Seymour will stop him somehow."

Maggie could hardly believe what she was hearing. She gasped out, "Are . . . are you sure about this?"

"I heard Cornelius talking about it enough," Rebecca insisted. "Why do you think he sent Seymour to Sweet Apple in the first place? He knew the town's reputation as a haven for lawlessness. He thought Seymour would wind up being shot within a week's time!"

"But instead Seymour became the marshal," Maggie said.

Rebecca nodded. "Cornelius was furious when he heard about that He sent two men to kill Seymour. When they failed, too, he decided to come himself, and bring more hired killers with him."

"Those three men who are supposed to be dry-goods salesmen?"

Again, Rebecca laughed scornfully. "Do they *look* like dry-goods salesmen to you? They're murderers. They've already tried to kill him a couple of times."

"Oh, God," Maggie breathed. "And Seymour doesn't know about any of this?"

"Not at all. If he's not dead already, they'll get rid of him at the first good opportunity. Cornelius even promised a three-thousand-dollar bonus to the man who actually kills Seymour."

Maggie didn't want to believe this incredible story, but Rebecca's voice had the ring of truth to it. She glanced across at Jessie and Sandy, and saw that the younger women seemed to accept what Rebecca was saying, too.

"Why are you telling me all this?"

"Because I can't keep this horrible secret any longer! If we're all going to die here, I don't want to die with that on my conscience." Rebecca's voice cracked a little from the strain she was feeling. "I . . . I'm fond of Seymour. I think he . . . could be a good man."

"He's already a good man," Maggie said. "You just don't know him well enough."

A bleak smile touched Rebecca's lips. "Not as well as I wish I could have."

"There was never . . . anything between you?"

Rebecca shook her head. "No. Not from lack of trying on my part. At first, Seymour was just hopelessly innocent. He had no idea what I wanted. And then he met you, and he knew what *he* wanted . . . and it wasn't me."

"I'm sorry."

"No need to be. You didn't do anything wrong." Rebecca pushed her tangled hair back from her face. "Anyway, none of it matters any more, does it? We won't be getting out of here alive, so neither of us will wind up with Seymour. I just wish . . . I wish I could warn him about his uncle." She looked intently at Maggie. "If you *do* survive . . . and if Cornelius hasn't murdered Seymour already . . . you'll tell him?"

"Of course," Maggie promised. "But don't give up. We may all come through this—"

The door of the hut swung open. The tall, brawny form of Diego Alcazarrio loomed there. He grinned at them and said, "Come out of there, Señoritas. You are about to make me a very wealthy man."

Hector Gallindo was among the guards who surrounded the prisoners as they stumbled out of the squalid shack where they had been confined. The young women squinted against the garish, late afternoon sunlight as their eyes adjusted after being shut up in the shadowy hut all day.

General Alcazarrio prodded them toward the center of the street. "Soon you will be free," he told them. "The ransom I demanded for Señorita Colton and Señorita Paxton will be paid, and you can return to your homes." He put a hand under Maggie O'Ryan's chin and tilted her head up so that he could grin down into her face. "And you and the other señorita will be freed, too, Señorita O'Ryan."

A chill went through Hector at Alcazarrio's words. He knew now that the general was lying. He had already promised Maggie and Rebecca to his men, whether the ransom was paid or not. He wasn't going to let *any* of them go, Hector realized.

That suspicion was confirmed a moment later when Florio Cruz passed among the guards and ordered in a low voice, "As soon as the mules carrying the ransom have drawn even with the prisoners, kill all the gringos except the women."

Only a bandit would do such a thing, Hector thought.

A true revolutionary would have more honor. He felt himself go hollow inside as he realized that all of Alcazarrio's bold words about freedom and liberty were lies. As Hector had begun to fear, the general was interested only in power and wealth, not in helping the common people. And Hector had thrown in his lot with such a man. He had *killed* for such a man.

And now he would have a hand in condemning four innocent young women to a short, miserable existence of pain and degradation. Hector felt physically ill, but he struggled not to show it. He hung on to his composure with every bit of his strength and tried to figure out what to do.

What *could* he do, except follow orders? It was too late for anything else . . . wasn't it?

Matt would have felt a lot better about things if Sam had showed up before he and the rest of the men had to take the mules on into Villa Rojo. But the main body of the posse couldn't be far behind, he told himself. He would stall as long as possible, just to give Sam and Seymour and the others time to get into position, but he was confident that once the shooting started, they would be there.

They had better be, a small voice in the back of his head warned, or else things were liable to get a mite tricky . . .

"All right," he said to the men who gathered tensely around him. "I don't trust Alcazarrio as far as I could throw him, and he's a pretty big hombre. He won't just exchange the prisoners for the ransom money. He'll try to pull *something*."

Colton grunted. "Hell, *we're* pullin' something. There

ain't a quarter of a million dollars in those chests. Maybe we should've paid the money."

"It's a little late to be thinking about that now, isn't it?" Paxton snapped. "If you wanted to pay, you should have said so before we ever left Sweet Apple."

"I never said I wanted to pay," Colton shot back at him. "There you go again, puttin' words in my mouth—"

"I never did that."

"The hell you didn't! What about those cows you accused me of wide-loopin'?"

Paxton shook his head. "You were the one who said you were going across the border to rustle some Mexican stock."

"The hell I did! For God's sake, Paxton, that was a joke!"

Paxton crossed his arms over his chest and said, "I didn't think it was funny when you said we ought to restock our ranch with wet cattle after that outbreak of disease cut our herd down . . . and then you went and did it!"

"I never did! I might've said it, but I never stole a cow in my life, damn it!"

Matt glanced around. The men from the Double C and Pax had gravitated behind their respective bosses, and they were glaring at each other now as if they were back in Sweet Apple, ready to resume the long-running feud. This was hardly the time or place for such a ruckus.

And yet, raw emotions colored the words tumbling out of the mouths of Colton and Paxton, and Matt decided it might be a good idea to let them spew some of it out before they rode into Villa Rojo. A fight with Alcazarrio was inevitable, and they would stand a better chance if everybody had clear heads.

"Then where did those cattle come from?" Paxton demanded.

"What does it matter? They saved the ranch, didn't they?"

"I know where they came from," Paxton said in answer to his own question. "You took some of the men, rode across the border, and stole them. Otherwise, why would you be so damned stubborn about telling me where you got them?"

"They weren't stolen, blast it! It's true that me and some of the boys drove 'em up from below the border, but I bought 'em fair and square from one of the Mex ranchers who had a spread down here."

Paxton obviously didn't believe it. "How could you afford to buy them? We were almost flat broke at the time from fighting that epidemic, remember?"

"I remember." Colton looked over at Matt. "We ain't got time for this, do we? We need to get on into that village."

"Alcazarrio's not goin' anywhere," Matt said. "You've got me a mite curious about all this, Colton. Jessie said everybody always wondered why you and Paxton split up and broke your ranch in half. I think I'd like to know."

Paxton said, "I can tell you that, Bodine. I insisted on it. I wouldn't be partners with a rustler!"

"I didn't rustle them Mexican cows!" Colton said. "I bought 'em with the money Carolyn got when she went off to San Antonio and sold her grandma's jewelry!"

Immediately, he cursed and rolled his shoulders and looked like he wanted to drag those words back in. It was too late, though. Everyone had heard them.

Paxton stared at Colton for a long moment, then said, "Carolyn . . . sold her grandmother's jewelry?"

"Yeah." Colton's reply was a grudging growl. "She

didn't tell me she was gonna do it. She just did it and came back and gave the money to me, told me to use it to save the ranch. I hated for her to have to make that sacrifice . . . but I didn't want us to lose the ranch. So I did what she said, and I was damn fool enough to make some joke about buildin' up our herd with wet cattle from below the border, so you wouldn't know what was really goin' on. And then you went and believed that I really *was* a rustler!"

"But . . . but you could have explained, Shad—"

Colton made a disgusted gesture. "Ah, hell. I ain't the sort of hombre who goes around explainin' himself. You oughta know me better'n that by now."

"Yes. I thought I knew you. I thought you'd never stoop to stealing, and when I believed that you had, I took it as a betrayal of our friendship. That was why I insisted that we split the ranch. That's why I refused to take even a single head of the stock you brought out of Mexico."

Colton shrugged. "You got all the cows we had left from before, I got the new herd from below the border. Seemed fair enough to me, if that was the way you wanted to do it. Now, I don't want to ever talk about this again." He started to turn away.

Paxton stopped him with a hand on his arm. "Your pride kept you from telling me the truth about where the money came from. You allowed our partnership to be destroyed rather than admit that you needed your wife's help."

"Get your hand off'a me, damn it." Colton pulled away.

"Shad . . ." Paxton took his hat off and ran his fingers through his thinning hair in sheer frustration. "Shad, you had to have heard the rumors. I wasn't the only one who thought you had stolen those cattle. And yet you never said anything to clear it up?"

"I never been the sort to worry overmuch about what folks think about me," Colton snapped. "Carolyn knew the truth. That's all I really cared about."

"What about your children?"

"Ah, hell, I figured they knew better. You were the only one who was dumb enough to really believe it, Esau."

"Dumb!" Paxton's nostrils flared with anger. "I'm better educated than you are, you big prideful lummox!"

"Book learnin' don't mean that a man's smart. It just means that he spent more time cooped up inside while all the real men were outside workin'!"

Both ranchers clenched their fists and thrust their jaws at each other belligerently. The men who worked for them followed suit.

Matt's powerful voice cut through the tension of the confrontation. "Before you two go to struttin' around like banty roosters about to fight, maybe you'd better think about why we're here. We came to get your daughters and those other two young ladies, remember?"

Colton and Paxton both looked at him and lost their hostile attitudes immediately. "You're right, of course, Bodine," Paxton said. "Truce, Shad?"

Colton shrugged and gripped the hand that his cousin extended to him. "Sure, we'll call a truce."

"I don't mean just for now," Paxton said. "Now that everything's out in the open, once we get back to Sweet Apple, I think it's time you and I started mending the fences between us."

Colton pulled his hand back and pointed a finger at Paxton. "You just keep your damn mouth shut about what I said." His furious gaze swept the other men, his own riders as well as the cowboys from Pax. "That goes for the rest o' you hombres, too!" he roared. "Anybody who says anything about what he just heard here will have to answer to me!"

"Save your bull-bellowin' for later, Colton," Matt said with a grin. "We got some prisoners to rescue." He jerked his head toward the horses. "Mount up. Colton, you lead the pack mules."

They swung up into their saddles and set off toward Villa Rojo. The red roofs of the village seemed to be on fire in the late afternoon sun.

As the gray stallion walked forward, Matt wondered again just how far away Sam and the other members of the posse were.

Maggie looked around, blinking against the garish light. Villa Rojo's single street ran east and west. The hut where she and the other prisoners had been held was at the western end of the street. The sun was only a short distance above the horizon now, so it flooded the village with red light that swept along the street toward the small, abandoned church at the eastern end.

The sound of hoofbeats made Maggie look in that direction. Her heart leaped as she saw the men riding into town. The tall, handsome, broad-shouldered man in the lead was Matt Bodine. Behind him were Shad Colton, Esau Paxton, and several cowboys from the two ranches owned by the cattlemen. Maggie's eyes searched among them for any sign of Seymour, but she didn't see him. That caused her excitement to subside slightly, and worry took its place. Maybe Seymour hadn't come along because something had happened to him.

Guards stood closely around the four women. Alcazarrio told the prisoners, "Do not move until I tell you to. Then you will walk down the middle of the street while the mules carrying the ransom walk toward you. Do you understand?"

Maggie and Sandy Paxton nodded. Jessie Colton said, "Sure." Rebecca was the only one who didn't respond. She stared dully at the ground instead, clearly refusing to have any hope that she was about to be freed.

Maggie didn't really believe it either. She fully expected Alcazarrio to pull some sort of double cross. But still, going through with the swap as far as they could represented their best chance of survival, Maggie thought. As Alcazarrio glared at Rebecca for not answering his question, Maggie grasped the Eastern woman's arm and said, "She understands. I'll see to it that she does as she's told."

"Very well." Alcazarrio stalked out into the middle of the street and raised his voice to call to the group of riders who had come to a halt down by the church. "Bodine! You have the ransom?"

Matt moved his horse aside and motioned for one of the other men to come forward. "Pa," Jessie breathed as Shad Colton came into view, leading the pack mules with heavy wooden chests strapped to their back.

Matt reached over and rested a hand on the first chest. "Here it is, Alcazarrio!" he called back. "You start the girls, we'll start the mules."

Alcazarrio laughed. "Mules are notoriously balky, hombre! How do you know they will cooperate?"

"The same thing could be said about women," Matt replied.

Alcazarrio found that funny, too. Maggie didn't particularly, but she didn't care what Matt Bodine said right now. All that mattered was somehow getting out of this death trap.

"Tell you what," Matt went on. "I'll lead the mules out."

"Bueno!" Alcazarrio agreed.

"And *you* bring the women."

Alcazarrio frowned as Matt's suggestion obviously took him by surprise. "That was not part of our arrangement," he argued.

"We'll be takin' an equal chance," Matt pointed out. "You bring the women to me, I'll bring the mules to you and hand over the reins."

Florio Cruz hurried forward and spoke in a low voice to Alcazarrio. The second in command looked upset, and Maggie wondered if this new wrinkle had ruined whatever plans Alcazarrio and Cruz had made beforehand. After a moment, Alcazarrio nodded and turned back toward Matt.

"My good friend and second in command Colonel Cruz will bring the women to you. Give the reins to him."

Matt hesitated. Then he must have figured that he couldn't push Alcazarrio any farther than that. He shrugged and said, "All right. Come ahead."

Maggie allowed herself to hope just a little. Maybe Alcazarrio really would stand by his bargain and let them go. Maybe they could get out of here without a lot of shooting and killing.

Deep down, though, she knew how unlikely that was. She knew that barring a miracle, within moments the air would be filled with the roar of gunshots and the stench of burned powder.

* * *

Cruz hurried over to the guards and whispered to them, "The plan is still the same. When the women are in the middle of the street with the mules, open fire on the gringos."

"But you will be out in the open, where they can kill you!" one of the men protested.

Cruz shook his head. "I will take my chances. Do as you are told, and pass the word to the others!"

Hector Gallindo heard that and swallowed hard. He had hoped against hope that the gringo called Bodine had maneuvered Alcazarrio into a corner so that the general would be forced to cooperate. But Alcazarrio would not abandon his plan. His pride, and his hatred of the gringos, would never allow him to do so. His men were posted in buildings all along the street. When the firing began, they would kill the gringos, including Señor Bodine. Nothing could save them.

But the women would be in great danger, too, because the gringos would fight before they died. The street would be filled with bullets. The chances were great that some or all of the prisoners would be killed in the battle, too.

Alcazarrio didn't care about that. All he cared about was the money—and killing gringos.

Florio Cruz started forward, herding the women in front of him like a flock of reluctant chickens. Maggie O'Ryan had to help the honey-haired woman called Rebecca. Jessie Colton and Sandy Paxton looked like they wanted to break into a run toward their fathers, but Cruz's sharply worded command held them back.

From the other end of the street, Matt Bodine rode forward, holding the lead mule's reins in his right hand. The other two mules were tied in a single file behind the first mule. The mules came along with him, not getting in any hurry. In fact, to Hector's strained senses, time seemed to slow down and drag out until the seconds were just creeping by. Hector's eyes darted right and left. He saw the men around him tightening their grips on their rifles, getting ready to raise the weapons and open fire. Hector heard everything, the soft shuffle of the women's footsteps in the dusty street, the *clip-clop* of the hooves as Bodine's horse and the mules carrying the ransom approached. Those hoofbeats sounded at first like distant drums to Hector, muffled at first, but growing louder and louder and louder . . .

Then the parties were together in the center of the street and Cruz was reaching for the lead mule's reins and Hector suddenly heard a voice screaming, "Get down! Get down! It's a trick! They're going to shoot!"

It was *his* voice, he realized as horror at the thought of what he had done filled him.

Then he couldn't hear anything except an earth-shattering explosion of shots.

Chapter 24

Matt had expected trouble all along, of course. He knew that Alcazarrio couldn't be trusted, that some sort of treachery from the bandit chieftain was inevitable.

Even so, a shock went through him as one of Alcazarrio's men yelled a warning. Was it a trick?

No, he realized as he saw Alcazarrio whirl around, a maddened look on his face, and shoot the young man who had cried out. Blood spurted from the man's chest as the bullet tore through it and knocked him backward.

"Kill the gringos!" Alcazarrio roared. "Kill them all!"

By now the four young women, being prodded along by Florio Cruz, were only about a dozen feet from Matt and the mules carrying the chests. Matt dropped the reins as he saw Cruz claw at his gun. "Get down!" he shouted to the prisoners, then slapped leather himself.

Both Colts flickered into his hands with blinding speed, but he had to hesitate as the women stood there in the line of fire, stunned and uncertain what to do.

Cruz didn't hesitate, though. His gun roared as he tried to line his sights on Matt.

At the same time, Maggie O'Ryan finally took

action. She had hold of Rebecca's arm already. She dove forward, hitting Sandy Paxton in the back and knocking the blond girl down as she dragged Rebecca with her. Jessie Colton hit the dirt beside them an instant later.

Matt felt Cruz's bullet tug at his sleeve. He triggered his right-hand Colt and saw Cruz's head snap back as the bullet smacked into his forehead, leaving a red-rimmed black hole. A finger of blood oozed from it as Alcazarrio's second in command stood there for a second, swaying slightly. Then the message that Cruz was dead reached his muscles, and he collapsed in a limp sprawl.

Matt was already firing again, emptying his left-hand Colt into the men standing near Alcazarrio. He left the saddle in a flying leap as lead buzzed around him. Shots came not only from the men in the street, but also from the adobe buildings, and he knew that Alcazarrio had planted killers there, just as Matt had suspected he would.

He landed on his feet, snapped a shot through a window, and saw one of the hidden riflemen thrown backward by the slug that blew half his head off. Back at the end of the street, Colton, Paxton, and the rest of the men with them had started shooting as well, spraying the bandits with rifle fire. Matt saw Alcazarrio throw himself through an open door, escaping the hail of lead.

Matt crouched next to the young women. "Run!" he told them. "Down the street! Stay as low as you can!"

Having grown up on the frontier and lived through battles before, Jessie and Sandy reacted first. They leaped to their feet and sprinted toward the group led by their fathers. Maggie would have been right behind them, but she had to haul Rebecca up. Rebecca started screaming hysterically as Maggie broke into a run and dragged her along.

Some of the Double C and Pax cowboys spurred their horses forward and raced along the street through the gunfire like bold young centaurs. When they reached the fleeing women, they leaned over and scooped them up, then whirled their horses and headed back the other way.

Matt retreated, too, stumbling a little as he was creased a couple of times. Even though the wounds were minor, they caused pain to flood through him. He fought back the red haze that tried to wrap around him and kept firing, picking his targets carefully, until the hammers of both Colts clicked on empty chambers. Then he turned and ran after the others.

Where the hell was Sam? The rest of the posse should have been galloping in by now, taking Alcazarrio by surprise and turning the tide of battle.

The horses carrying Jessie and Rebecca and the cowboys who had picked them up suddenly fell, hit by bandit slugs. The riders flew into the air and disappeared in a welter of dust kicked up by flailing hooves. Matt holstered his gun as he plunged into the cloud. He found the two women and jerked them to their feet. "Go!" he urged them. "Keep movin'!"

One of the fallen cowboys surged to his feet and joined the fight, the gun in his hand roaring. The other puncher stayed down, and the grotesque angle at which his head was cocked told Matt that he would never get up again. His neck had been broken in the tumble.

Despite being heavily outnumbered, Matt harbored a faint hope that he and his companions could fight their way clear. Something must have happened to delay Sam and the others, he thought, but they were probably on their way right now. They might even be close to Villa Rojo. If Matt and the men with him could bust out of the village, the bandits would give chase. But they might get a hotter reception than they expected if they ran into Sam and the posse.

Matt thumbed fresh cartridges into his guns, each Colt in turn, as he ran along the street. When both revolvers had full wheels again and the dust had cleared a little, he resumed fighting. Twisting, whirling, veering right and left, falling and rolling, running a gauntlet of death in this abandoned village, he never stopped firing, and each time flame spouted from the muzzle of one of Matt Bodine's Colt, a bandit would double over in agony or spin off his feet as lead ripped through him. It was one of the most dazzling exhibitions of gunfighting skill and sheer nerve that the world had ever seen.

All the prisoners had reached the group of men led by Colton and Paxton, who were bloody from being nicked but still fighting furiously. Jessie and Rebecca were swept up on horseback again, and the riders turned to charge out of the village with guns still blazing. A shrill whistle brought Matt's gray to him, and he caught the saddle horn and swung up as the stallion went past him, hardly slowing. They were going to make it, Matt thought.

Then disaster struck again, as a solid line of riflemen appeared beyond the edge of town, sent there by Alcazarrio to block the gringos' escape. A volley rang out and half a dozen of the horses went down, mortally wounded. Other mounts tripped and fell over those who had fallen. What had looked a second earlier like a possible escape was suddenly floundering chaos.

Matt managed to stay in the saddle, but he saw that most of the rest were unhorsed. And they were cut off from freedom by Alcazarrio's men who had circled around the village. Only one bit of cover was close enough to offer sanctuary.

"Into the church!" Matt shouted as he leaped off the stallion again and sent shots rolling like thunder into the onrushing bandits. "Into the church!"

Colton and Paxton scrambled up from where they had fallen, grabbed their daughters, and hustled them toward the old mission. The door was rotten and falling apart, and some of the roof had collapsed as well. But all four walls still stood, and the thick adobe would stop bullets just fine.

The other cowboys who had survived the fighting limped and ran after their bosses. Matt spotted Maggie O'Ryan still helping Rebecca Jimmerson along. A large red stain blotched the Eastern girl's dress, so Matt knew she had been hit hard. But she was still able to move with Maggie's help.

He fell in behind them and gave them covering fire as they hurried toward the church. They disappeared through the doorway, and Matt was the last one in. Something slammed into his side as he ducked through the opening. The impact knocked him off his feet, but he recovered quickly and flung a couple more shots at Alcazarrio's men as he scrambled up and stumbled to one side, out of the direct line of fire through the door. He planted his back against the cool wall next to the opening and tried to catch his breath. He felt warm wetness on his side and knew that a slug had plowed a furrow along his ribs. He didn't think any bones were broken, but it hurt like hell.

He pushed the pain down in his mind and risked a look out the door. Alcazarrio's men were closing in, but a pair of swift shots knocked two of them off their feet, and that blunted their charge. They peeled off and sought shelter instead.

More shots came from within the church as Colton, Paxton, and their men found windows and places where chunks had fallen away from the walls, creating openings. They were digging in to defend the old mission against heavy odds, just as other valiant Texans had found themselves in an old mission called the Alamo, over in San Antonio.

That effort hadn't ended all that well, Matt reminded himself with a wry grin as he started reloading yet again. But maybe this one would be different. Maybe this time the Mexicans wouldn't overrun the place and slaughter everybody in it.

That was sort of up to Sam, Seymour, and the rest of the men with the posse, Matt thought as he snapped the cylinders closed, swung into the doorway again, dropped to one knee, and started squeezing off shots, the Colts bucking in his hands, left, right, left, right . . .

Sam already had the posse moving at a fast pace, but as the sound of gunshots came to his ears, he called to Seymour, "The fight's started!" and leaned forward over his paint's neck to urge the horse on to greater speed.

Ever since they left the ranch where Maria's family lived, impatience had gnawed away at Sam. He was angry with himself for delaying the posse and putting the young women, Matt, and the rest of the men in even more danger. And even the knowledge that his blood brother would have done exactly the same thing if the circumstances had been reversed didn't help all that much. But he knew that Matt wouldn't have been able to turn his back on folks in trouble either.

Seymour had his dun galloping for all it was worth, and lines of fear were etched on his face. Not fear for himself, Sam thought as he glanced over at the young lawman, but for Maggie O'Ryan and maybe a little for Rebecca Jimmerson, too. Sam didn't know if Rebecca was aware of the fact that her employer, Cornelius Standish, was plotting to kill his nephew, but it was at least possible. But Seymour didn't know anything about that.

Sam glanced over his shoulder. The posse was strung out behind him. Standish and the other three Easterners were having the most trouble keeping up, so they were bringing up the rear. That was just fine with Sam. The farther those treacherous varmints were from Seymour, the better. Seymour would soon be in enough danger without out the threat of being shot in the back by hired killers.

Because the posse was in sight of Villa Rojo now, and since the sun had begun to sink below the horizon, enough shadows had gathered in the village so that gun flashes were readily visible, like a circle of fireflies around an old building at the eastern edge of town. The crumbling bell tower told Sam it had been a church at one time.

And the spurts of muzzle flame coming from inside the building told Sam that somebody was forted up there, trying to hold off the bandits led by Diego Alcazarrio.

Matt, Sam thought as a savage grin touched his lips. He had no doubt that his blood brother was one of those making a last stand in the old mission.

He drew his Colt and sent the paint thundering forward in the dusk, anxious to give Alcazarrio one hell of a surprise.

* * *

Even though Matt Bodine hadn't gone to college, he had studied enough military history on his own to know that the Plains Indians were some of the finest light cavalry in the world, as they had demonstrated with bloody eloquence in battle after battle, including the one on the bluffs above the Little Big Horn.

Sam Two Wolves was half-Cheyenne, so he came by his fighting expertise naturally. As the sound of gunfire outside the church suddenly rose dramatically, Matt risked a glance through the window where he had retreated when shots forced him away from the door, and he saw riders flashing into view seemingly from all directions at once. Sam had arrived and split his forces so that he could hit Alcazarrio with stunning surprise from all quarters.

Matt let out a triumphant whoop. "The posse's here!" he shouted to his companions. "We'll get out of this yet!"

Ignoring the pain of his wounds, he ran to the winding staircase that led up into the bell tower, which was open on all four sides except for a short wall. He bounded up the steps, taking them two or three at a time, until he reached the top and came out in the little area where the mission's bell had once hung. Colton and Paxton followed him, along with Jessie and Sandy. All four of them carried rifles, and from this vantage point they opened fire on the bandits as the posse's charge trampled some of them and forced others into the open.

In the fading light, Matt caught a glimpse of Sam and Seymour riding side by side down the street, firing to the left and right, trailed by several other members of the posse. They didn't know it, but they were closing in on the building where Alcazarrio had taken cover, along with some of his men. That would be the toughest nut to crack.

But they wouldn't have to do it alone, because coming up right behind them were Cornelius Standish and his three men, Welch, McCracken, and Stover. They all swung their guns to bear . . .

What the hell! Matt suddenly thought. It looked like the four men were drawing a bead on—*Seymour!*

It seemed like Maggie's ears would never stop ringing from all the gunfire. The explosions burst continuously around her as the defenders tried to keep Alcazarrio and his men from overrunning the old church.

She had to force herself not to pay any attention to that as she tried to staunch the bleeding from the wound in Rebecca Jimmerson's side. Maggie was no expert on such things, but she could tell that the bullet had gone in and not come out, meaning that it was still inside Rebecca's body somewhere. The Eastern girl's face was drained of color. She had lost a lot of blood and was only partially conscious. Her eyelids fluttered and she looked around from time to time, but she didn't really seem to know where she was or what was going on.

"You'll be all right," Maggie said to her in a low voice as she pressed a pad made from torn petticoat to the wound. "You're going to be just fine, Rebecca."

Then Matt Bodine shouted that the posse had arrived. Maggie's head jerked up. That meant Seymour was here, she thought. But she had just enough doubt that she had to see for herself.

That wasn't the only reason she had to get to Seymour.

She had to warn him about what Rebecca had said earlier. She had to let him know that it was his uncle and those three phony dry-goods salesmen who wanted him dead.

"Rebecca! Rebecca, hold this cloth on the wound! I've got to warn Seymour!"

Rebecca didn't respond. Maggie grimaced and stood up anyway, leaving the other woman where she was propped against one of the walls of the church. She hurried toward the doorway. The old door itself had been riddled with bullets, and only a few rotted pieces of it remained, hanging askew from its hinges.

Maggie took a deep breath and looked outside. Not many shots were striking the church anymore. Alcazarrio's men were too busy trying to defend themselves from the posse, who had swept into town in the dusk on a storm of fire and lead.

Suddenly, Maggie saw Seymour and Sam Two Wolves gallop past. Her heart leaped in her chest at the sight. Seymour appeared to be all right as he fought fiercely at Sam's side.

Then four more men rode by, coming up fast behind Seymour and Sam, and as Maggie recognized them, her blood seemed to freeze in her veins. They were Cornelius Standish and his hired killers.

Maggie was about to run out of the church and shout a warning to Seymour, heedless of any danger, when a form flashed past her. Somehow, Rebecca Jimmerson had gotten onto her feet and made it over to the door in time to see what was happening. Even through the pain of her wound, she had grasped that Seymour was in danger, and now she ran toward him, screaming, "Seymour! Seymour, look out!"

She stumbled as she was hit again and then again by flying lead, but she stayed on her feet and continued to cry her warning. Seymour and Sam reined in and wheeled their horses around. So did Standish and his three men. With his face contorted by hate, Standish shouted, "You bitch!" and fired at Rebecca. She was jolted backward by the slug driving into her body.

At the same time, Standish's men opened fire, but Sam Two Wolves was ready for them. The Colt in Sam's hand roared as shot after shot rolled out from it. Warren Welch was driven backward out of the saddle by one of Sam's bullets, while Daniel McCracken folded up as a slug tore through his guts. Ed Stover was the strongest, and even with one of Sam's bullets in him, he stayed in the saddle long enough to get off a couple of shots. One knocked Seymour's hat off and another clipped some of the fringe on Sam's buckskin shirt, then another slug from Sam's gun crashed through Stover's brain and killed him.

Meanwhile, Cornelius Standish had swung around and was trying to bring his gun to bear on his nephew, who stared at him in shock. Maggie knew that Seymour probably couldn't believe what he had just seen. He had watched as his uncle gunned down a helpless, already badly wounded woman—and now Cornelius was about to shoot *him*.

Instinct took over. Seymour's Colt came up and roared an instant before the shot exploded from Standish's gun. Standish's shot went wild as Seymour's bullet rocked him back in the saddle. His eyes widened in pain and horror as he looked down at his chest and saw the rapidly spreading bloodstain there. Then he looked up at Seymour, dropped his gun, and slipped from the horse's back to thud into the street and lie there motionless i death.

Maggie realized she had stopped breathing. She starte again as she cried, "Seymour!" and began running towar him. He saw her, and his face lit up with relief.

Behind Seymour and Sam, Diego Alcazarrio and sev eral of his men burst out of the building where they ha holed up, and more gunfire exploded in Villa Rojo' single street.

The gunfight pitting Sam and Seymour against Stan dish and his men was over so fast that Matt hadn't had chance to take a hand in it. But as Alcazarrio launched hi last-ditch attack, Matt knew Sam and Seymour wouldn' have a chance on their own. Alcazarrio had the drop o them.

Matt had reloaded both Colts just before he charge up the stairs to the bell tower, so he didn't hesitate. He rolled over the low wall, dropped to the slanting roo below, slid along the red tiles, and flew into the air. landing in the street with both fists filled with thunder ing, death-spewing six-guns.

His slugs smashed into Alcazarrio's men, and into the bandit leader himself. From the top of the tower, Colton and Paxton and their daughters joined in the fight with their rifles. And Sam and Seymour swung around and opened fire as well. The withering hail of lead scythed through the bandits, knocking them off their feet and sending them flying like tenpins.

Alcazarrio was the last one standing, and he was shot to pieces. His clothes were sodden with blood, and crimson covered his face. He struggled to lift the guns in his hands as the firing slowly died away. His lips pulled back from his teeth in an ugly grimace. Only his hatred was keeping him on his feet. In a blood-choked voice, he rasped, "I hate you . . . damn gringos—"

A final shot blasted, but it came from behind Alcazarrio and threw him forward. He landed on his face and didn't move again. Matt saw one of Alcazarrio's own men try to rise and then fall back, smoke curling from the barrel of the gun that slipped from his fingers. Alcazarrio had been finished off by one of his own followers.

Matt rushed forward, joined by Sam, who hurriedly dismounted. Seymour practically flung himself off his horse as well, but he grabbed Maggie and held her as if he would never let go of her, instead of joining Matt and Sam.

The blood brothers went to the side of the man who had just shot Alcazarrio. Even in the fading light, his round face with its drooping mustache was familiar, and after a second Matt exclaimed, "Hector! Son of a gun, Sam, this is that hombre Seymour helped out up in Sweet Apple."

Sam knelt next to Hector, checked for a pulse, and then shook his head. "He's dead. Wonder why he shot Alcazarrio like that."

"Because Alcazarrio shot him." Maggie's voice came from behind them. Sam stood, and they both turned to see her standing there with Seymour's arm around her. "He's the one who called a warning and tried to help us. He was Alcazarrio's spy in Sweet Apple and told him when to attack so that he could kidnap Jessie and Sandy, but he was doing it for the revolution. He believed in that, and it must have changed something in him when he realized that Alcazarrio was nothing more than a common bandit."

That made sense to Matt, but something else still had him as confused as hell. "What was that business with your uncle and his men, Seymour?" he asked.

"I can answer that, too," Maggie said. "Mr. Standish wanted Seymour dead. Those men of his were really hired killers."

"Yeah, I'd figured that out, too," Sam agreed. "I shouldn't have let them slip up on us like that, but things were a little hectic."

Seymour looked into Maggie's eyes and asked, "How do you know that? About my uncle, I mean?"

"Rebecca told me."

They all looked around and saw Rebecca's body lying in the street a few yards away. The four of them moved to her side. Her face was smooth and peaceful in death. All the pain she had endured was over now.

"My God," Seymour said. "She knew?"

"But in the end she tried to help you," Maggie said, squeezing his arm. "That has to count for something."

Seymour shook his head slowly. "I . . . I think I still have a lot to learn about women."

"Well, about one woman anyway," Matt said with a grin as he clapped a hand on Seymour's shoulder and inclined his head toward Maggie. "I got a hunch this one's gonna be more than enough for you, Seymour."

A week later, Matt Bodine tipped his chair back against the front wall of the marshal's office, rested a boot heel against the railing along the edge of the boardwalk, and watched a peaceful evening settle down over

Sweet Apple. Beside him, Sam Two Wolves assumed a similar position.

"You know," Matt said, "as much as we get shot up, I reckon we could support a sawbones all by ourselves."

Sam grunted. "We keep the undertaker pretty busy, too."

"That's true, more's the pity."

Both of the blood brothers were still sporting bandages and stiff, sore muscles. But they were getting better with each passing day, and today, in fact, each of them had felt a familiar stirring inside.

Judge Simon Clark came along the boardwalk, limping a little on the cane he was still using. The burly judge paused and said, "Evenin', gents. Heard the news?"

"What's that?" Sam asked.

"Shad Colton and Esau Paxton are havin' papers drawn up to merge their ranches again. I haven't been around here very long, but I wouldn't have thought it was possible for those two old pelicans to patch up their differences."

"Anything's possible, Judge," Matt said with a smile. "You wouldn't think a dude from New Jersey would become a gun-totin', fightin' frontier marshal, would you?"

Clark chuckled. "No, but that boy's going to be a good one. Is it true what I heard? Halliday, Akin, and Keller have signed on to be his deputies? Three notorious gunfighters pinning on badges as lawmen?"

"They've fought side by side with Seymour a couple of times now," Sam explained. "They've seen what a good man he is."

"And they're gettin' a mite older, too," Matt added. "Fella can't be a gunslinger his whole life, I reckon."

"What about you?" Clark asked.

Matt's smile widened into a grin. "I'm young yet."

"And still full of wild oats, the both of you. I can see the look in your eyes. You're going to be ridin' on, aren't you?"

"Seymour doesn't need us anymore," Sam said. "He's got some real deputies now, and he can handle just about anything Sweet Apple can throw at him, I'm betting."

"Besides, we weren't cut out to stay in one place for too long," Matt said. "There are too many places we haven't been yet."

"You'll at least stay for the wedding, I hope."

"Wedding?" Matt and Sam said together.

Clark nodded. "That's right. Next week. The marshal's going to make that pretty little schoolteacher his wife. Ought to be the biggest thing in Sweet Apple for a long time. I expect there'll be quite a party afterwards. Everybody in this part of the country will be there."

Matt and Sam looked at each other. "We sort of owe it to Seymour . . ." Sam said.

"Yeah," Matt agreed. "A big fandango like that, he's liable to still need a couple of unofficial deputies to go along with the official ones. Especially since he's gonna be a little busy gettin' married and all."

"And we're still a little too banged up to be riding a lot anyway. But after that . . ."

"Yeah," Matt said. "After that."

The blood brothers nodded, happy in the knowledge that soon they would be on the trail again, a couple of untamed hearts answering the call of the untamed frontier.